UNFORGETTABLE

Praise for *Casting Lacey*

"*Casting Lacey* is a compelling, sexy, angsty romance that I highly recommend to anyone who's into fake relationship books or celebrity romances. It kept me sucked in, and I'm looking forward to seeing more from Elle Spencer in the future."—*The Lesbian Review*

"This is the romance I've been recommending to everyone and her mother since I read it, because it's basically everything I've been dying to find in an f/f romance—funny voices I click with, off-the-charts chemistry, a later-in-life coming out, and a host of fun tropes from fake dating to costars."—*Frolic*

By the Author

Casting Lacey

Unforgettable

UNFORGETTABLE

by
Elle Spencer

2018

UNFORGETTABLE

ISBN 13: 978-1-63555-429-8

THIS TRADE PAPERBACK ORIGINAL IS PUBLISHED BY
BOLD STROKES BOOKS, INC.
P.O. BOX 249
VALLEY FALLS, NY 12185

FIRST EDITION: NOVEMBER 2018

CREDITS
EDITORS: BARBARA ANN WRIGHT AND STACIA SEAMAN
PRODUCTION DESIGN: STACIA SEAMAN
COVER DESIGN BY TAMMY SEIDICK

Acknowledgments

There are many people who played a part in bringing this book to life.

Many thanks to Rad, Sandy, and the entire Bold Strokes team for everything you do and for making me feel so welcome. I don't know what I ever did without you.

Thanks also to my editor, Barbara Ann Wright, for her insight and guidance and for making my first editing experience such a wonderful one. I'm beyond happy to have you on my side.

To my copy editor, Stacia Seaman, thank you for your amazing attention to detail.

To my wife, Nikki, who never stopped believing in me. Thank you for being behind me, pushing me every step of the way; for being in front of me, pulling me along when I didn't think I could do this; and for being by my side for all the good stuff. You and me, baby.

Paula (Counselor)—Thank you for being the best, most loyal, crazy-fun friend I've ever had. You teach me something new every day. You bless my life with constant love and support. I'm lucky to be on this ride with you. (Even if you have effectively doubled the number of bossy women in my life.)

Finally, thank you to my readers for being on this journey and for reaching out to let me know my work has touched you in some way. That means everything.

For Nikki—my map, my compass, my true north.

UNFORGETTABLE

FORGET HER NOT

CHAPTER ONE

I told myself I wouldn't do this anymore.

When I hear the shower turn on, I'm annoyed that my one-night stand seems to think my hotel room is an appropriate place to get ready for the day. What's next? Cuddling? Then I realize this isn't my hotel room.

Fuck. My head hurts.

Like I said, I told myself I wouldn't do this anymore. I'm pushing forty, for God's sake. It's time to settle down—and by that, I *don't* mean become someone's other half. I'm not the marrying type. Too independent and too stubborn, or so I've been told. No, I just mean I need to stop sleeping around so much.

Not that I'm some raging whore who opens her legs for just anyone. I have a discerning palate. Certain requirements. For one, he has to make me laugh. Tall, dark and self-deprecating—that's what I'm drawn to. And I can tell by the way certain parts of my body feel right now that we had a good time last night. I can't remember a damn thing, but the less you remember, the more fun you had, right? Or maybe you were just that wasted, Samantha.

Shit. I really need to stop doing this.

I manage to crack one eye open. I reach over and pick up One-Night Stand's watch off the bedside table: 7:55. Shit. I'm definitely going to be late if I don't get my ass out of bed. I sit up and grab my head. I glance back down at the watch. A Rolex. It's nice, but a tad feminine if you ask me.

"Drink this, you'll feel better."

That is not the voice I expected. I don't move. I don't flinch. My facial expression doesn't change one bit. This is not a reflection of my steely resolve. It's only because I'm so fucking hungover my body can't actually react to anything in less than thirty minutes. Inside, my mind is blown. From the way my body feels, everything else is blown too, but that's not the point.

My eyes follow long, smooth legs up to black panties. Smooth legs? Black panties? I take the water bottle from her hand and try to hide my shock. I take a sip and look a little further up to a tan, toned stomach and black bra. I swallow hard and look her in the eye. She's smiling at me. "I had fun last night." She picks up the watch and puts it on her wrist.

"Yeah, um…" I try to clear my dry throat and look behind me, hoping I'll find a man in the bed.

Fuck. The empty bed makes me turn back around to her, confusion written all over my face, I'm sure. "Was there…" Her eyebrows rise while she waits for me to say something halfway coherent. "I mean…surely there's someone…" I glance at the bathroom, hoping to see a light on under the door. "Did we…"

Have a threesome? I don't say it out loud. Instead, I scan the floor looking for a used condom. Please God, tell me I wasn't so drunk that I forgot to have him use a condom. And also, God— please tell me there was a *him* involved in this—whatever it was.

"Yes, we did." She's nodding and smiling. I think she finds this funny. I watch her eyes go lower and realize she's checking out my tits. My God, what have I done?

"Who, um…" I casually pull the sheet up to cover my bare chest.

"Who? I'm not sure what you're asking."

"Was there…" I take another sip of the water, wondering if I look as bad as I feel right now. "You know…a third person at this party?"

"A man, you mean?"

I nod.

She rolls her eyes. "I'll let you get dressed."

Damn. I think I pissed her off. My eyes follow her as she walks away. She's gorgeous—you know, as women go. Long, wavy brown hair and a very nice ass—you know, as women's asses go.

Did I touch that ass last night? Well, fuck if I can't even remember my first lesbian experience. Just my fucking luck.

I'm zipping up yesterday's trousers when she comes out of the bathroom. I give her a little smile and then look away in case I start blushing. Why do I suddenly feel so shy? We obviously had some awesome gay sex last night or she wouldn't have been so friendly this morning. And my body is telling me it might have even gotten a little rough. I haven't looked in a mirror yet, but I noticed a good-sized love bite on my lower abdomen, aka an inch above my pussy. What. The. Fuck?

Maybe the reason I feel so shy right now is because chances are really good that this woman had her head between my legs last night. God, I'm such a slut. I steal another glance at her as she slides into a nice pair of heels. She's wearing a very sexy yet businesslike skirt and top. I'd ask her where she shops if I didn't feel so embarrassed.

I slide into my own heels and put my purse on my shoulder, not sure what to say or do next, which is kind of strange for me. I usually run my fingers over scruffy whiskers and say "thank you for a great time."

The face touching is so I don't have to kiss them good-bye. It shows just the right amount of warmth, so they don't feel like they just fucked a coldhearted bitch. I hate being misunderstood, even by complete strangers.

I'm not cold-hearted as much as noncommittal. Men are clingy and needy and want me to have their babies. Well, they used to anyway, when I was younger. I didn't want to ruin my body then and I certainly don't want to now. It would never recover. Not at this age.

She opens the hotel room door, and I say *she* because I can't remember her name. I really should get her name before I leave so I don't feel like a complete asshole. But how exactly do I do that without sounding like a complete asshole? I duck my head and walk to the door. She grabs my hand as I walk past her. "Samantha…"

Damn. I guess she remembers my name. Our eyes meet and she intertwines our fingers. I look down at our hands, enjoying the way her slender fingers fit perfectly with mine. I'm racking my brain for her name while I wait for her to say whatever she was going to say. Her brow knits together and then she smiles. It's almost as if she's warring with herself for the right words. Then she suddenly lets go of my hand and points back into the room. "I forgot I need to make a phone call before I go."

I can read people pretty well, and I'd bet a thousand dollars she doesn't actually need to make a phone call. She just doesn't want to endure the awkward elevator ride with me. I don't blame her, and honestly, I'm kind of relieved. I give her a nod and walk out. When I hear the door shut behind me, I let out a big sigh. God, I'm a fucking moron.

❖

I'm currently vacillating between wanting so damn bad to remember every second of whatever the hell happened last night and wanting to pretend I didn't just wake up in another woman's bed for the first time in my life.

A *woman*! Christ.

This coffee isn't helping me remember anything. Neither are these scrambled eggs. Why do hotel restaurant chefs think they have to cook every last bit of moisture out of the eggs? Even when I ask for a wet scramble they're... Oh God, she just walked in.

She really is beautiful. And she seems very put together, almost as if she knows exactly what her next move will be; her whole life planned out and written down somewhere. Ten bucks says I wasn't a part of that plan.

She certainly wasn't a part of mine. Not that I have anything planned beyond the next two weeks. Whatever brought her to Chicago has probably been on her calendar for months now. Or maybe I'm completely off base and I just happened to sleep with a hooker last night. One of those *high-end* prostitutes. This is a nice hotel, after all, with the bathrobes and complimentary slippers. I take a quick look in my wallet, just to make sure the same amount of cash I started with last night is still there. And then I shake my head at myself. Like I'd pay to have sex with a woman! The thought almost makes me laugh out loud, but I control myself so as not to draw the attention of my beautiful, exotic-looking lover. Yes, I just said that in my head. Hey there, lover. Yeah, I said that, too. Don't judge.

I wish I knew how we came to be in the same bed last night. What were the circumstances that took me to her hotel room? What words did I speak? Was I suave? Was I forward? Did I kiss her first? All questions I might not ever get answers to unless I speak to her again. All joking aside, I'm not sure I want to do that. How would I even begin that conversation? *Sorry I'm such a lush and can't remember a goddamned thing, but hey, mind telling me why we screwed last night?*

And we definitely did. Like I said before, my body is sore in unmentionable places. And that only happens when I go at it all night. God, I wish I could squeeze even just one memory from this thick, foggy brain of mine. I rub my temples again, trying to ease the hangover. It doesn't help.

She's taken a booth across the restaurant from me. She'll have to look to her far right to notice me, which means I'm basically hidden from her view. It makes me smile that I can watch her while I nurse my second cup of coffee and pray this jackhammering in my head goes away.

Who is she? Where is she from? Neither of us is from Chicago, obviously. So, where did this beautiful creature come from and how did I end up in her bed? I know I keep asking that question, but this is a serious matter. I don't sleep with women! Not ever. Not once. Not even in my youth when I would get so drunk, I couldn't remember…fuck.

The truth is, I wish I could remember what she feels like. Surely I ran my hands over her body. Touched her smooth skin and kissed those full lips. When I woke up in her bed this morning, I was mortified by the thought of it, but looking at her now, I'd say I scored. Big time.

She just put on a pair of black-framed reading glasses, and my tummy did a flip-flop. Why do I have butterflies? I haven't had butterflies in a million years. Now I wish she'd look my way. Hey, baby, what's your name? Wanna talk?

Coffee and a muffin while she works on her tablet—that's her breakfast. I wonder if that's her normal routine. God, I wonder if she's married and this was just an out-of-town romp in the hay. Maybe she does this on all her business trips. I usually look for a wedding ring or signs of a wedding ring (tan lines where a ring should be). I don't sleep with married men. I learned that lesson a long time ago. Did I think to look for a ring on her finger? I doubt the thought even crossed my mind. Because why the hell would it?

I can't eat my dry eggs. My stomach is too tied up in knots now.

"Is something wrong with the eggs?"

My server is seriously blocking my view of Sexy One-Night Stand. I lean to the side, trying to look around the rotund woman. I don't want to lose sight of her. "No. Just the check."

"If there was something wrong with the eggs, I'd be happy to get the chef to—"

"No!" I look her in the eye. "Just the check, please."

By the time she's glared back at me and then shrugged her shoulders, Sexy is halfway out of the restaurant. So, I have a choice. Do I wait for the check and lose her forever? Or do I throw some cash on the table and run after her?

Yeah, I agree.

"Mia!" I stop dead in my tracks. I have no idea what part of my brain suddenly remembered her name. God, I hope that's her name. Turn around, Mia.

She's smiling at me. And slowly walking toward me. That's what she did last night! I can see her in my head, smiling the way she is right now. I wish I could remember what happened after that. Like, for instance, how the hell I ended up in her bed.

"Hello again." She's standing close enough that I can smell her perfume. It smells familiar. And delicious.

"Hi."

And that's where my communication skills end. Because how

do I casually ask who she is and did she get me drunk just to have sex with me, and by the way—did I like it? God, how I want to know if I liked it. The way she's smiling at me makes me think we had a very good time.

She turns and glances at a group of people standing by the hotel entrance. "I need to go or I'll miss my ride." I just nod, still not sure what to say. "But if you'd like to meet up later…"

"I'm…I'm leaving tonight." God, now I'm stuttering.

She nods and smiles again, showing off her cute dimples. "Okay. Well. I really don't know what to say."

We both giggle. "Neither do I." Her brown eyes are warm and kind, and for a second, I get lost in them. I look down and clear my throat, hoping I'll find some courage in the next three seconds and string some words together. "I could…maybe…change my flight. Leave tomorrow morning?"

She's studying my eyes, wondering if I'm serious, I would guess. It's so crazy, but I'm dead serious. For some reason, I can't leave it like this. I have to know more. I have to know—why.

She looks back at the group again. Some of them are looking our way. They look like coworkers. Not family. Not friends. "See what you can do. And leave a note for me at the front desk. I'll be back around six." Our eyes lock for a few more seconds and then she gives me another huge grin. Her eyes sparkle a little bit when she smiles. "Okay, then. Maybe I'll see you later."

"Yeah" is all I can muster. She gives me a final nod and turns to walk away. And yes, my eyes fall to her ass. My fucking eyes fall to her fucking ass.

CHAPTER TWO

After an unsuccessful client meeting (I was off my game), I'm ripping yet another page off the hotel notepad. I crunch it up, shoot, and miss. It shouldn't be so hard to write a simple note, should it? *Hey, I changed my flight. Let's hook up again.* That would work, wouldn't it? At least it's honest.

I've been racking my brain, trying to remember more about last night. I know I checked in late, around eight. I had the bellman take my luggage to my room and headed straight for the hotel bar. I was dressed in business casual. Nothing flashy. Nothing that said *hey sexy lady, take me to bed and screw me.* I'm not even sure what that outfit looks like.

Anyway, I ordered my regular martini with olives. Nothing out of the ordinary there. It's not like I tried something different and got so drunk I couldn't think straight. Heh. I have to laugh at that one.

The only memory I have of her is seeing her walk toward me with that smile—as if she knew me. As if she were meeting me there. I focus on the notepad again, and as soon as I write her name, another memory from last night pops into my head.

You don't remember me, do you?

She said those words to me and then waved at the bartender. She ordered the same thing I was having and leaned her elbows on the bar, still smiling as if she knew a secret and couldn't wait to share it with me.

Mia Rossi.

That's the name she said when she offered me her hand. I took it and told her my name.

I know. God, you really don't remember me, do you?

I drop the pen, lean on the desk, and rub my temples. Did we sit and reminisce and drink until we couldn't walk? Obviously, we could walk. I'm pretty sure she didn't carry me to her room. "Mia Rossi. Mia Rossi. Who the hell are you?"

You dated my brother. I had a total crush on you and he used to tease me about it.

My eyes shoot open. High school? Fucking high school? Fucking twenty plus years ago, and she remembered me?

You're still beautiful. You haven't changed a bit.

I stand up and start pacing the room. I don't remember a little sister. I dated Gabe Rossi almost my entire senior year and I have no memory of a little sister. So I do the only thing I can think of to do. I pick up my phone and call my own little sister.

"Sam?" Juliet says my name all tentatively, like we haven't spoken in years.

"Don't sound so surprised."

"Oh-kay. How should I sound?"

I roll my eyes. It hasn't been that long since I called her. Or maybe it has. Shit, I'm a terrible sister. "How are the kids?"

"All grown up."

She was always such a pain in my ass. "I know they're grown up. I'm just asking how they are. How's…" Damnit, what is that oldest kid's name? "Nathan! How's Nathan?"

"Sam, why are you really calling?"

I look at the ceiling and shake my head. Why did I call her, of all people? She'll want to know everything and then she'll judge me. Juliet always judged me. She's still judging me from her perfect little home in the suburbs. "It's about Gabe Rossi."

"Nathan's football coach?"

"We dated in high school, remember?" She doesn't reply. "Juliet?"

"I know his wife, Samantha. My God, what did you do?"

"What are you talking about?"

"*He's married!*"

"*Good for him!*" Now we're shouting at each other? Just for old time's sake? Wait—she thinks I slept with Gabe? I have to laugh because it's so much worse than that.

"You really think breaking up a marriage is a laughing matter?"

"No, Juliet. Believe it or not, I don't. And that's not who I…" Shit. I need to slow down. I take a deep breath and clear my throat. "Do you remember him having a little sister?" Silence again. "Juliet? Do you remember Gabe's little sister?"

"She was a couple of years younger than me, but yeah, I remember her."

"How much younger?"

"You and Gabe were seniors. I was in ninth. Mia was, like, sixth, I think. But then she skipped a couple of grades. She was the smartest kid in our school. Last I heard, she was a lesbian doctor, but not like a doctor, doctor. More like a medical researcher or something."

"A lesbian doctor?" I can't keep the sarcasm out of my voice. "Like they need their own doctors?"

"You know what I mean. She's a lesbian *and* a doctor. But not a doctor, doctor…"

"Yeah, I get it, Juliet." I cover my eyes with my hand so I can think for a second.

So, she's only about six years younger than me. That's good news. And she's a lesbian, which means I didn't coerce a straight woman into bed. Also good news. Maybe the good lesbian doctor seduced me. That, I could definitely live with.

"Sam, why are you asking about Gabe's little sister?"

Shit. "Uh, I'm in Chicago on business," I answer in an upbeat tone as if that will clear everything up for her.

"And?"

"Aaaand…I saw her in the hotel bar. I mean, I didn't see her, she saw me…and we…met. You know, had a drink."

It takes Juliet several seconds to say anything. And then finally, "Why do you sound so flustered? Did something happen?"

"Like what? What could possibly happen?"

"I don't know. You just sound flustered. And defensive."

"I do not!" I clear my throat again, hoping my voice will drop down to its normal range. "I do not."

I always hated this about my little sister. You see, in our family, the first child was actually the second child and vice versa. Juliet was always the pragmatic, sensible, favorite child. And I was…wild.

Not this wild, though. I never fooled around with girls. This will definitely be something new for Juliet and my mom to talk about for months on end. I can hear my mother now. *Where did I go wrong?* And then Juliet trying to comfort her. *It's not your fault, Mom. Samantha is just Samantha. She always has to push the limits.*

That's probably true. I've never been a respecter of limits. And people who try to place them on me get thrown to the curb pretty quickly. Gabe Rossi was the first non–family member who learned that lesson. Get married right after high school graduation? Was he fucking kidding? I was eighteen, blond, tan, and gorgeous. I had beaches to visit, and Eiffel Towers and pyramids to climb, and hot foreign guys to fuck. Marrying Gabe Rossi that summer or any other was not going to happen. And I didn't let him down very gently. I'm sure he hates me to this day.

"Sam?"

"Yeah. Sorry. I'm here."

"Did you and Mia…you know…I mean, she's kind of young for you and she's a woman, but…"

"But what?" I need her to finish that thought.

"I wouldn't judge, is all I'm saying."

I have to laugh out loud. Juliet not judging me would be like the sun not rising.

"She'd be a total catch," she adds. "Gabe…Coach Rossi and his wife, Janey…they can't say enough about her. Gabe is so proud of his little sister."

It's a trap. She'll pull me in, get me to admit the truth, hang up on me, and call Mom. I know her tricks.

"Sam, you wouldn't have called me if this wasn't important."

She's right about that. And I'm so thrown by Juliet's reaction, I don't know what to say to her. Would she really be this open to me dating women? Surely not. Hell, I'm not even open to me dating women.

"Talk to me, Sam."

As much as I don't want to admit the truth to Juliet or anyone else, I could really use some advice right now. If it comes back to bite me, so be it. My mother is already disappointed in her eldest child. Always has been. This won't change anything. "I don't remember much, just bits and pieces." I take a deep breath and sit on the edge of the bed. "I got to the hotel late and went straight to the bar." I stop, because when have I ever described my sexual escapades to my little sister? Never, that's when.

"And Mia was there? At the bar? Did you have a few drinks and then fall into bed with her?" She's giggling. "It doesn't surprise me that she'd find you attractive."

What? Did Juliet just compliment me? My looks were always the bane of her existence. She hated how much attention I got. She used to say I stole all the sunshine from the room. She's literally never, ever complimented me on—anything!

"That's what happened, isn't it, Sam."

"Something like that...yeah." And now I wait for the real Juliet to show herself.

"Maybe this is what you need."

"What I need?" I ask, my voice rising again. What the hell does she mean by that? I soften my tone, hoping she'll actually respect my wishes. "What I need, Jules, is for you to not tell Mom about this." I use her nickname so she'll understand how serious I am and maybe cut me some slack.

"See her again, Sam. And I won't tell Mom, but you should totally pursue this. I mean, if you...you know...enjoyed it."

God, who is this person? "I can't remember if I enjoyed it. I'm racking my brain trying to remember, but I must've had too much to drink because I don't even remember flirting with her."

"What does she look like?"

"Gorgeous. I mean, you know...she's pretty." I think that answer fell from my mouth a little too quickly because she's giggling again. "I just mean, I saw her this morning, and she's..."

That moment when she took my hand in hers while we stood at her door comes to mind, making me feel all warm and fuzzy inside. "I think I liked it," I whisper, more to myself than Juliet.

"Did you get her number?"

Okay, now I just have to ask. "Juliet, why are you being so cool about this?"

"I don't know. I guess I'm just glad I was your first call. I'm never your first call." I squeeze my eyes shut. She's right about that. "Also, I want you to be happy. I want you to find someone who's good enough for you. My big sister has terrible taste in men, but her taste in women is kind of awesome."

"Huh. For some reason, I thought you'd see this as just another screwup on my part."

"Only if you screw it up," she says with a laugh.

I don't say anything.

"Sam, listen to me. Sometimes I've wondered if there wasn't some deeper reason why you've struggled your whole life with relationships. Why you couldn't ever commit yourself to anyone. Even that great guy you dated for a year and then suddenly out of the blue just broke up with him. What was his name?"

"Mike," I tell her, knowing exactly who she's talking about.

"Mike. That's right. Anyway, I've wondered if maybe you were…"

I wait for her to finish and then roll my eyes. "Gay, Juliet? You've wondered if I'm gay?"

"You grew up in this town with me, Sam. Every gay kid had to leave and never come back. And the only people I know who openly talk about their gay relative are the Rossis. Everyone else likes to pretend that their sister or brother or son or daughter doesn't exist. It would be natural for you to suppress those feelings if you had them. And…it would explain why you never come home."

As much as I appreciate her openness on the subject, it's just not true. "I really don't think I've repressed anything. I've never even looked at a woman in that way before."

"Before Mia, you mean?"

I guess I can concede that point. "Okay, yes. Not until Mia."

"So, give it a chance. Stop worrying about the fact that she's a woman and focus on how she makes you feel."

I still don't know if I trust Juliet, but she's being so nice. I guess it won't hurt to tell her about tonight. "Yeah, um...I'm going to stay an extra night so I can have dinner with her."

"Yes!" She lets out a little whoop and now I'm the one giggling. "You have to call me later and tell me how it goes. Or text! Just send a text if you can't talk, okay?"

"Okay. I will."

"Okay. Love you, Sam."

"Love you too." I end the call and stare at my phone for a moment. I don't understand how a single second of that phone call could've just happened, but I do know that I haven't told my sister I love her since we were little. It felt good to say those words again. I stand up and go back to the desk and the notepad.

Mia,
Call me when you get in. I'd love to take you to dinner.
Room 733
Samantha

CHAPTER THREE

I didn't want to overdo it with the clothes and makeup. The last thing I want is to look like I'm trying too hard since I'm not even sure what I want to have happen tonight. I went with skinny jeans, heels, and a silk blouse that isn't too low cut. I step out of the elevator and see her standing a few feet away with a handsome man who looks to be about my age. Our eyes meet and she smiles, putting her hand out as if she wants me to hold it. "Samantha!"

"Hi." I gladly take her hand.

"I'm sorry, I haven't even gone upstairs to freshen up yet. Samantha, this is one of my colleagues, Dr. Mark Roberts."

I let go of her hand and shake Mark's. He's totally someone I would flirt with in a bar, with his full head of dark, wavy hair, piercing blue eyes, and sharp jawline. "It's a pleasure, Mark."

"The pleasure is all mine. Unfortunately, Mia beat me to the punch last night. I was just about to send a drink your way when she jumped up and said—I know that gorgeous woman!"

I glance at Mia, who seems to be glowing with pride now. "And I was right. On both counts."

"Well," Mark inclines his head, "I'd invite myself to join you two beautiful ladies tonight, but I have a feeling three would be a crowd."

Mia motions with her head toward the elevators. "Get outta here," she tells him with a wink. Mark walks away laughing and Mia turns her attention back to me. Her eyes slowly wander down and then back up my body. "Hello, beautiful."

"Hi." I lean in and kiss her cheek, letting my hand rest on her waist like it's the most natural thing in the world to do. And a second ago, it was, but now I feel embarrassed that I did it, so I take a step back.

"I haven't had a chance to change. Do you mind if I meet you in the bar in a few minutes?"

I suppress a laugh. "Last time that happened…"

"Yeah, um…I guess we both had a little too much to drink last night. I don't usually…"

I duck my head. I wish I could say the same, but the truth is, most of my short-lived relationships started in a bar. "I'll just wait in the lobby." That's my way of telling her I'd like to get to know her before we, or if we, get drunk and sleep together again.

"If Mark tries to buy you a drink, just tell him…"

"Don't worry about Mark," I quickly reply. On any other night, handsome Mark might be a threat. But tonight…well, tonight, I want to have dinner with a beautiful woman and see how I feel. Thank you for the advice, Juliet.

❖

I'd like to think that I slept with Mia last night for the very same reason that I can't take my eyes off her right now. She'd be gorgeous wearing anything, but these cute little cropped trousers and V-neck sweater are especially adorable on her. They make her look even younger and scream *I can put any old thing on and look smokin' hot*. I stand up, and once again, my hand makes its way to her waist. "I hope you don't mind, I put our name in at the restaurant next door."

"Not at all." She has a brilliant smile that makes her eyes light up. "And I'm sorry you had to wait for me. Sometimes my colleagues don't know when to stop talking shop."

I'm not sure if I should try to hold her hand as we walk, so I tuck my hands in my jeans pockets. "I hope you like seafood."

She rests her hand on my back, letting me walk through the revolving door first. "Good choice. I love it."

Once we're outside, she puts her hand on my back again and keeps it there until we're at the front door of the restaurant. Then she opens it for me and lets me walk in first again. It makes me wonder if she does this with all her dates, or just me, because I'm straight and it's what would feel most natural to me.

Did I tell her that I'm straight before we had sex or after? Or ever? I hate that so much of last night is missing for me, but one thing is pretty clear—having her hand on my body feels extremely natural to me. Comforting, somehow. And warm. She's warm.

I'm still feeling a little uneasy about Juliet's reaction to all of this. I've always felt like my little sister wanted me to be something I wasn't. A better role model. A better person in general. Someone she could emulate and look up to. But I didn't want to be her or anyone else's role model. And now she wants me to be gay, as if that would explain everything—and then she wouldn't have to see me as the loner/heartbreaker she thinks I am.

I need to stop thinking about Juliet and focus on Mia. Even though I'm the one who made the reservation, she's the one talking to the hostess. She turns around and gently takes my elbow. "Do you mind if we sit at the bar until our table is ready?"

"That's fine." I could definitely use a drink right now. I love being in Mia's presence again, but at the same time, it all feels a little bit surreal that I'm actually on a date with a woman. I still can't fully wrap my head around it. I keep hearing Juliet's words. *Focus on how she makes you feel.*

I'm trying, Juliet. I'm trying.

We're sitting at the bar, turned toward each other on the stools, sipping on a lovely bottle of wine she ordered. It's always a turn on for me when someone knows their wine. Score one for the cute girl.

"You know, you broke Gabe's heart. Are you going to break mine, too?"

Well, that came out of nowhere. My eyes shift to my glass of wine. I pick it up and take a sip before I answer because Jesus, she actually just said those words.

"I'm sorry," she quickly says, putting her hand on my knee. "That was a really stupid thing to say. We're not...we haven't…"

"It's a fair question." I look up and find her eyes. I can tell she'd like to take the words back, so I lean forward, resting my elbow on the bar. "Gabe and I were so young. Way too young to get married, which is what he wanted us to do."

Her eyes widen in surprise. "I didn't know that. He asked you to marry him?"

"Yeah. And he didn't give up easily. At eighteen, Gabe knew exactly what he wanted in life, who he wanted to be, how many kids he wanted to have. He had our lives planned to the very last detail. So…I ran. And while I don't regret that decision, I'll always regret hurting him."

The interesting part is that we hadn't been seated for more than a few minutes when she asked me that question. I still don't know where she lives and she definitely doesn't know anything about me yet. I haven't even admitted that I don't remember much about last night. I don't know how to broach that subject without hurting her feelings. And hurting her is the last thing I want to do. I'd much rather tell her it was the best night of my life and that we'll be together forever.

The doctor and the art dealer. She doesn't even know I'm an art dealer and that I spend more time in hotel rooms than I do in my tiny New York apartment. She doesn't know that I don't have a cat or a dog or even a damn bird. She doesn't know that the only thing I'm capable of taking care of in this world is—me.

I have lots of acquaintances. Hell, I probably know at least one person in every country in this world. Well, maybe not all of Africa, but you know what I mean. I've been traveling my whole life, ever since I left Gabe and my family behind two weeks after high school graduation.

So, yeah. Lots of acquaintances and lovers. But right now, I'm suddenly petrified that she's going to ask me delving, personal questions about my life, my friends; the people I hang out with. The people who have my back and I have theirs. And I'm sure I could come up with a few names. And there are probably some who believe that I'm their friend. And I am, but not in the true sense of the word. What I'm saying is I probably wouldn't have their backs because I'm too busy having my own. And on top of that. I haven't seen my mother or my little sister in well over a year.

And none of this…not any of it…especially that last part…is something I ever want this smart, beautiful woman to know. So I need to do what I always do. Because it was indeed a fair question—and she wouldn't like the answer.

"Excuse me." I stand up and put my napkin on the bar. "I'm sorry. I need to go."

"Go? Go where?"

"It was great seeing you again." I pick up my purse and throw a few bills on the bar while trying not to look her in the eye. "Say hello to Gabe for me, would you?"

"Samantha." She reaches for me, but this time I don't let her touch me. I just give her a forced smile and then walk away.

Good God, what was I thinking? This was a train wreck from the start. Yes, I will most definitely, at some point, now or later, break her heart. And although it's killing me to walk away from her—like, gut-wrenchingly painful—I'm glad she asked the question. If Juliet and Gabe and everyone else think so highly of her, she definitely deserves better than me.

Mark seemed perfect for me. I should find Mark and spend the night with him, just to prove my point, if for no other reason. Hotel bar, here I come.

It doesn't take Mark long to notice me. He leans on the bar and gives me a smile. "Don't tell me Rossi stood you up."

I look him up and down, letting him know I'm interested. "Does it matter?"

He smells freshly showered and his face is clean-shaven. He's definitely down. "I guess not." He waves to the bartender to make us both another drink. "That just doesn't seem like something she'd do, is all."

"And why is that? Is Dr. Rossi beyond reproach?"

Mark laughs. "Well, let's just say she's a much better person than I am."

Better than both of us. I touch his hand with one finger, making little circles around a knuckle. "We sound perfect for each other."

And that's about all it takes to get a man in bed. I still have to wonder what it took to get me in bed last night. Did Mia touch me like this? And why am I still thinking about her? I meet Mark's gaze, trying to focus all my efforts on him again. "What do you say we…"

"Yes," he says, before I can finish. "Your room or mine?"

He's slowly leaning in, our mouths getting close enough that I can tell he drinks whiskey. Yes. This is who I am. Just as I'm leaning in for a taste, he quickly stands up straight, looking over my shoulder. "Hey, Mia. Join us?"

Oh God. I don't even want to turn around. I take a rather large gulp of my martini and hope she walks away.

"Um…" Mark is staring at her. "I think maybe I should…" He looks at me again and then heads for the door.

I turn and watch him chase after Mia, wrapping his arm around her shoulder when he reaches her. Fuck. I focus on my drink again and wave my hand for another.

❖

Is it too late to apologize? Why do I even care? And why do I look like I'm about to cry? I shake out my shoulders and stand a little taller as I look at myself in the bathroom mirror. Mark didn't come back and I couldn't stomach anyone else's advances. Two drinks and I was outta there.

No doubt Gabe will eventually hear about this and hate me even more than he already does, along with my mother and, of course, Juliet. *Samantha screwed up again.* It might as well be the family motto.

I pace in my room for a few minutes, trying to decide if I should call her room and try to explain myself. But how would I explain away my actions as those of a reasonable, rational person? And do I even want another chance, just so I can screw it up again? No, maybe it's better left where it is; a bad decision on both our parts. Something to get past and move beyond. Something to forget—as fast as humanly possible.

I decide to look at my calendar. I'm pretty sure I'll be in Europe next week and a million miles away from my current situation. A million miles away from her. I dig through my purse but can't find my phone. "Shit." Did I leave it somewhere? I sit on the bed and pick up the hotel phone, dial my number, and hope I'll hear my cell phone ringing in the room somewhere. Instead, I hear a woman's voice.

"You left it on the bar. And Juliet's been texting. She wants to know how our date went. I told her it was over before it even started and I have no idea why."

"Mia…"

"Juliet hasn't replied, but I'm sure she'll tell me to run like hell while I still have the chance."

"Mia…"

"And what the *hell* were you doing with Mark? I mean, my God, Samantha…were you trying to hook up with him?"

Okay, I don't need this shit. "Look…"

"No! We had something last night. I know I wasn't the only one who felt it. *You* felt it too…even if you don't want to admit it. But that's why you changed your flight, isn't it?"

"I can't honestly say what I felt last night since I don't remember most of it. But Juliet's right. She's always been right about me." Shit. Here come the tears. What the fuck is going on with me? I just need to get my phone back and move on.

"Wait. You don't remember last night? We talked for hours. And then we…you don't remember any of it?"

I clear my throat and try to sound detached. "I remember waking up naked in a stranger's room. And while that's not so unusual for me, waking up with a woman was."

"So, I was just a big, awful mistake and it suddenly hit you right before dinner?"

"Look, you don't know me and you don't really want to. I'm not a good…" I cover my mouth for a second, trying to hide my emotions. "You don't want this. Trust me."

Long silence.

"Can I get my phone back, please?"

"I'll leave it at the front desk."

Before I can even say thank you, she ends the call.

And I guess that's that.

CHAPTER FOUR

Europe felt lonely. I met with four dealers, bought five paintings for my clients in New York, dined in several very fancy restaurants with some very wealthy people, bought an expensive bottle of wine for my collection, and I ignored the advances of one of the most handsome men I've ever met.

And it felt lonely.

Whatever happened that night with Mia has changed me. I barely even know the woman, but she's always on my mind. I kept wishing she were there with me, sharing every moment, inspecting magnificent works of art, taking in the sights and sounds of the Old World, dining in amazing restaurants, holding my hand as we walked the narrow cobblestone streets, sharing a glass of wine that she no doubt would've loved, based on the bottle she ordered for us at the bar.

In Europe, I realized what an incredible life I have, and while it was always enough to experience it alone before, that is no longer the case. Thanks to her.

When I got my phone back that night at the hotel in Chicago, I could see that Juliet had indeed texted several times but Mia hadn't actually replied to her. So I did, simply telling Juliet that I'd blown it. I knew she'd buy that without any further explanation, and she did. I haven't talked to her since, even though I really could use a sympathetic ear right now. Unfortunately, I think the supportive Juliet would be replaced with the Juliet I've always known and resented. She'd tell me to grow up or something just as insulting.

In a few minutes, I'm meeting with the man who brought me into the art world and taught me everything I know. We had an affair when I was in my early twenties. He was much older than me and married. I'm not proud of it, but that affair ended up giving me a great career, and honestly, I don't know who I would be if I hadn't met him—what other paths I might have taken.

He's one of my clients now, since he considers himself too old to search the world for pieces on his own anymore. He just wants to enjoy them. He doesn't want to have to find them.

"François."

"My lovely Samantha." François takes both of my hands and kisses them, then leans in and kisses my cheeks. He's worn the same cologne for as long as I've known him. It always brings back such wonderful memories of the time we shared together in the south of France. He was an incredible lover. From him, I learned what I enjoy most in bed, and he was always more than happy to oblige.

Time has taken its toll, but he's still a tall, handsome, distinguished-looking man. If anyone in this world *were* to have my back, I guess it would be François. Although I've never put that theory to the test.

"You missed my seventy-fifth birthday," he tells me, his voice a little less powerful than it used to be. "You know how Simone loves to celebrate my age. It makes me wonder if the celebration was a little *too* real."

We share a laugh and I give him a hug. "You know how much Simone loves you, François. And I'm sorry I missed it."

Simone, François's third wife, is younger than me, believe it or not. I think they've been married for about five years. The crazy part is that she really does seem to be madly in love with him. Then again, maybe it's not so crazy. Maybe you meet your person and nothing else matters. Not age, not gender. God, there I go thinking about Mia again.

"What did you find for me? Something that will make me jump for joy, I hope."

It takes a lot to make François jump for joy, but I think I've found something he'll love. It's a painting that's been in the same family for over two hundred years. I heard through an acquaintance of mine in Eastern Europe that the family wasn't interested in a public sale, but that they would consider private offers. I flew out of Paris the next day and made a preliminary offer on François's behalf, knowing he'd buy it, given the chance.

I pull out my tablet and show him a photo. "It's in Slovenia. A private sale, but I'll need to make the call today."

His smile tells me he's very pleased. "Let me show Simone." He gives me a wink, letting me know Simone's opinion doesn't really matter. We both know it's a done deal as he walks out of his study. He gets a few steps out and turns back, giving me a concerned look. "Is everything all right, Sam?"

Jesus. Can he see right through me? Is the loneliness and confusion etched across my face? "Can we talk for a few minutes?" I almost want to take the words back, but I purse my lips together, waiting for his reaction. He nods and then walks away. I guess I'm going to see if he really is my only true friend.

❖

"So, you're confused. You had sex with a woman and now you're confused."

We're sitting in François's garden at a small round table, drinking white wine. The garden smells like lavender and looks like France, even though we're not even ten miles from New York City.

"I really don't know what I am," I tell him. "Confused, I guess would be accurate...since I don't remember what took place with her that night. I just know that it left a hole inside me. And I've never had holes."

François holds up his glass in agreement. "No, you haven't." He takes a sip and then studies me for a moment. "For as long as I've known you—which is a rather long time—you've never given your heart to anyone, including me, hard as I tried to earn it. So, why now? And why this woman?"

"I didn't say I'd given her my heart." Is he insane?

"Maybe not. But there's a piece of you missing now. A piece this woman seems to own."

He might as well have punched me in the gut the way the air just left my body. He reaches across the table and pushes my jaw back up so my lips meet. And here come the tears again.

"My sweet, precious girl." He has mirth in his eyes and I want to tell him this isn't even close to being funny. "Don't fight it. Give in to the gift God has given you. It's not every day you find the one." He smiles and wipes a tear from my cheek. "It's never the person you think it should be. Love isn't perfect, but it's so worth it."

I quickly wipe my tears away and take a deep breath. I don't like crying in front of people. I don't like feeling this vulnerable. François moves his chair next to me and wraps his arms around me. "And don't try to make sense of these tears, either. Just let them go."

I rest my head on his shoulder and do as he says. I let them go. And I don't try to make sense of them, either.

❖

Mia had put her number in my phone. I found it while I was in Europe but I couldn't bring myself to do anything about it. François changed that. I've been texting her for the last few weeks, slowly telling her the story of me. The first text was an apology. I simply said, *I'm sorry.*

I don't know why I panicked that night. I was so ready to have dinner with her and talk to her, find out who she is, how she lives her life. But I ran before I could even ask the most mundane of questions. Where do you live? Where did you get your education? Do you enjoy fine art? Why did you want to sleep with me? Those questions and a thousand more are what I think about every night before I fall asleep.

I didn't get a reply to that first text, but that didn't stop me. Every few days I've sent her a picture of where I was or something interesting I'd seen that day. I even sent her a picture of an incredible meal I had in San Francisco. It wasn't lost on me that I'd eaten it alone and imagined her sitting across from me through the entire meal.

It's like Instagram and she's my only follower, sans the likes and comments. She still hasn't replied to anything I've sent. So, I'm left wondering if I should stop altogether or send a selfie. I have to giggle because now I'm picturing myself sending her a daily *naked* selfie. I wonder how many I would have to send before I got a reply. Maybe one good shot of my tits would do the trick. I'm not ruling it out.

I'm on the rooftop of my building trying to get the perfect shot before sundown, and no, I'm not naked, but I do suck at taking selfies. Luckily, a man from my building joins me on the patio. I've seen him a few times. He's a hot, thirty-something Wall Street guy. "Hey," I greet him, noticing he's got a raw steak and two beers sitting on a plate. "Dinner?"

He laughs. "Yeah, I guess it is. I was hoping to fire up the barbecue if there's any propane left."

"Would you mind…before you do that…taking a quick photo of me? I'm losing the sun."

"Sure!" He takes my phone and offers his hand. "I'm Adam, by the way."

"Hi, Adam. Samantha." God, this man has a gorgeous smile. I've never seen such straight, white teeth before in my life. He must have had a good orthodontist in his youth.

"Okay, so where do you want to be?"

I walk over to the edge of the building and lean on the wall. "How about here? Is the light still good?"

"Um…I don't think the light matters. You'd be gorgeous in any light."

I smile and motion with my hand for him to hurry. "Sweet talker."

He takes a few shots and then hands me my phone. "See what you think."

I scroll through them and choose one. "Looks great, thanks." I quickly type *New York City—right now* and send it off to her, the woman who rules my world now.

Adam stuffs his hands in his pockets and bounces on his toes. "Hey, do you want to have a beer with me while the steak cooks?"

I shrug my shoulders. "Sure. Why not?"

He's sweet and funny and I can tell he'd love to ask me out. My beer is long gone and even though it took him a while to get the barbecue going, his steak will be ready soon. I wouldn't mind going out with him. I'm pretty sure there's a six-pack under that T-shirt, and he smells nice. Has nice feet, too. He's wearing flip-flops, even though it's not summer anymore, so I noticed.

I should give him a sign. Maybe linger on his eyes for a minute, so he can ask and I can accept and he can go home and eat his steak before it overcooks. But something stops me. Something always stops me these days.

I don't know why I expected a reply from Mia this time. It's not as if she'd look at that picture and like what she saw. I'm just a bitch to her. A very bad, horrible mistake. The girl who broke Gabe's heart and the woman who hasn't changed much. I look at Adam and force a smile. "Thanks for taking the pics." I stand up to walk away.

"Who are they for? I noticed you sent one immediately."

"Just a girl. Thanks again." I give him a little wave and make my way to the door. Halfway there, I stop abruptly when my phone dings. It's her. My God, it's really her. And then I panic for a second. What if she tells me to just stop and leave her alone? Can I? Will I be able to put her behind me? I'll have no choice, I guess. I hit the button and bring up her message.

New York is beautiful.

I quickly look at the photo again. Yeah, you can see a few buildings behind me, but the shot is mostly—me. She thinks I'm beautiful! I'm so excited, I jump up and down a few times and yes, I even let out a little squeal.

"She's a lucky girl...whoever she is."

I turn back around, embarrassed that Adam just witnessed my reaction. I try to regain my composure. "Thanks again, Adam." I casually walk the rest of the way to the door and then I run down the stairs and sprint to my apartment.

CHAPTER FIVE

I wait a few minutes so I can catch my breath. I have one chance to make this right. One chance to tell the truth and hope she'll see me again.

Once I feel fairly calm, I pick up my phone and call her. Three rings and I'm worried she won't pick up. I can leave a message. A quick message. Just say hi and then…

"Hi."

I almost choke when I hear her voice. "Uh…hi. Hey. Um…hi."

Long silence.

"I, um…" *Get control of yourself and just talk to her.* "I was a jerk. And I panicked…because you asked if I would break your heart…and um…no one has ever asked me that before, so I panicked. And I'm so sorry."

Another long silence.

"But the thing is…whatever you did to me that night… whatever spell you cast on me…it worked. And so you either need to break the spell, or you need to give me another chance…because I can't live like this." I hear a little giggle. "This isn't funny. I'm dead serious."

"Okay."

"Okay? Okay, what?"

"Okay, I'll break the spell. Just say my name over and over again while you turn around in a circle three times and the spell will be broken."

"That's not funny."

"But you said you wanted me to break the spell."

"No. I said I wanted you to give me another chance." This time, the silence is hers to break. I'll wait.

"The question still stands."

I take a deep breath. "I don't like making promises I can't keep, but I have no plans to break your heart. I just want a chance to get to know you. We never really talked."

"We did talk. For hours."

Her voice is gentle. She doesn't seem mad at me still. That's such a relief. But I have to be honest now. I have to come clean. "I don't remember that. I don't remember touching you. I don't remember kissing you, and it's making me crazy, because my mind may not remember it, but something inside me remembers it…and can't let it go."

Again, I wait for a reply. I know it's a shocking statement. I half expect her to hang up on me and send a text in all caps telling me to FUCK OFF!

"I remember everything. Every second of it. Would you like to know what you told me?"

I stop pacing and sit down. "God, yes. Tell me how I ended up in bed with you."

"Oh, that." She giggles and I practically swoon, because talking to her like this is what I've spent weeks hoping for. "Well, I was shamelessly flirting with you. And had I known you were that drunk, I never would've…" She pauses for a second. "Did I…take advantage of you, Sam? Maybe I'm the one who needs to apologize."

I'm not going to let her take the blame for this. I've never been a fall-down drunk. I can hold my liquor pretty well and it wasn't her job to monitor me anyway. And besides, I'm sober now. And I want this. Wherever it may go, I want it. "No one has ever taken advantage of me. I've never been so drunk I couldn't walk away. So please don't worry about that."

Another long pause. "Okay. So, anyway…"

"Wait, Mia." I feel like I need to slow this conversation down. Maybe talk about lighter things first. Ease into the heavy stuff. "Have I told you I'm an art dealer? I travel a lot."

"Yes, I know."

"And I don't go home enough. I don't see my family enough." So much for keeping it light, dumbass.

"I know that too. And you feel bad about it, but being at home doesn't feel good to you, so you avoid it. I also know your favorite color used to be pink, but now it's blue, like the ocean. And you hate the little mole on your shoulder. I kissed that mole several times. I think it's kind of cute just sitting there on top of your shoulder like a little friend."

I close my eyes and groan loudly, partly because I'm embarrassed about how much she knows and partly because I really fucking wish I could remember what that kiss felt like. She giggles at my groan and then continues. "You were in love once, with an older man. I think his name was François. But you walked away when you found out he was married. You still feel bad about that, even though you were really young when it happened. You apologized to his wife and she called you a little whore, among other things. They got divorced…"

"Okay, stop."

I've never admitted to anyone that I was in love with François. He had it wrong, what he said the last time I saw him. He *did* own my heart. It killed me when I found out he was married. I was so broken, I considered going back home. But I knew if I told my mother that I'd fallen in love with someone older than her, and a married man no less—well, let's just say there was no way I was going home.

"My family doesn't know about François," I gently tell her, hoping she'll understand that I don't ever want them to know about François.

"Samantha." Her voice is suddenly intense. "You gave me all of you that night. And you warned me. You told me that when the sun came up, you'd put your walls back up. And you did. And I accepted that. I let you walk away. So, why did you come back? Why did you call to me in the hotel that morning? And why did you want to take me to dinner?"

Because I need you? Because I don't fucking know how to

forget you? I don't say it out loud. Instead, I make a joke. "Oh, well, that's easy. The sex was so great, I wanted more."

Her silence tells me my joke fell flat. But then she says, almost whispering, "It was pretty great."

"What was that?" I heard her. I just want to hear it again. Maybe she'll elaborate and tell me I'm an awesome lay. I wonder if I had an actual orgasm.

"You came twice. Not that I was counting."

"Huh." I never come twice. I have to be pretty aggressive and bossy to even come once with a man. They need direction. A lot of direction.

"You don't remember?"

"God, I wish I did."

I hear a big sigh. "Me too. But maybe it's better this way."

She's frustrated. I can tell by the tone in her voice. I would be too if I were her. The problem is, I don't want her to end this call. I want to keep her on the line as long as possible. Even more than that, I want to see her again. "Do you think…" God, this is hard. I don't want her to say no. I need to see her if I'm ever going to figure out why she has this strange hold on me.

"I've loved your texts, all the photos you sent." She interrupts my unsuccessful attempt at trying to find the right way to ask her on another date.

"You have?" This surprises me since she never replied to a single one until tonight. "The next one was going to be a shot of my tits."

"Damn," she says with a giggle. "What do I have to do to get that one?"

"Hey, I was getting desperate. You hadn't replied to a single one."

She clears her throat. "I'm just going to hang up now and pretend this conversation never happened so you can send that pic."

"Don't. Please don't. I'll happily send you another selfie. Just don't hang up on me, okay?" I know I sound desperate, but I don't care. Desperate is exactly how I feel. I can't lose her again.

"Okay." She pauses for a second. "I won't hang up."

"Thank you," I breathe out.

"Anyway," she continues. "I was too busy with medical school to ever really travel. It's been nice seeing the places you go. I especially liked that photo of—"

"Let me take you there," I interrupt. "Wherever. Just let me…I don't know…start over."

Long silence again. I wait and wait and just when I'm about to beg, I hear her clear her throat. "I'm free this weekend."

I practically jump off my sofa. "I'm going to Spain on Friday. Do you have a passport? Where do you live? I'll get you on a flight."

"Yes, I have a passport. And I'm working at a research facility in Atlanta right now…and no, I can't go to Spain with you."

Okay, maybe Spain was a stretch. Coffee somewhere near her home would be more appropriate. "What do you research?"

"Cancer. It took my favorite person in the world. My grandmother."

"Mine too. My dad died of cancer when I was fourteen."

"I'm sorry. That must've been rough."

I'm somewhat surprised she doesn't already know since I apparently bared my entire soul to her that night. "So, in my drunken state, I didn't cry about losing my dad, the only friend I had in my family?"

"No. That never came up."

"Well, I'm glad you're working on cures or medicines or whatever it is you do. Thank you for that." I don't like to think about the long months we spent watching my dad waste away to nothing. He was my hero, and I prefer to remember him in his prime. He was a good father. A good man. And now I want to talk about something else before I become a blubbering idiot. "I'll delay my trip to Spain. How about coffee Saturday morning?"

"I need to say something first."

"Okay." I'm hoping she's going to pivot and that we don't have to dwell on the sad stuff. Maybe one day I'll tell her about my dad, but not today. One thing I've learned is that this girl enjoys long pauses. I patiently wait for her to work through her thoughts. I have to smile because it's these kinds of things—like the fact that she's a deep thinker—that I desperately want to know about her.

"I don't sleep around," she finally blurts out, and I breathe a sigh of relief. Not because she doesn't sleep around, but because she pivoted. "And what happened between us was as big a surprise to me as it was to you. And the next morning, I just kind of told myself it was God making one of my childhood dreams come true."

We both giggle at that.

"But it was more than that," she continues. "I knew it the second you called my name that morning after breakfast. And even though it feels really intense, this thing between us…we don't have to fear it because we became friends before we slept together. I know you don't remember it, but we did. I told you a lot of things, too. Things I don't usually talk about. And if friends are all we're ever meant to be, and the sex thing was just a fluke because you were drunk, I need you to understand that I'm fine with that. I'm the lesbian in the room, so I just want to be clear about that."

"So, I wasn't that good in bed?" I jokingly reply.

"Fuck," she says under her breath. "No, that's not it."

I lower my voice an octave. "Did you come too, Mia?"

Phone sex isn't what I had in mind when I called her, but I'll be damned if I'll let her take future sex off the table. I hear her sigh and swear under her breath again, so I continue my little seduction. "Answer the question."

"Yes," she whispers.

I pump my fist, congratulating myself. "And this childhood dream of yours. Tell me about it."

"Hmm…maybe one day."

"Not tonight?"

"Not tonight."

Damn. "Okay, just tell me one thing. Was it as good as you imagined it would be?"

She sighs. "Okay, fine. My childhood dream was me imagining that you'd choose me over my big brother and we'd get married and have two kids, and basically, you were my Princess Charming. Not exactly what you wanted to hear is it?"

I'm pretty sure all the blood just left my face.

"This is where you take off like a bat outta hell."

She said it matter-of-factly, like she knows me or something. "No...um...that's not...God." I sigh in frustration. It was going so well, my little seduction.

She's laughing at me now. "I was like, twelve, Samantha, and you were my brother's beautiful girlfriend who I used to stare at when you weren't looking and one day, you did look at me and you smiled at me...and I was too shy to talk to you, but I never forgot that smile and how it made me feel. And then, there it was again, in a bar in Chicago. And I was no longer too shy to talk to you. But I can assure you that the very adult things we did to each other that night weren't even on my radar when I was twelve."

We listen to each other breathe for a minute, me wishing I would've given her more than just a smile when we were young. I wish I would've talked to little twelve-year-old Mia. I'm sure she would've blown my socks off with her smarts and her wit, even at that age.

"It's my fault you can't remember anything," she quietly states. "We were having so much fun talking, I didn't want the night to end. I'm the one who kept ordering drinks."

"And then what happened?" I lie on my bed, hoping I can keep her talking all night.

"When the bar closed, I invited you to my room. Shameless, I know."

"And I accepted this invitation?"

"You did. God, you did. And I..."

I roll onto my stomach. I have a feeling this conversation is about to get very intimate. "Tell me."

"I asked if it would be okay if I kissed you...because those lips were just so...and I'd had too much to drink, which made me not care if you were straight. I just had to know what it would feel like to kiss you."

I cover my eyes with my hand and shake my head. "This is so unfair." I hate that I can't remember any of it.

"You were incredible," she says. "Amazing. Unforgettable."

Butterflies.

"You were unforgettable too. My brain can't remember, but my…" *Heart? Soul? Pussy?* "Something inside me…remembers."

"Come to Atlanta."

I breathe the biggest sigh of relief I think I've ever breathed. I also say a silent prayer, thanking God for giving me something I know I don't deserve. "I'm already on my way."

CHAPTER SIX

Getting out of a taxi in front of a very busy coffee shop in downtown Atlanta is making me even more nervous than I was five minutes ago. Everyone sitting at little tables on the outdoor patio has turned to see who will exit the cab. It's human nature to people watch, but I don't need all those eyes on me right now. I run my card through the little machine and look around for her. Is she sitting at a table inside or am I early? And why am I such a fucking bundle of nerves? I look at my watch and then the cab door opens.

"Hi." She leans down so we're eye to eye. God, that smile. "Give me your bag."

I give her my weekender bag and thank the driver. I step out onto the curb and she's standing there with her arms open, waiting for me to fall into them. Which I do. And it feels like heaven.

My arms are wrapped around her waist and our cheeks are touching and there's that familiar scent again. I realize we've been much more intimate than this, but this feels extremely intimate to me. I turn my head slightly and gently kiss her cheek. "Hi."

"I missed you," she whispers in my ear.

She's not letting go and neither am I. It makes me wonder how long two women can stand on a curb hugging like this before someone catcalls. I pull back slightly so I can see her face but still hold on tightly around her waist. I don't want her going anywhere just yet. She touches my cheeks with her fingers and then rests her forehead on mine. I feel her sigh, almost as if the tension of the last several weeks was something I didn't experience alone and she just released it all for both of us.

I loosen my grip on her and take a step back, looking her up and down. She's dressed very simply in black skinny jeans and a low-cut white T-shirt, but God, she's gorgeous. "You're so…" Fucking gorgeous!

Before I can finish, she picks up my bag, slings it over her shoulder, and takes my hand. "This place is too crowded." I realize at that moment that I would follow her just about anywhere. "I should've known the coffee shop would be busy on a Saturday morning."

"Anywhere is fine. I just want to be with you."

She turns and gives me that megawatt smile. "I know just the place."

She throws my bag in the back of a cute little sports car and we slowly walk hand in hand up the sidewalk. I have no idea where we're going and I couldn't care less. I just want to *feel* every second I have with her. Because who knows what the future holds?

She's soft. Her fingers are slender and interlock perfectly with mine. For some reason, this walking hand in hand business doesn't feel new to me. It feels right and perfect and like we were always meant to be these people. And the silence isn't awkward. I think we're both taking in the significance of this moment.

"Are you freaking out right now?" She glances at me, looking concerned.

If she only knew everything that was going on inside me. I'm making plans and none of them include running away from this. I release her hand and move in closer, wrapping my arm around her waist. She rests hers on my shoulder. We fit like a glove. "Not in a bad way," I tell her. "Just surprised at how right you feel."

That causes another smile. I think my new goal in life will be to make her smile at least a thousand times a day.

"Tell me how you like your coffee." We walk up to a street vendor parked outside a city park. I give her a look. "Trust me, it's good coffee," she says with a smile.

That's not what the look was for. I just told her how right she feels and she changed the subject. I want to repeat myself but I'm pretty sure she heard. "Cream, no sugar. And one of those bagels. I didn't eat breakfast."

We find an empty bench in the park to enjoy our late breakfast. She was right, this is much better than trying to talk in a noisy coffee shop. But as we sit in veritable silence, only commenting on what's going on around us—the cute baby in the stroller that just went by and the dog that just broke away from its owner and is chasing a squirrel—it suddenly feels heavy again. Heavy and fragile. Like, one wrong word and it'll all fall apart on us. So, before it breaks, I try to fix it.

"Mia..." She looks at me and I get lost in those deep brown eyes again. There's so much going on behind them. So much I desperately want to know. "I don't know what this is." I can't hold her intense gaze. I have to look down and focus on my coffee if I'm going to get this out. "I didn't come all this way just for a booty call, that much I know." God, that sounded stupid. "I'm not even gay." Aaand that was even worse. I quickly stand up, needing some space.

"Don't do this, Sam." I turn around and meet her gaze. "Don't make this like Chicago where you tear us apart before we can even..." She looks away and shakes her head.

I stand right in front of her until she looks up at me. "That's what I'm trying to avoid. I don't want that to happen, either. So if you know what this is...please explain it to me."

"Obviously, this is all too much for you. The gay thing."

"I didn't say it was too much. It's just confusing, the way I feel about you. I mean, it's crazy, right?"

She's staring at me. So, I stare back. "What would you think this was if I were a man?"

The truth is, I would think I was falling in love with Mia. But that's impossible since I barely know her. I turn away from her and fold my arms tightly around my body, not replying to her question. She stands up and rests her hands on my shoulders, and my eyes shutter closed at the touch. "The way you just walked down the street holding my hand makes me think you don't really care about labels," she says.

"You're right about that. I don't."

"And from everything you've told me, it seems you've always lived your life on your own terms." Her hands run down my arms and onto my hips. I can feel her body melding into my backside and it's making me feel tingly inside. "So, if you tell me that's what this is really all about, I'll respect that...but I think it's something else. I think that when we're this close, it scares you, how much you feel...and you want to examine it and break it down into little pieces and have it all figured out within minutes." She wraps her arms around my waist and rests her chin on my shoulder. I can feel her warm breath on me. God, it feels good. "But that's not what I want. Because honestly, that's what I do all day. I literally put everything under a microscope."

I look down at the hands that are resting on my tummy and gently cover them with my own. "What do you want, Mia?"

"I want you to believe that whatever is supposed to happen between us—will. And I want you to relax. Because there's no pressure. Remember what I said on the phone? We can just be friends if that's what you want."

I'm such a mess. I'm all tied up in knots, even though she feels so amazing. I don't want to hurt her again. I don't want to run from this. I want to be with her and get to know her and maybe—who knows?—make love with her. I just can't have that be the ultimate goal. It scares me too much. And it pisses me off that I'm afraid of it. I've never been afraid of sex. But the two of us together, breathing the same air, feels like nothing I've ever experienced. Maybe with François, but that was so long ago and I was so young, it's hard to compare.

I take a deep breath and turn around in her arms, resting my hands on her biceps. She's so soft and smooth. And that scent of hers—it brings something to the surface for me. I can almost taste the memory, if that makes any sense. "I'm sorry I'm so frustrating. I don't mean to run hot and cold. I just..."

"It's okay." She brushes a strand of hair away from my face. "I don't understand it all, either. But I know I want you in my life... however I can have you. I don't have a lot of friends. Mostly, just work buddies. How about you?"

I shake my head. "No. I travel a lot." I don't want to lie to her. "That's not why. I just...don't let people get that close to me, I guess."

She takes my hand and leads me back out of the park. "Let's go shopping like best friends do. I haven't been shopping in ages. I need new clothes. Work clothes, casual clothes..."

I'm listening to her tell me about all the clothes she needs and how she usually wears jeans under her lab coat and all I can do is smile, because she's taking our minds off of the heavy stuff but she's still holding my hand and gesturing with her other hand, and my fucking God, she's so pretty and sweet and funny and I really need to get my act together so I can kiss her.

I think she was exaggerating about her lack of clothing. She made it sound like she dresses like a total slob most of the time, but I find that very hard to believe after watching her shop. The girl has expensive taste and I can't wait to see what her closet really looks like. I have a feeling that clothes and shoes are where she spends most of her fun money.

And as we walk into yet another designer store, I'm almost positive it was all just a ruse to help take the pressure off me. She immediately finds what she wants and leads me to the chairs by the dressing room, dropping all the bags at my feet. "Stay here. I won't be long."

A minute later, I utter the word *"Whoa!"* rather loudly when she comes out in a sexy little black dress. And it wasn't a good whoa, more of a neutral whoa that leaves everyone wondering why you said it at all.

She stares at me for a second and then looks in the mirror. "I would need new heels, but what do you think?"

"Where are you going to wear that?" I ask because the neutral whoa wasn't quite bad enough.

She puts her hands on her hips and frowns as she looks at herself in the mirror. "Do you like it or not?"

"I…yeah, it's nice." I turn my attention to a rack of blouses I don't even like and search for my size.

God, what is wrong with me? I should tell her to buy it because her tits look incredible and what that dress is doing to her ass should be illegal in most states. Why the hell can't I say the words? I think, if I'm really honest with myself, it's because I'm feeling rather jealous of whoever she's buying that dress for.

"We have reservations at a very fancy restaurant tonight and I have nothing to wear, so, could you maybe help me out here?"

My eyes shutter closed at my own stupidity. I gently hang the ugly blouse back on the rack and turn to her.

"This dress is for you," she says. "So, you know…I'd like to know what you really think. Is it too much? I can find something less…"

All I can do is stare at her because now that I've really looked at her in that dress, it leaves me speechless. And the fact that she'll wear it for me tonight both thrills me and scares me shitless.

"Never mind." And she's back in the dressing room before I can say another word.

I go over to the dressing room door and knock. "I love the dress, Mia. But I didn't bring anything that fancy. So, maybe we could find something for me to try on, too?" She doesn't answer, so I try a different tactic. "Don't take that dress off. I'm going to find the perfect heels. What size do you wear?"

"Eight."

"Okay. Promise you won't take it off? I'll be right back." I don't wait for an answer. I run to the shoe department and scan the shelves. She needs something high but not too high. It's ridiculous what women try to walk around in these days. There. The perfect heel for a little black dress. Black satin with a three-inch heel. I grab the sales associate. "A size eight, please."

It feels like it takes forever for her to find it but when she finally does, I run back to the dressing room and shove the box over the top of the door. "Here you go."

Mia takes the box but doesn't say anything.

"Do you like them?"

"Yeah, these will work. Thank you."

"Aren't you going to come out and let me see?"

"No. You'll see them tonight."

"Ugghh." I plop down in a chair next to a man who's been patiently waiting for his wife.

"Nice save, but let me give you a piece of advice," he says, leaning in and almost whispering. "Don't ever hesitate. When she walks out of that dressing room, even a second of hesitation means she looks terrible and fat and any other number of things her mind will conjure up in that split second. Just be firm and whistle if you like it. And if you hate it, say so immediately, but in nicer terms, like 'you look so good in red. Do they have it in red?'" He winks at me. "And your girl looked smokin' hot in that dress. Just sayin'."

He was watching us the whole time? I'm just staring at him with my mouth hanging open because I have no idea what to say. Next thing I know, his wife walks out of the dressing room and he whistles. "Gorgeous, honey." She gives him a swoony look and then goes back in. "See?" he says. "I've been doing this a long time. Going on fourteen years."

"You ready?" I look up and see Mia standing there with her dress and shoes in hand. "We'll find something for you in the next store."

I stand up and glance back at the man. He gives me another wink. It's like I'm in the gay twilight zone where everyone knows Mia is my girlfriend. Everyone except me. I give her a quick nod and a smile. "Yeah, let's go."

I felt something when she came out of that dressing room. But it wasn't a good feeling. It was a mixture of *holy fuck, that dress was made for you* and *holy fuck, I'm jealous of whoever you'll be wearing it for*. And then she said she would be wearing it for me.

And my brain couldn't catch up. Because a part of me still doesn't want to accept that this is happening.

Talk about a mind fuck.

And then that asshole mansplaining to me about how to treat a woman. I fucking know how to treat a woman because I am one. I've worn dresses like that before. For only one reason, and we all know what that reason was. So, is that what's happening tonight? Mia is hoping to get laid? Oh, for fuck's sake. If truth be told, I'd like to get laid tonight, too.

So, why am I so scared?

She doesn't take my hand this time as we walk to the next store. Why doesn't she take my hand, I wonder? Bags. She's carrying bags, dummy. I rest my hand on her lower back and glance at her. She gives me a little smile but I can tell it's somewhat forced. I open the door for her and let her walk in first. "Thank you," she says. I can tell by the tone in her voice I've blown it again. Fuck. Me.

She sits in a chair by the fitting rooms and pulls out her phone, seeming completely uninterested in picking out a dress for me. That's fine. I'll find one myself. *And* the shoes. I think that as hard as she was trying to convince me we could be just friends, her true feelings came out when she put on that dress. She wants dinner tonight to be a date. And why wouldn't it be?

I have several options for said date in my hand, along with a few summer sundresses and bikinis and bathing suit covers, because why not? As long as I'm here, I might as well pick up a few things I'll need in the next few months. Winter is on its way, after all, and I don't do winter in New York, if at all possible.

"Going somewhere warm?"

I can't believe she noticed since she's trying so hard not to care. I shrug my shoulders and hang the items in the dressing room. "Christmas in the Caribbean sounds nice."

"You don't spend Christmas back home with your family?"

Not in years, but I don't tell her that. "Not usually. Do you?"

"If I can swing it. Definitely this year. Janey's due right before Christmas."

"Janey?" I lean against the doorframe and fold my arms, wanting to hear more.

"Gabe's wife. It's their fourth. They thought they were done, but surprise! And it's a boy. Gabe is over the moon. I mean, he loves his girls, but he always wanted a little football player."

"You and Janey are close?"

"Yeah. She's great for him. Gabe and I...we had a lot of expectations placed on us as kids. My grandparents were immigrants and my parents never let us forget the sacrifices they made to come to this country. They expected us to grab the American dream with both hands, you know? And because of that, sometimes we forget—me, mostly, but Gabe too—we forget that living the American dream isn't just about making our parents proud, it's also about our own happiness."

"You both work too hard. Is that what you're saying?"

"I'm saying Janey keeps Gabe balanced. And I'm grateful to her for that."

"And who keeps you balanced?"

She drops her phone back in her purse. "Enough about me. Let's see those bikinis...I mean, dresses."

I narrow my eyes at her. "It's not like you haven't already seen my body."

"You're right. Sorry."

I was just teasing, but she took me seriously. It seems we're both confused about how to treat one another. We're both somewhat fearful of what our words and actions will do to the precarious state of our relationship. I want to sit next to her and pull her into my arms and take away that look of fear on her face, but I'd be lying if I told her everything will be okay because honestly, I don't know if we can be just friends with all the sexual energy that exists between us. And I don't know if we can be more than that, either.

Sex is one thing. A relationship—a gay relationship—and it suddenly hits me that it's not the sex I'm afraid of. Not at all. It's the longing I see in her eyes for something bigger than that. My knees want to buckle, so I quickly shut the dressing room door and sit on the bench. She takes a phone call and as I hear her voice trail off as she walks away, I will myself to not run away again. I came here because I couldn't stop thinking about her. She's in my soul now. A part of my life I can't just put behind me. I take a deep breath and pull my shirt over my head. It's time to try on a red dress.

CHAPTER SEVEN

We're pulling into the garage at her apartment building. For some reason, I didn't expect she'd live downtown. I assumed she was more of a suburban girl, since we grew up in a small town in Ohio, out where there's plenty of room to roam.

"I've only been here a few months, so don't judge my lack of home décor."

"I'm not here to judge." I give her a reassuring smile.

"I know. I'm not sure why I said that."

It's the art dealer thing. People automatically assume I have a critical eye when it comes to just about everything. It's true that I notice when artwork is hung too high or in a place that's not well suited for its size, but I try really hard to not be a snob. I'd prefer to give a gentle suggestion and educate people rather than judge them. I've never had it go unappreciated and we usually end up moving the artwork together, be it a few inches or to another room entirely.

It's a nice apartment Mia lives in. She's right about the lack of décor. In fact, I don't see a single piece of artwork on her walls. The furniture is nice mid-century modern and there are a few small, framed photos on the sofa table. I drop my shopping bags and head straight for those.

"Oh my God, they're so sweet." A photo of Gabe and his little family is the first one I pick up. He has three beautiful girls and his wife is a dark-haired beauty. I can't believe how far we've both come since high school. So much life we've lived away from each other. I also can't believe that I'm getting emotional again. I never had reason to cry until I met Mia. Now I can't seem to stop. I put the picture down and try to hold back the tears so she won't see. But she's right there, turning me around to face her. "I loved your brother," I quickly tell her. "He was a good man. I knew he'd do well in life."

"Why the tears?" She wipes one away and I take a step back.

"I don't know. I guess I just feel bad for hurting him the way I did."

"You're too hard on yourself. You were a kid."

I pick up my shopping bags and my overnight bag. I need a little bit of alone time to decompress. "Where am I staying?"

She points down the hall. "Guest room. First door on the left." I'm halfway down the hall when she calls my name. I turn back around.

"It never would've worked between you two, Sam. Gabe is a homebody. He's never even been on a plane. The biggest trip they've taken was to Disneyland, and they drove. Yes, he's a good man. The best of men, in my opinion. But he would've held you back. And that would've been a terrible thing to watch. Because…also just my opinion…but I think you're exactly who you were meant to be. I also think you're the most interesting, funny, smart, stunningly beautiful woman I've ever met."

How is it possible that she would know exactly what I needed to hear? Now it's my turn to give her something. "How long until we need to leave for dinner?"

She looks at her watch. "You have an hour."

"Perfect." I give her a smile and then open the guest bedroom door. It's time to get all gussied up for this woman.

❖

My hair isn't very long. It barely brushes my shoulders, but I manage to pull it back into my version of an updo. I have to say it makes my blond highlights look great. The gold hoops are a perfect complement to my tight, but not too short, dress. I don't belong in those dresses that barely cover a woman's ass. I'm almost forty, after all. This one hits me just above the knee, and I have to admit it looks pretty good.

I chose a red dress with matching strappy heels. I hope Mia likes red. I've always been told it's my best color. I've never been one for red lipstick, so I go with an almost nude lip gloss. I look at my phone and see that it's go time. I take one more look in the mirror and breathe in and out to calm my nerves. "It'll be fine. Whatever happens, it'll be fine," I tell myself. It has to be. I refuse to lose her again.

Mia's waiting for me in the living room. My God, she looks amazing. Her hair is curled into long ringlets. Her makeup is perfect. Her dress is absolutely stunning. And those heels are perfection. She is by far the hottest date I have ever had. "Look at you."

She covers her mouth with both hands and shakes her head. Then she opens her mouth, but nothing comes out. I think she's incapable of putting a sentence together. Mission accomplished. "My God," she whispers. "I don't stand a chance."

"You're the only one who stands a chance tonight." I run my hand down her arm and intertwine our fingers, noticing the pretty silver ring on her middle finger. She even has expensive taste in jewelry. "The only one." I say it again, knowing she might be remembering what I did to her in Chicago, when I left her and almost hooked up with her friend, Mark. I want us both to forget that happened. I give her hand a squeeze. "Shall we?"

❖

She wasn't kidding. It's a very fancy restaurant. I look into the dining room and notice a sommelier pouring wine for an older couple and my mouth starts to water. Mia takes my hand and leads me to our table. I'm used to getting a few double takes, but we're getting double and triple takes, most of the eyes ending up on our joined hands. The older couple takes an especially long look at us.

We're barely seated when the male half of the older couple comes up to our table. "Dr. Rossi. How nice to see you out and about." He's a distinguished-looking gentleman with a nice haircut and a thin mustache.

Mia quickly stands up and shakes the man's hand. "Dr. Roberts. It's good to see you, too. Is Betsy here?"

The man motions toward his table with his hand. "We were just finishing up. Otherwise, I'd have you join us."

"No, of course." Mia smiles and waves at the woman. Dr. Roberts glances at me and then back at Mia. "Sorry, Dr. Roberts, this is Samantha King. Samantha, this is my boss, Dr. Roberts."

I stay seated, offering him my hand and a smile. "Pleasure to meet you."

"The pleasure is all mine." He takes my hand and kisses it, which would've seemed very chivalrous except for the way he ogled my chest while he did it. "And please, call me Andrew."

I take my hand back and turn my attention to Mia, hoping he'll do the same, but his eyes stay on me. "Are you from Atlanta, Samantha?"

I start to answer, but Mia interrupts. "Samantha is from New York City, but we grew up in the same town. She's an art dealer."

Dr. Robert's eyebrows almost lift off his forehead. "An art dealer? Is that so? I'm a big collector." He puts up a hand. "Well, my wife would tell you it's only in my imagination that I'm a big collector, but it's definitely a passion of mine."

This guy can't stop looking at my chest. "What is your weakness, Dr. Roberts?" Besides tits.

"Early Westerns. I have a few small pieces, but I'm looking for something larger for my den. Maybe something Dixon-esque."

"I love Dixon's work. I'll keep my eye open for you." Over the years, I've learned that every art collector has one style or even one specific piece they'd pay almost any price for. It's my job to find that piece. I've made a very good living finding that piece.

"I'd appreciate that. Here, let me give you my number. Maybe we could meet sometime for lunch and chat about…art."

Dr. Roberts hands me his card. I politely take it. Normally, I would jump on the offer and think nothing of it. It wouldn't hurt to have another wealthy client, and I can tell this doctor likes to spend his money. Everything from his shoes to his cufflinks tells me that. But the way he's acting is making me uncomfortable. Not that he's different from any other man I know—it's just that he's doing it in front of Mia, which is how I would feel if he were acting this way in front of my boyfriend or husband. Holy shit!

"I'm only here for the weekend," I tell him. "But like I said, I'll keep an eye out for you and let you know if I come across anything."

I can tell he'd like to push the issue, but Mia stops him. "Good to see you, Dr. Roberts."

"Good to see you, Mia." He gives me another once-over. "Samantha…till we meet again."

We both watch him walk away. I don't know how Mia feels, but I feel like I want to wash my hand. He pulls his wife's chair out for her and she glances at me before she makes her way out of the restaurant. More of a leer than a glance.

"It's amazing what you learn about people outside the office," Mia says, pulling my attention back to her. "He's Mark's father. The guy you met in Chicago."

"Yes, I remember Mark." Unfortunately.

"I guess we all have the same taste in women." She stares at me for a few seconds and then picks up the menu. "Should I pick a wine for us?"

I reach across the table for her hand. "Mia."

She doesn't take my hand or even look at me. "That man has several medical patents that have made him a multimillionaire. He'd be a great client for you. Red or white?"

I pull my hand back and wait until she looks at me. "I'm sorry about what happened with Mark. I know he's a friend of yours."

"Not anymore."

"Mia…he didn't do anything wrong. He assumed you'd stood me up and I let him think that. And his dad…look at me." She reluctantly does. "His dad won't ever hear from me. Ever. Okay?" I rip his card in half and toss it on the table, so she knows I'm serious.

She huffs and then shakes her head. "I thought he was faithful to his wife. Mark loves his parents. He'd be devastated if he witnessed what I just witnessed."

"It wasn't that bad," I say, which gets me a glare. "Okay, it was...kind of obnoxious, but I don't want it to ruin your working relationship with him."

The waiter comes up to the table with a bottle of rather expensive champagne. "Courtesy of Dr. Roberts."

Mia rolls her eyes and I cover my mouth to hold back a giggle.

❖

Once she'd had a glass of champagne, Mia loosened up again. I definitely learned more about her over dinner. The most important thing I learned is that she loves her work, but she's tired and needs a vacation. Whether we end up being friends or lovers, I'm definitely planning that vacation.

I keep glancing at her while we wait for the valet. She doesn't look tired to me; she looks absolutely beautiful. I'm surprised Dr. Roberts hasn't tried to make a move on her. But then again, she's gay and everyone knows it.

"You're looking at me," she says with a sideways glance.

"Yeah. I can't help it."

She turns to me and almost knocks me over with that smile again. "Are you flirting with me?"

"All night long."

She takes a step closer. "I was going to take you to a nightclub, but I really don't want to have to fight for your attention all night."

A nightclub. That could mean dancing and holding and possibly kissing. I've been wanting to kiss her all night. "You won't have to fight for it."

Her eyes widen. "Oh, but I will. From the moment we walk in the door. Unless..." She narrows her eyes.

"Unless?"

"How would you feel about going to a gay bar?"

That's an interesting suggestion. I've never been to a gay bar before. I mean, I've been in bars with gay men, but they weren't exclusively gay bars. It could be fun. But I'd rather do something else. I'd rather...

"Well?" Her eyebrows lift while she waits for an answer. God, she's so cute.

"What if we go back to your place…get comfortable and turn on some music…drink some more wine and make out on the sofa instead?"

"Like we're in high school?" she says with a giggle.

"The wine will be better quality…but yeah…just like high school."

Her smile could light up the world. I think she likes the idea. "Yeah. Let's go."

❖

We've had two more glasses of wine and laughed about anything and everything. We're both feeling loose and happy, sitting on opposite sides of her sofa, playing footsie. Now is as good a time as any to ask the question I've been wondering about. "Does Gabe know about us?"

"No." She lowers her gaze.

"Why not?"

"How do I tell my brother I slept with his first love?"

She has a point. It's not something you just bring up in casual conversation. No, that would require a special phone call and it would still be awkward. "He was my first love, too. Also, my first time. Your brother took my virginity," I tell her with a wag of my eyebrows.

"Oh yeah? How was it?"

"As good as you might imagine it would be. It sucked. But we learned together."

She's studying me, now. "You really did love him, didn't you?"

"It was a young, naïve love. But yes, I loved him."

"What does that mean…young, naïve love?"

I ponder that for a moment. "I guess what I mean is I used to give my heart freely. Too freely. I broke hearts and others broke mine. I didn't think before I fell in love, is what I'm trying to say."

"And now?"

"Now…it's not part of the equation…usually." I look away, hoping she won't read my mind. It wasn't part of the equation until she showed up in my bed. Or, I guess it was her bed.

"That's not the woman I experienced that night. She wasn't closed off and aloof. She was right there with me, feeling everything I felt."

I have to take her word for it since I still don't remember much about our first time together. "I guess it was different with you."

She tilts her head. "How so?"

Good question. And one I don't have the answer for, so I put the focus back on her. "Tell me about your first love. Your first time."

She pushes air through her lips and sighs. "My mom walked in on my friend and me. We were sixteen. It didn't go over well."

"A girl?"

She nods. "There was a lot of drama. I worked my ass off to graduate high school early just so I could get out of the house. If it weren't for Gabe, I would probably be estranged from my parents, but he fought for me. And family is important to me, so I overlook what I can't change."

"And they're proud of you now?" They should be so proud of her. I'm not a parent, but surely, she's everything a parent would want their child to be.

"Being a doctor helps."

I can see sadness in her eyes and it makes my heart sink a little. "But it was rough for a while, trying to be true to yourself and also please them?"

"It sounds like you speak from experience." She's putting the focus back on me.

"I'm still fighting that battle. I don't, and never will, live the life my mother would've chosen for me. To her, there is only one way for a woman to live her life—the way my sister, Juliet, lives hers."

Mia sits up and crosses her legs underneath her. "Are you sure that's still true? Have you given your mom room to grow and change her opinions? Parents do that sometimes. The good ones, anyway."

I shake my head in disbelief. "I don't think her opinions have changed. They're pretty much set in stone. But honestly, I haven't had an authentic conversation with her in years. It just hasn't seemed worth it, you know? All the guilt trips about not settling down and giving her grandchildren."

She grabs my toes and grins. "I think you should go home with me for Christmas."

Is she crazy? "Absolutely not."

"Thanksgiving, then. Just a couple of days. One day, even. Just enough time to see Gabe again and meet his family and maybe, if it feels right, have that conversation with your mom."

I smirk at her. "You want to take me home to meet the family? Like someone would do if they were, oh, I don't know…dating someone?" Her shoulders droop. And now, she's nervously biting her thumbnail. "What's wrong?"

"I made a rule for myself a long time ago that I wouldn't date straight women."

"But apparently, you don't mind sleeping with them."

"No." She wags her finger at me. "That was an unusual circumstance."

"How unusual?" I suddenly want to know everything about her previous lovers.

"It broke all of my rules. I don't pick up women when I'm on a business trip. I don't sleep with…or date…straight women. I don't…"

I set my wine glass on the coffee table. "Yeah, me either." I'm done talking about this. So, we both have our doubts about what this is and what we're doing. That doesn't mean I can't crawl across this sofa.

"I guess we're both breaking all the rules for each other."

My lips are hovering over hers. "Let's break some more."

I've spent a lot of time thinking about how I would feel the first time her lips met mine again. I'm not disappointed. Her lips are soft and plump and as her tongue searches for mine, I decide to tease her a little and not give it to her. That doesn't last long. She grabs my head and delves her tongue into my mouth and it feels like fireworks going off inside my body.

I'm lost in the sensation of her tongue and teeth sucking and biting on my neck, just below my ear. I feel her hand work its way under my T-shirt and up my side to my breast. Her hand squeezes it firmly but not too firmly. It feels incredible, but I want more, so I sit up, and straddling her, I pull my T-shirt over my head.

"Fuck, you're beautiful," she tells me, her eyes darkening with lust.

Her hands are squeezing my thighs and her eyes are roaming over my body. They land on the zipper of my jeans. Yes, we've done this before and she can't wait to have more of me. God, that is such a turn-on.

I'm about to take my black bra off when she grabs my hands. "Let me do it." She slides her fingers under the straps and slowly pushes them down. The bra gets caught on my hardened nipples, causing them to bounce a little as she pulls it all the way down. The slight whimper that slips through her lips makes me smile. "You're exquisite," she whispers.

She sits up and wraps her arms around me, squeezing my ass and pulling my pussy closer to hers. The first flick of her tongue against my nipple causes my hips to jerk. I run my fingers through her hair and pull her against me, needing more pressure. Her fingernails dig into my back and her name falls from my mouth like a breathless prayer. She releases my nipple and looks up at me, expectantly. I cup her cheeks and gaze into those gorgeous brown eyes.

This isn't how it normally goes. I don't stop and look my lover in the eye. I don't try to memorize their face so I won't ever forget this feeling. And I certainly don't say things in my head like, *I'm yours. I can't live without you now. Please love me forever.*

I don't know why I said her name out loud. I'm feeling so many things right now, my heart and my pussy both feel like they want to burst. Grateful and turned on. That's how I feel. "Thank you for giving me another chance," I tell her with a smile. And then I stand up and hold out my hand to her. "I want to be in your bed."

CHAPTER EIGHT

I remember everything this time. Every beautiful sound that I elicited from that sexy mouth of hers. Every touch, every kiss. It's all there, stored nicely in my brain. I no longer have to wonder why I so desperately wanted more of this. Or why I yearned for something I couldn't even remember.

It's her.

She's everything I've wanted but couldn't quite find. Granted, I was looking in all the wrong places, but I found *her* in a bar, too. No, it's not how or why we met that's important, only that we finally did.

I snuggle in behind her and gently kiss her shoulder. I have to taste her sweet skin on my tongue again, so I suck a little bit, making a little red mark where her left arm meets her shoulder. I wrap my arm around her waist and snuggle in even closer, breathing in her scent. It's euphoric, this feeling, this desire to stay in bed and never let her go. I can't say I've ever experienced it with anyone else before. I would remember this feeling.

I seriously can't get close enough to her, no matter how hard I try. I want her to wake up so she can feel me wrapped around her, so she can wake up in my arms and feel safe and at home with me in her bed. I want her to want more of this. I want her to crave my skin and my body and my tongue the way I crave hers now.

She suddenly sits up and puts her feet on the floor. I'm shocked by the sudden movement, so much so that I push back from her to the edge of the bed. She slowly turns around and looks at me like she's never seen me before. "Did we…you know…" Her eyes search the room. "Was this a three-way?"

I lightly slap her shoulder. "You ruined a perfectly lovely moment."

She gets on her knees and kisses my tummy. "Oh, come on. It was funny."

She's working her way lower, but I pull her up and have her lie on top of me. I need to kiss those lips again. "You're beautiful in the morning," I tell her and then kiss her gently.

"No regrets?"

I feel like I should stop saying things in my head and actually say them out loud. "I think I kind of fell in love with you last night."

She lays her forehead on my chest, not saying anything. I run my fingers through her hair, hoping I didn't just blow it again. "Is it too soon to say things like that?"

She rolls off of me and shakes her head. "No. It was just unexpected."

"I left you speechless?" I lie on my side and rest my hand on her tummy, rubbing little circles around her belly button.

"Last night left me speechless. You, saying that to me…" She rolls on her side so we're face to face. "Do you really mean it, or are you saying it because the sex was great?"

"It *was* great," I say with a wag of my eyebrows. "But I said it because telling you that I love you wasn't something I could wait another second to do."

"We should date exclusively," she says with a serious look on her face. "I mean…would you…want to date me…exclusively?"

I roll on top of her. "What happened to no pressure? Just being friends if that's what I want?"

"Oh." She opens her legs and wraps them around me, digging her fingernails into my ass and grinding against me. "So, I guess now that you've had me again, and you remember it this time around, you're good to go back to men?"

I rise up on my arms and press my pussy against hers. "I am soooo not good to go."

I start to grind my hips and she opens her legs even further. "Fuck," she says as she closes her eyes. She pulls her knees higher, holding them with her hands, and I grind harder. I can't take it anymore. I have to taste her again, so I slide down her body and suck her clit into my mouth.

"Fuuuuck," she says as she bucks her hips. I wrap my arms around her legs and rest my hands on her stomach as I flick and suck, taking her higher and higher until she stills for a second and then comes completely undone. I let her catch her breath and then crawl back up and kiss her gently. "Yes, I want to date you exclusively. Which means you don't get to wear that little black dress for anyone but me."

She wraps her arms around me and I lie on her chest, listening to her breathing even out. "I love you, too."

I smile and kiss her chest and say things in my head again. Things like *I have a girlfriend. I'm Mia Rossi's girlfriend. And I'm so okay with that.*

❖

Mia Rossi is nothing like her brother. Granted, they're both good looking and have a great sense of humor, but Mia doesn't dictate everything the way Gabe did when we were young. He wanted to tell me who I was and how I should live my life, but I wouldn't let him. I wanted the freedom to find out who I was on my own.

I realized today that I don't really like who I've become. I'm distant and unyielding with my family. I use men for sex. And I basically do what I want, when I want. I'm self-indulgent. But Mia sees me differently. She says I'm interesting and honest and smart, even though she has about twelve more years of schooling under her belt than I do. She also says I'm loving and kind and tenderhearted and affectionate and a generous lover. I think that last one means she comes just as much as I do.

It's because of this that I *want* her to dictate the terms of our relationship. I want her to spell it out for me so I can follow the rules and live up to—no, exceed—her expectations. She brings out the best in me, and I love her even more for that.

The problem is she's being vague and almost nonchalant about how we're going to make this long-distance dating thing work. I know she has opinions and I know she cares a lot more than she's letting on. I'm just not sure how to tell her that I will do anything she wants—I'm just that whipped. I'll even go back home with her.

Wait, that's it! I quickly scroll ahead on my calendar. "So…for Thanksgiving, do you want to meet at the airport and then share a rental car and hotel together?"

She sets her coffee cup down and stares at me intently. "I usually stay with my parents."

"Oh." I tap my pen against my lips for a second. "Just the car, then?"

"You're really willing to go home for Thanksgiving?"

"Yes." I could elaborate on why, but I'll leave it at that.

"And we're really…you know…a couple?"

That makes me smile. "Yeah. If you're willing to date a straight—possibly more bi than straight girl."

"Just so we're clear…" She looks so serious. "You, Samantha King, would be going back to our hometown as my girlfriend. And anyone we see, run into, whatever…I can introduce you to them as my girlfriend?"

I giggle. "You make it sound like I would be a trophy of sorts."

"Of sorts," she says with an insincere shrug. "I mean, not that I would gloat about getting the hottest girl ever to walk the halls of James Madison High School."

I reach for her hand. "You're adorable. And yes, you can introduce me to everyone as your girlfriend."

She stands up and walks around the table, leaning down for a kiss. "Then my parents couldn't possibly expect us to share my little twin bed." She kisses me again. "Car, hotel, and the rest of our lives if I have anything to do with it."

"That's more like it," I whisper as she goes over to the coffee-maker.

"What was that?"

"I just said…I like it."

And I do like it. I know she wants this as much as I do. I also know she has fears, just like I did. My fears are gone now, but it seems like hers have magnified. I just need to prove to her that she has nothing to be afraid of.

Mia seems proud to be with me, but she has no idea how proud I am to be with her. To think that I would be anything but happy to go back to our little hometown as a couple is so absurd to me, it makes me want to laugh out loud.

I can't hide this. She's mine now, and I plan on keeping her.

On Sunday evening, we say our good-byes. And now I'm waiting for my flight to board. Normally, I would be sitting in one of the bars with a glass of wine until the very last minute. Now all I can do is pace and check my phone. I know she's driving home and can't text me, but I'm desperate for some connection. Something that will tell me she misses me too, even though it's only been half an hour.

What a mess I am.

And then a feeling washes over me that is so foreign to me I'm not even sure it's real. Call Juliet? Why would I want to call my little sister? I scroll for her number and hit the call button before I can stop myself.

"Samantha?"

"Hey." I ignore her surprised tone this time. I know I should call her more often.

"Hi. I'm just getting dinner on the table. Can I call you back in a few?"

"I'll be on a plane. This won't take long. I just…I wanted you to be the first to know, Jules."

"Oh, God. What's wrong?"

"Nothing's wrong."

"You sound sad."

"Only because I just left her."

"Who?"

It's going to feel so good to say this out loud. "Mia Rossi. We're dating. Exclusively...dating."

"Oh my God! Really?"

"Really."

"This is huge, Sam!"

"I know. But I don't want you to say anything yet. I think Mia should be the one to tell Gabe."

"No, you're right." She pauses for a second. "What about Mom?"

"Well, that's another thing I wanted to tell you. Mia and I are coming home for Thanksgiving."

"*Oh my God!* I love this woman already!"

"Yeah. I love her too." And I can't stop smiling about it.

"Okay. Your secret is safe until Thanksgiving. Have a safe trip home."

"Thanks, Jules. Love you."

"Love you too."

I end the call and see that there's a text waiting for me from the good doctor.

My apartment smells like you. Call me when you land.

P.S. Nine days is too long.

❖

It was the longest nine days of my life. I stayed in New York for most of it, trying to decide if I should give up my apartment and move to Atlanta. Mia makes me want to be a better person, and part of that is being less selfish. I'm the one who should move. It makes sense. My best contacts and also the best galleries are in New York, but that doesn't mean I have to live there.

When she rushed into my arms at the Cincinnati airport, the first words out of my mouth were "I can't do this long-distance thing." And then we held each other for the longest time. Long enough that her bag was the only one left on the carousel.

Now we're sitting in the local diner sharing a burger. Tomorrow we'll see our families, and Mia looks worried. "You have a lot on your mind," I casually state, hoping she'll share her thoughts with me.

"I just wonder if it's too soon to think everything I'm thinking. Like, for instance, did I rush this whole meeting the family thing?"

"We don't have to. I can spend tomorrow with my family and you can spend it with yours."

"Is that what you want?"

I reach across the table for her hand. "It would make for a terrible and very long Thanksgiving. So, no, that's not what I want."

"That's not what I want, either." She takes her hand away and looks out the window. "Can you believe we're back here together?"

She's trying to change the subject, but there's so much going on behind those brown eyes, I can't let it go. "Are you worried about what Gabe and your parents will think about us dating? Talk to me, honey."

She slowly shakes her head. "No. I'm worried that you'll pull away from me and try to slow things down if I tell you that I want to move to New York."

"Samantha King? Is that you? Well, I'll be damned."

I have no idea who this jovial woman standing at our table is. She's wearing a uniform, but she's not the woman who took our order.

"You don't remember me, do you?"

Those are the exact words that Mia said to me not too long ago. We ended up having hot, drunken sex, but I don't see that happening with— "I'm sorry…" I try to read her name tag, but it's half covered by a festive turkey made out of clay. Or maybe it's Play-Doh.

"It's okay. After four kids, I'm not the cheerleader I once was. How about you, Samantha? Any kids?"

I shake my head. "No." I look at Mia, hoping she'll save me, and she does.

"I remember you, Renee. You dated Gabe after high school. I'm Mia, his little sister."

My head jerks back to the woman. She narrows her eyes at Mia. "Right. I've heard of you. You're the…"

"Doctor. She's a doctor, Renee." I use her name forcefully, now that I know it.

"Riiiight," she says, dragging out the word. "Well, anyway, I think the whole cheerleading squad dated Gabe after high school, but none of us hometown girls could snag him, right, Sam?"

"Riiiight." The word comes just as slowly out of my mouth as it did hers.

"So, no kids. How about a husband?"

"Nope." I shake my head and give her a tight smile.

"Well, what the heck have you been doing all these years?" She doesn't wait for an answer. "Juliet sure found herself a gem. And those kids of hers! Every time your mom comes in, all she can talk about are her grandkids. Nathan is on the honor roll. Did you know that? My son, on the other hand…"

She only stops talking when another customer raises his hand, needing service. But it's too late. We now know that her son is a juvenile delinquent and her husband keeps getting laid off, which is why she has to work in the diner, but somehow, she still manages to consider herself more successful in life than either of us.

She didn't say that, of course. Not out loud. But she did manage to give me a sympathetic pat on my shoulder and tell me she was sorry I hadn't found someone to share my life with. She left out the part that I'm probably too old to have kids now, but I know she was thinking it.

Mia and I just stare at each other, both feeling a little shell-shocked. This is why I never come home. I don't fit this town's version of what a woman should do with her life. I never have. "Well, that was fun," I finally say.

"Did you happen to notice that once she found out who I was, she had nothing to say to me? She knows I'm gay. The whole town does. So, what could Renee Johnson possibly have to say to a gay woman? 'Hey, any kids yet? How about a wife? No? That's too bad.'"

"How about congratulations for becoming a doctor?"

Mia shakes her head in disgust. "Without a husband and kids, being a doctor equates with choosing a career over family. And even if I have kids one day, it'll be a woman I have them with, not a man. And then I'll be considered an inadequate parent. Worse than a single parent. I mean, how dare a gay person bring a child into this world to suffer under their deviant care?"

I haven't seen Mia this angry. So, I have to wonder. "Why do you come back here?"

She sighs deeply and stares out the window for a moment before she answers. "Because I love my family, and I'm not going to let this town's backward attitudes keep me from visiting them." She leans in and lowers her voice. "And before she so rudely interrupted us, I told you that I want to move to New York."

"Ah. Yes, you did." She's eyeing me closely, waiting for a reaction. Probably a negative one. "What about your job in Atlanta?"

"I only moved there so I could work with Dr. Roberts, but my respect for him has diminished since we saw him at dinner that night. I look at him now and all I see is a—" She stops herself, but I can imagine what she wanted to call him. "He's a married man, and the way he looked at you…"

She seems frustrated, but she still gives me her hand when I reach for it. "You're a good person, you know that?"

She runs her thumb back and forth over my hand. "I think about you all the time, and my work is suffering. I need to be closer to you."

"I want that, too. In fact, I've been considering moving to Atlanta, but if you want to come to New York…"

"I do. Atlanta isn't home to me." She glances at our hands and smiles. "I know it sounds silly, but I want to date you the way normal people do. Go out on the weekend and spend Sunday mornings together. I also want to travel with you and learn more about your job. I want…"

I squeeze her hand. "Do it. Move to New York. The sooner the better."

"Really?" she squeaks, her face lighting up in that way that makes me feel giddy inside, because I'm the reason.

"Really."

She throws money on the table, stands up, offers me her hand, pulls me to her and kisses me, right there in front of God and everyone. "I love you," she whispers in my ear. "And that was for Renee Johnson. Is she by any chance looking at us right now?"

I don't even have to look to know. "I think the whole diner saw that kiss."

"Good. Now, let's go to the hotel so I can *really* show you how I feel."

CHAPTER NINE

How she feels—is perfect in my arms. Perfect in my life.

I wasn't aware that a person could miss someone they didn't even know, but that's how it feels to me. It feels like my soul has longed for her, ached even, for the essence of her. I guess sometimes you don't know how cold you are until you feel the heat of the sun on your face, the warmth washing over you and filling your soul with light. Mia is my light.

I'm holding her again, waiting for her to wake up. I slide my hand up her belly and gently cup her breast. I love her body. It's so soft and smooth and smells heavenly. She takes my hand and pulls me even closer. "God, I love this," she says. "Can we stay like this all day?"

"No. We have food to eat and parents to meet, remember?"

"And brothers," she adds.

And then her phone beeps. She looks at the message and hands it to me. It's from Gabe.

Samantha King???? WTF!!!

"Renee Johnson has a big mouth," I reply with a frown.

She pulls the sheet up over her head. "I'm staying in bed today."

❖

Of course, we didn't stay in bed. The tradition in the Rossi family is to eat all day with extended family dropping in at any time. My family has Thanksgiving dinner at four p.m. sharp. So we opted to visit her family first and then show up at my sister's house at three thirty.

After seeing Gabe's message, we're both feeling a little worried about how things will go. "You didn't want to warn him before you brought me home?"

She takes the keys out of the ignition and pauses for a moment. "I probably should have. But it's not his call who I bring home." She pats my hand, assuring me everything will be fine. "Come on. It's time to meet the family."

When Gabe and I were dating, we didn't spend much time at his home. His parents were stricter than mine, so we mostly hung out at my place or his best friend Mitch's house. I don't ever remember meeting the twelve-year-old Mia, but that doesn't mean I didn't. I was definitely a selfish teenager wrapped up in her own world. But I do remember their parents. They didn't have much to say to me, but Gabe told me they approved of me and that's all that mattered to him.

I enter the house behind Mia, and the intense aroma of Italian cooking hits my nose. This is a meal I will definitely enjoy. "Mama?" Mia yells.

"You made it! Your father ran to the store for me, but he'll be right back. He can't wait to see his little girl!" Mrs. Rossi comes out from the kitchen and stops short when she sees me. "And who is this?" She's looking at me with questioning eyes, trying to figure out how she knows me.

Gabe walks into the living room and answers before Mia can. "Samantha King. You remember, Mama…we dated in high school."

Gabe's body is stiff and unwelcoming. He's not happy to see me, but I greet him with a nod. "Gabe."

He's a nice-looking middle-aged man. It's apparent he works out with the high school football team he coaches. His pecs and biceps are noticeable under his shirt. He looks good. Healthy. I can't say that he looks particularly happy, though, since he's scowling at me.

"Yes," Mrs. Rossi says. "I remember Samantha." She doesn't

look so happy now, either. And why would she be, since I broke her young son's heart?

Mia goes to hug her brother, but he shies away from her. "Really, Gabe?" she says to him. "Please don't ruin Thanksgiving." This is quickly going from bad to worse. I take a step backward toward the door.

Mrs. Rossi's eyes dart between her two children. "What's going on here?"

"Your daughter..." Gabe practically spits the words out. "Forgot to inform us that she was bringing a guest."

"I can go," I quickly tell them. "Really, Mia, I don't want to cause any trouble." I tug on her coat sleeve, but she ignores me.

"Is this a game for you?" Gabe stares me down like he would a criminal who had just entered his home. "Since when are you gay?"

"Gabe!" Mrs. Rossi and Mia shout in unison.

Fuck. Since when am I gay? Your sister made me gay, Gabe. Okay? She has special powers or something. Fuck if I know how it happened! Of course, I don't say any of that out loud. "Maybe we could talk in private?" My eyes are imploring him. "Please, Gabe."

"Help me get the grill ready. We're having steak." He turns on his heel and is out the door before I can follow him.

Mia reaches for my hand. "You don't have to do this."

"Yes, I think I do." I squeeze her hand, trying to reassure her. Mrs. Rossi is standing right there, frowning at me. "I'm sorry for the interruption," I tell her before I go out the sliding glass door. I'm relieved to see that the grill is on a cement pad about twenty feet from the house. I have no idea what I'll say to him or what unkind things he'll say back, but I'm glad the whole family won't be privy to our conversation.

Gabe is vigorously scraping the grill with a metal brush when I walk up to him. "You fuck me over and now you want to do the same thing with my sister."

It wasn't a question. He's already made up his mind. I look back to make sure the sliding glass door is closed before I answer. "We were kids, Gabe. Are you really going to hold what happened twenty years ago against me?"

"No!" He jabs the metal brush at me, coming within inches of my face. I flinch, but I don't back away. "Don't make it sound like we were nothing. I loved you! I wanted to marry you!"

"And I love your sister."

He steps closer so we're eye to eye and almost chest to chest. "You don't even know my sister," he growls out. "I know my sister," he adds, tapping on his chest. "And she would never willingly subject herself to this."

This—meaning me. As if I'm some sort of torture device. "Don't do this, Gabe. You're the one who's hurting Mia right now. Not me."

"I would *never* hurt her! *Ever!*" He chucks the metal brush at the grill, making a loud, clanging noise. I turn to see who's watching. I can make out bodies behind the glass door, but I can't tell who it is.

"Gabe…" I don't know what to say, what to tell him so he'll understand. "I was surprised too, that this happened, but it did. And I know you love your sister, but this isn't your decision. It's hers."

"What's her favorite color?" He's coming closer again, his face red with anger. "Her favorite junk food?" His breath smells like beer and it takes everything in me not to back away. "Her favorite candy bar? What was the toy she slept with as a child? What's her favorite band? *Tell me!*"

I turn my head because he's practically on top of me and yelling, but I don't back away. I don't want him to win. So I look him in the eye. "Yours is blue, mac n' cheese, Zero bars, and I don't remember you ever telling me what toy you slept with, but your favorite band is…was…No Doubt. I know yours and I'll learn hers."

I don't think that was the answer he expected. He takes a step back and shakes his head. I can't tell if he wants to laugh or cry, but his demeanor has totally changed. He no longer seems threatening. In fact, I'm pretty sure those are tears in his eyes.

"Pink," he says, his voice softer now. "Grilled cheese sandwiches. Almond Joy. A teddy bear named Henry, and the Beatles."

I have to smile. "I forgot about Henry."

"I never…" His emotions are overwhelming him now. He can barely talk and he's gasping for air. "I never forgot about you, Sam."

Oh, God. "Gabe." I don't want to hurt him again. I want to hold him and apologize until he doesn't hurt anymore. "I'm sorry. I was too young. I was selfish. But that doesn't mean I didn't love you. You were my first…everything."

He's on me before I can stop him. His arms are wrapped around me so tight I can barely move. He's crying and apologizing and telling me he never stopped loving me. It's obvious his anger has nothing to do with him wanting to protect his sister and everything to do with who we used to be. Who he wishes we still were. Shit.

I hesitate to return the hug. I'm not sure who's watching us and I don't really want to look, but I wrap my arms around his waist because I really do care about him. "It's okay, Gabe. You don't have to apologize."

Holding him like this doesn't feel familiar at all. He's definitely not the skinny boy I once knew. His back is strong now and he smells different. I'm trying to place the cologne because I've certainly smelled plenty of it in my day, but I don't recognize this one.

He turns slightly and breathes me in, his nose grazing my ear, and right as I feel his lips brush against my neck, the sliding glass door opens. Gabe pulls away and wipes his eyes and I don't dare look to see who it is, but he does. "Shit," he whispers and then turns away from the house and back toward the grill.

I look over, expecting to see Mia, but it's another woman standing there, looking very pregnant. She also looks like she wants to punch someone. Me, probably.

Mia says something to the woman who I assume is Gabe's wife and then stomps her way over to us. "Your wife is wondering why you seem to have a love/hate relationship with my girlfriend. We'll go now so you can explain yourself to her."

Gabe shoves his hands in his pockets and ignores his sister, keeping his eyes on me. Mia takes me by the arm and pulls me toward the side gate. I can't help but look back at Gabe as I'm being dragged away. I hope I didn't just ruin his life for the second time.

❖

We drove back to the hotel in dead silence and now we're sitting in the car in dead silence. I didn't appreciate being yanked away like that as if I was somehow the bad guy, but I don't want to start a fight. The situation was horrible for everyone. I don't really know where to go from here. We're supposed to be at my sister's house in two hours, but I don't think either of us can handle more drama right now.

"I know I was kind of abrupt," she finally says, keeping her eyes on the steering wheel. "But I had to get us out of there. When he grabbed you like that…"

"He didn't grab me. He hugged me." She looks at me, so I say it again. "He hugged me."

"Well, Janey came out of the bathroom and saw it all. And now I'm sure he's trying to explain to his wife why he's still in love with his high school sweetheart."

"No," I say, shaking my head so it won't be true.

"He yelled at you and then he hugged you. And not just hugged you—*intimately* hugged you. Those are some pretty strong emotions from someone you haven't seen in twenty years."

"He's just looking out for your best interests," I lamely tell her. We both know that's not what it was. And now she's glaring at me, telling me with her eyes she knows that's not what it was. I reach for her hand and she pulls it away, so I put mine up in defense. "This isn't my fault. I didn't do anything wrong here." I get out of the car and start walking. I feel terrible about the whole thing. Thanksgiving is ruined for her whole family, Gabe is in trouble with his wife, and apparently, I'm in trouble with Mia.

My gut reaction is to get as far away from this as possible. Go back to the airport and find a bar where I can forget that I slept with Gabe's sister and broke his heart all over again. Then fly out first thing tomorrow morning. The hotel bar will have to do for now. I find an empty stool and order a martini.

"I'll have what she's having." Mia sits on the stool next to me.

She waits until she's had a sip of her drink before she looks at me. "Won't hurt to take the edge off before we do this again."

"Yeah, about that. I'm not sure."

"You promised your sister you'd be there. Even if you don't want to take me, you should go."

"And leave you alone in a hotel room on Thanksgiving?" She chuckles and then takes another sip of her drink. "What?" I ask. "What's so funny?"

"You forget that I kind of know you now, and I'd bet twenty bucks you're looking for a way out of this."

"Only twenty? Sounds like you're not that confident."

I hear the confidence leave her body, along with the air. After the big sigh, she downs the rest of her drink, throws a bill on the bar and stands up. "Let me know what you decide to do."

I don't stop her. Instead, I wave at the bartender for another round. All I'm going to do right now is have another drink. After that, who knows?

Not even twenty minutes go by before another Rossi pulls up a stool next to me. "I'm glad I found you. I need to talk to my sister."

"Well, hello to you too, Gabe." I'm just tipsy enough to not give a damn about his needs.

"Can you tell me where she is?"

"I think if she wanted to talk to you, she'd find a way."

"Don't act like you know her, Samantha. She's *my* sister!"

"Oh, no." I shake my head. "We're not doing this again. You're not going to accuse me of…God knows what."

He looks around the bar, probably to see if anyone he knows is watching us. Then he turns his whole body toward me, leans in, and pushes my drink away. "Look at it from my point of view, Sam. Someone saw you kissing my sister last night and then you show up with her like it's no big deal. Like it's the most normal thing in the world. And I'm just supposed to accept it? I'm supposed to what… sit back and watch you ruin her life?"

I turn and look him in the eye. "You don't know me anymore. I haven't seen you since high school, so stop being so judgmental and give your sister a little credit."

"I know enough. I know you've never settled down. I know you have a new boyfriend every year. Juliet and your mom have stopped trying to keep up with whoever your latest conquest is."

Fucking Juliet and my dear mother. I see they're still commiserating with each other and, apparently, the whole town about my awful lifestyle. Fuck them. And fuck Gabe. He may think he still loves me, but the truth is, he's happy I've never found anyone to replace him. He's enjoying this little story he's telling. I reach for my drink. "Are you done?"

He puts his hand on mine, stopping me from taking another drink. "Why, Sam? Why is your life such a disaster? You had everything going for you. You were loved by everyone, you got good grades, you had me…"

Jesus fucking Christ. "A disaster? That's really what you think? Well, let me clarify a few things for you. I'm pretty sure I make more money than you, Gabe. I've seen most of the world. I've brokered deals on works of art worth millions of dollars and I have a rather large collection in storage that I could sell at any time, making me a millionaire. In fact, I could retire right now if I wanted to. But if thinking that I have nothing and that no one loves me helps you sleep at night, then by all fucking means, keep that thought."

I get up to leave, but he stops me, grabbing hold of my arm. "And you don't regret not having children? Where's your legacy? Who will bury you and speak at your funeral? Who will tell the story of your life to future generations? Who will remember you ever existed?"

I try to pull away, but he holds me there with both hands. "My sister deserves to leave her legacy, too. Her time is running out, so if you really love her, don't let her waste her childbearing years on someone who never wanted a child in the first place."

I don't have a clever comeback for that one.

"Samantha, she's a doctor. She could save millions of lives with her research. God gave her a gift, but he also gave her a burden. She's vulnerable. She's always been vulnerable. She sees a pretty girl and falls madly in love without thinking. Without considering the consequences. She's been hurt so many times and I can't watch it happen again. We both know who you are. You're a vagabond. You have no roots. No one can hold you down, and anyone that tries gets trampled under your feet as you run away. So, please…let her go."

It takes a moment for his words to sink in. Long enough for my throat to go dry and my heart to break. He slowly loosens the grip on my arms and I try like hell to fight back the tears. "She's in room 405."

He backs away and it takes everything in me to stay on my feet. I watch him walk away, knowing I should do the same.

CHAPTER TEN

I'm in a taxi headed back to the airport when I get a text from Juliet, asking me to call her if I'm alone.

I'm definitely alone.

Gabe went to the hotel room to convince Mia to dump me, and I, well, I left before she could. I have no doubt that was his plan. And whatever his motives—be it to save his sister from a world of hurt, or save himself from having to see us together—it doesn't really matter. The truth is, he has me doubting everything again.

I want to ignore Juliet's request, but I should tell her we won't be showing up for dinner. I owe her that much. I put the phone to my ear and squeeze my eyes shut. It was so nice being able to talk to her freely without hearing that judgmental tone in her voice. I guess those days are gone now. She'll blame all of this on me. And so will my mother. "Hey, it's me," I say, barely holding it together.

"Sam." I hear her take a deep, shaky breath. "Um…"

"What's wrong, Jules?"

"Janey, Gabe's wife, was just here looking for you…and her husband."

I can't fucking believe this. "Tell her he's with Mia at the hotel."

"Listen, Sam. Mom's pretty upset about it. Maybe it would be best if…"

"Yeah. No problem. I'm on my way back to the airport anyway."

"Janey said some horrible things about you. I told her to get the hell out of my house."

I squeeze my eyes shut again, trying to hold back the tears. This is just one more example of what a fuckup Helen King's eldest daughter is. "There was an incident…" I start to explain but really, why bother? Everyone has already made up their mind about whose fault this whole thing is. "It doesn't matter. Just tell Mom I'm sorry."

"I'll tell her. I can't really talk right now with everyone here."

"Yeah, okay." I quickly end the call before the tears start to fall.

❖

I barely caught the last flight out. They just closed the airplane doors and I have to send Mia some sort of message before we take off. I've typed at least twenty messages and then deleted them all. The only one that seems worth sending is this one:

It was never going to work.

I'm so sorry we hurt your family.

I wish you a good life.

It may be the cowardly way out, but eventually, one way or another, I would've hurt her even worse than I already have. There's no use trying to pretend otherwise. Sometimes the things people say about you are true. And sometimes the lies you choose to believe about yourself are just that. Lies.

❖

I turned my phone off after I sent the message and didn't bother to turn it back on once I landed. It seemed better not to know how much more pain I've caused. I've been hiding out in my apartment for two days, sleeping, crying, and barely eating. I can't talk to Mia or I'll lose my resolve. I have to be strong about this. I know it's for the best. She needs to find a nice drama-free 100 percent bona fide lesbian she can have a family with. She's never specifically stated that a family is what she wants, but how could it not be what she wants? Family is everything to her. Gabe is everything to her. His kids are everything to her.

It's for the best.

I keep repeating the mantra as I make myself some toast and coffee. I have to eat something, and toast is the only thing that sounds even remotely good.

When I was sick as a child, my mom always made dry toast that she would dip into a soft-boiled egg and hand-feed to me. Believe it or not, I was actually looking forward to seeing her again. I felt like with Mia by my side, I could show my mother that I've changed. I've become someone she could be proud of. I'd found a doctor who loved me. Surely that had to count for something. Surely it could erase all the years of disappointment, even if that doctor happens to be a woman.

Then again, maybe nothing could. And now it doesn't even matter because her daughter is an opportunist who has no shame. She'll even stoop so low as to sleep with a woman if it means getting something she wants. You'd thought you'd seen the bottom, but no. Samantha King could go lower.

So much lower.

The dry toast tastes nothing like my mother's did, so I toss it in the trash can and climb back into bed.

❖

On Monday morning, I have no choice but to turn on my phone. I can't avoid the world forever. I have two text messages and a missed phone call from Juliet, asking me to let her know that I'm okay.

And nothing from Mia. Not a phone call, not a text, not an email. Absolutely nothing. I had imagined at least twenty of each. I drop my phone and run to the toilet. It's nothing but dry heaves since I haven't been able to eat anything. Not even a reply to my text? I wipe my mouth with a tissue and crawl under the covers to cry a few million more tears.

❖

It was all a little too easy. Too easy for me to walk away and too easy for Mia to let me go. I wish I knew what that meant. Were we kidding ourselves? Were we really not in love? Did we wreak havoc on the Rossi family for little more than a sexual fling?

And then I remind myself that it wasn't easy at all for me to walk away. It was quite possibly the hardest thing I've ever done. And God knows I've never in my life cried over someone the way I have Mia.

I want her back. I don't care if I'm not the right person for her. I don't care if I'm keeping her from having the American dream. I don't care if she never sees her family again. I don't care if I'm not gay and will probably never be able to identify as such.

I want her back.

But she never called or texted or emailed. And that means she doesn't want *me* back.

And I can't blame her. I fucking broke up with her via text message. Go me.

❖

I haven't had a drink since I left Mia, I'm not even sure how many days ago, so I can't figure out why my head is pounding. And then I realize it's someone pounding on the door. I throw the covers off and crawl my sorry ass out of bed.

"*What!*" I yell, as I'm walking to the door in my robe.

"*Delivery!*" some guy yells back. I open the door and he slides my suitcase across the threshold. I stare at it blankly until he pushes his little signature pad at me. "Sign here."

I sign it and then close the door. Mia sent my suitcase back to me via FedEx? All I can do is stare at it as tears fill my eyes again. I open the coat closet door and shove the suitcase in with my foot, and then slam the door as hard as I can. Fuck my suitcase. And fuck her.

❖

I'm going to Puerto Rico for Christmas. I can't spend another day in this apartment. I'll die here if I do. I need sunshine and sandy beaches and a reason to start living again. I'm finalizing my plans when my phone rings. It's an Ohio number, but not one I recognize. I take the call but don't say anything. Whoever is calling can be the first to start this conversation.

"Samantha? Samantha, it's Gabe."

"What do you want, Gabe?"

"Mia's forgiveness."

"I can't help you with that. And how the hell did you get my number?"

"Juliet gave it to me. Not easily. I had to beg."

"I'm hanging up now."

"Wait! I talked to your mom. I apologized for the things Janey said to her...calling you a whore and a home-wrecker. She never should've done that."

In my mind, I can hear François's first wife saying those exact words to me. God, I was so young and stupid. I should've asked him if he was married. I should have found out on my own somehow. It just never crossed my mind that he would be. Apparently, I've never known what I was doing when it came to love, and I still don't.

"Tell your wife she had it right, Gabe. Tell her she didn't say anything my family didn't already know."

"Samantha..."

I end the call and block his number. Then I send a text to Juliet.

Please don't give my number to anyone else.

Her reply is almost immediate.

He was desperate. Mia won't talk to him. He was crying in my living room. What was I supposed to do?

This is insane. With me out of the picture, they should be busy repairing their relationship. Why won't Mia talk to him? Yes, he was an ass that day, but that was almost a month ago. Let it go, Mia. Be a family again!

Fuck it. I will not be held responsible for this shit for the rest of my life. I pick up my phone again and send a text to Mia.

Please forgive your brother. He misses you.

It takes a few agonizing minutes to get a reply.

I'm sure he'll be thrilled to know you care. Or maybe he already does. Funny how you were able to drop me like a hot potato the minute he showed up at the hotel.

"*What the fuck?*" I stare at my phone in shock. "*What the fuck are you insinuating?*"

Before I know it, I'm calling and yelling at her instead of my phone. "*Are you fucking insane? I have not seen or talked to your brother!*"

"Stop yelling at me! I'm at work!"

"*I don't fucking care where you are…how dare you insinuate… whatever the fuck it is you're insinuating!*"

"Hey, it got you on the phone, didn't it?"

I'm dumbfounded. If she wanted to talk to me, why didn't she just call? "What the hell are you talking about?"

"I was respecting your wishes. That doesn't mean I accept them or that I don't miss you every single hour of every day. It just means that I understand that I'm maybe not the right choice for you, given the circumstances and all the complexities and how vastly different your life would be, and I know I rushed things with saying I'd move to New York…so maybe…you know…respecting your choice to leave…and also not putting us both through the pain and humiliation of me begging you to be something you're not…"

"Stop talking," I tell her, waving my hand in the air. "Just stop with all the rationalizing and putting it under a fucking microscope. Just…" I drop the phone to my side for a second because I have to decide right now, right this second, what I really want. I put the phone back up to my ear. "If you want me, fight for me." I end the call before she can reply.

CHAPTER ELEVEN

I don't even know if I want Mia to fight for me. I mean, it would be nice to know that I meant something to her and that maybe she shed a tear or two for me, too. But is it worth it, to go through it all again? From day one, it's been an emotional roller coaster for me. I'm not sure I'm up for more, the way I feel right now.

I'm so lost in thought I almost jump out of my skin when the doorbell rings. I look through the peephole and see my mother standing there with flowers in her hand. My mother has never, not even once, come to my home. And it's been over twenty years since I moved out of *her* home.

I look down at myself. Nothing matches. My oversized tan sweater doesn't exactly go with my green bunny pajama bottoms or my fluffy purple socks. And my hair is pulled back in a messy ponytail. I look like hell and probably smell even worse. I open the door a few inches, leaving the chain locked in hopes I can convince her to stand out there while I can clean myself up a little. "Mom?"

"May I come in?"

"Why are you here?"

"Please don't make your mother stand out in this drafty hallway."

Shit. She's right. I unlock the door and open it wide for her.

"Where should I put these?"

She's holding a large vase of flowers. Did my mother bring me flowers? I can't imagine her ever splurging on such an extravagant, useless gift. "Just on the table over there."

"I signed for them in the elevator. The young man was thrilled he didn't have to bring them up twenty floors." She hands me the card and then opens her arms for a hug. "I'm sorry Thanksgiving didn't work out."

I let her hold me, even though I'm scared to death about what comes next. She lets go and I look at her for a moment. She's wearing nice dress pants and a thigh-length double-breasted wool coat. I've never seen her look so fancy. Normally, she's wearing mom jeans with a turtleneck and walking shoes. She's always kept her figure, but she's never shown it off well. "What are you doing here?" I hesitantly ask again, not sure I want to know the answer.

"Why don't you see who the flowers are from first?"

I pull my untrusting eyes away from her and open the card.

> *Samantha,*
> *I'm a fool.*
> *I should never follow my head when it comes to you.*
> *Only my heart.*
> *Love,*
> *Mia*

I try to swallow the large lump in my throat so I can speak. "They're from…Mia…um…Gabe's sister." I whisper that last part, trying to hold back the tears.

"I know who she is." My mom holds out her hand. "May I?"

I set the card in her palm and search her eyes for answers to why she's here. She smiles at me and puts her reading glasses on. Then she closes the card and gives it back to me. "Good," she says. "That whole family owes you an apology. Especially that Janey woman… barging into Juliet's house the way she did on Thanksgiving Day, and saying those horrible things about my daughter. I don't care how out of whack your hormones are from being pregnant, you don't say such things to another mother."

All I can do is stare at her in shock. I assumed she would've wholeheartedly agreed with everything Janey had to say. My mother was never one to get the entire story before she passed judgment. I was regularly grounded for things I could've easily explained away if she just would've given me five seconds of her time, but she always put her hand up, which meant stop talking or the grounding period doubled. Explaining yourself was never worth it.

"Can we sit and have some coffee? I just want to relax for a little while before dinner. You're taking me somewhere fancy that has nice wine and fish." She takes off her coat, and underneath it is more fancy clothes. She's wearing tan trousers with a navy-blue silk blouse and a thin gold belt. There's also a gold bracelet on her wrist. Who is this woman?

I pour her some coffee, make a dinner reservation, and quickly jump in the shower. I take Mia's card with me and set it on the bathroom sink so I'll have it there to look at while I get ready. As I'm drying off, I read it again.

Samantha,
I'm a fool.
I should never follow my head when it comes to you.
Only my heart.
Love,
Mia

I also had to stop following my head after I met her. I had to listen to my heart, because it was screaming at me, telling me it wanted her. Begging me to let it love her. A lot of good it did me.

My head is currently the one screaming, telling me to back out of this dinner with my mom. It's bound to get ugly. She'll make a scene and I'll want to crawl under the table and disappear. What was it Gabe said? Oh yeah. If I disappeared, who would even know I ever existed?

Sounds pretty good to me right now.

I set Mia's card on my dressing table and clasp my hands together while I stare at it for a few more minutes. "I miss you," I whisper. "I wish you were here right now. I need a buffer. I need you to tell my mom I'm not the horrible person she thinks I am."

My mother may not have wanted to hear it from Gabe's wife,

but I know she doesn't think very highly of me. I stop whispering and set the card face down on the table. I can't cry right now. I just did my makeup, and my mom is waiting for me. I kiss my finger and then touch the card. "Wish me luck."

My mom gets up from the kitchen table when I walk out of the bedroom. She stares at me long enough that I have to look down at myself. I chose a very conservative look for tonight; black leggings with tall leather boots and a red turtleneck sweater under a black blazer. "Is something wrong?" I ask.

"No." She shakes her head and smiles. "Now I understand Gabe's reaction when he saw you. I'd fall in love with you all over again, too."

"Mom…"

She puts up her hand. "Don't make me cry before dinner."

"I don't want you to cry, I just…I need to know why you're here."

"Because my daughter needs me."

I suck in air and then bite my lip to keep myself from crying. Can it really be true that she's here not to reprimand me, but to comfort and support me? I could definitely use a little of that right about now.

She picks up her coat and wraps her arm around me. "Let's go have a nice dinner, shall we?"

❖

It's been mostly small talk through dinner. Mom wanted to know all about my life as an art dealer, the places I've seen…things she's never shown much interest in until today. But now she's staring at me intently, so I know the conversation is about to turn serious.

"I was hard on you," she admits. "Especially after your father died. You were the oldest, and you were such a free spirit, I thought it was my job to tame you. That's the way I was raised and it was the only way I knew. But I see Juliet with her kids…the way she loves them and treats them like they have their own brains, their own opinions. And each child is different, so she adjusts how she deals with them." She shakes her head and sighs. "It's no surprise that you ran as far away from me as you could."

"Mom." I grab her hand and squeeze it, because she's right, she's always been hard on me, but she's still my mom, and right now, seeing her vulnerable like this, isn't easy for me. I'd rather she turn on the tough act and rip me a new one for never giving her grandchildren. That, I can handle.

"Let me say this and then you can tell me to go fly a kite if you want." She grabs her napkin and wipes a tear from her cheek. "I failed when you were young, but I'm still your mother. That will never change. Not even…" She pauses for a second, her bottom lip quivering. "Not even if you're gay."

Ah. It all makes sense now. I let go of her hand and she wipes away a few more tears.

"Juliet says she's a lovely woman. A doctor. And if we were to judge it by the size of that bouquet of roses she just sent, I'd say she loves you very much."

I pick up my spoon and stir my coffee. "The situation with Gabe complicated things. I kind of…broke up with her."

"The situation with Gabe is his to deal with, not yours."

I glance at her, because every word out of her mouth is a shocking new surprise. And then I lower my gaze again. "Family is very important to her. Gabe, her only sibling, is important to her. If he and I can't even be in the same room…"

"It's my understanding that she isn't speaking to Gabe right now. I think that speaks volumes about who and what is important to her." She shrugs her shoulders and picks up her coffee cup. "And besides, that just means I'll get more holiday time with the two of you."

I stare at her and shake my head in disbelief.

"I know. This isn't what you expected from me."

"What happened, Mom? When did you become so open-minded?"

"When I saw that town trying to rip apart the reputations of two good women. I can't go anywhere and not hear about how my daughter and that awful Rossi lesbian had the gall to kiss in public! And home-wreckers my ass! Gabe Rossi needs to get his shit together and grow up!" She throws her napkin on the table and leans back in her chair. "Okay, I've said my piece. Take it and do with it what you will."

All I can do is smile from ear to ear. It took my mom thinking that I'm gay for her to accept me as I am, but hey, I'll take it.

❖

I drop Mom off at her hotel with plans to have breakfast together tomorrow morning. She'd like me to show her some of the city, and with how well it went over dinner, I'm actually excited to spend some time with her. After that, I need to pack for my trip to Puerto Rico.

Now I'm relaxing in bed with a hot cup of tea. I took a photo of the flowers Mia sent. I want to send it to her along with a message.

You didn't waste any time. They're gorgeous.

I didn't have to wait long for a reply.

Don't want to waste another second. And I don't want a pic of the flowers, I want one of you.

I already sent one to you. On the roof in NYC. Remember?

I know. I look at it every day.

I pull up a photo I had the waiter take of my mom and me at dinner and send it.

My mom showed up today. Shocked the hell out of me.

You both look happy. And you're fucking gorgeous. God, I miss you.

I'm leaving town day after tomorrow, but maybe after the New Year we could meet somewhere and talk.

Your Christmas trip?

Yes. Puerto Rico.

I can't wait that long. That's why I'm getting on the first flight out in the morning.

And don't try to stop me.

I sit up in bed and stare at the message. And then I smile.
Breakfast is at ten. My place.

❖

My mom is thrilled that Mia will be here any minute. She
knows the whole story now, how we met and had sex. How I couldn't
remember a damn thing the next morning but knew I needed to see
her again. How confusing and complicated it all is. I didn't hold
anything back. If she's serious about accepting me, she'll listen
without judgment. And much to my surprise, she has.

"I've been miserable without her, Mom. I've never cried so
much in my life."

"You both gave up too easily. You let other people control your
destiny. That doesn't sound like my daughter. She lives her life on
her own terms. Always has."

"Is that your version of a pep talk?" I say it with a smile as
I'm dropping chocolate chips into the pancake batter. When we
were little, my mom made smiley faces with the chocolate chips.
It's funny how I can remember more of the things I loved about
her now. It's like the thick fog of resentment has been lifted and the
good memories have returned.

She nudges me out of the way so she can take over. "Think
past today and tomorrow. Think about next year and five years from
now; where you want to be and who you want to be with. If you
see yourself with her—happy, content, being a family—then make a
commitment. A real one. When it's right, it's right, and anyone who
says you should wait some predetermined amount of time has never
known that kind of love."

"Did you have that kind of love with Daddy?"

She stops what she's doing and wipes her hands on a dish towel.
She turns to me and holds my cheeks in her hands. "We knew the
minute we laid eyes on each other. We were forced by my father to
wait six months until we could get married, and it was pure agony.
You were conceived in the fifth month of that long wait, and if you
ever tell anyone…especially your sister…I'll…"

I pull her into a tight hug before she can finish. I can finally see my mother for the beautiful human she is. "I love you, Mom."

The doorbell rings and she winks at me. "I'll finish up breakfast."

I put my hand on the door handle and take a deep breath, telling myself to be brave. I open the door and move to the side so Mia can walk into the small hallway. Neither of us says anything. I take the carry-on bag from her hand and set it by the closet. Then I look at her. And in an effort to not break down crying right then and there, I open my arms. "Come here," I whisper.

I'd almost forgotten how right she feels in my arms. I hold her close and let my cheek rest against hers. "My mom is here," I whisper. She nods and I feel her hands slide up my lower back a little. They weren't on my ass, but they were close. I pull back so I can look at her again. I don't dare kiss those lips for fear I won't want to stop. Instead, I take her hand and kiss it before I lead her into the kitchen. "Mom, this is Dr. Mia Rossi." I don't let go of her hand. "Mia, please meet my mother, Helen King."

Mia offers her right hand, keeping hold of mine with her left. "It's a pleasure to meet you, Mrs. King."

Mom's eyes fall to our joined hands. She smiles. "The pleasure is all mine. Now, sit. We'll get to know each other over breakfast."

❖

Every time my mom thinks Mia isn't looking, she winks at me or nods emphatically or gives me some other sign that she approves of her. When she gives me two thumbs up from the kitchen, I roll my eyes at her and she giggles. Mia leans in and whispers, "You should listen to your mother. She's a smart woman."

After breakfast, Mom grabs her coat and puts it on. "I'm going to go now and give you two some time alone."

"What about the city?" I ask her. "Don't you want to see some sites before you leave?"

"Well, I'm hoping this won't be my only trip to New York, and besides, the hotel has a sign-up sheet for one of those bus tours that they do for old people and tourists. I can always hop on one of those today if the mood strikes."

"If you're sure."

"Please don't leave on account of me," Mia says, getting up from the table. "I'd be happy to tour the city with you and Samantha."

"My dear," Mom goes up to Mia and rests her hands on her arms, "not that you need it, but you have my permission to marry my daughter." Mom puts up her hand to shut me up. "Sam, let me finish." She takes Mia's hand in hers and reaches for mine as well, holding on to both of us. "Take it from someone who lost their one and only true love far too soon. Life is short. Too short. So, live now and ask each other for forgiveness at least once a week, because you'll need it." She kisses our hands and then hugs Mia and then me. "I love you, Samantha."

"I love you too, Mom. I'm sorry I haven't said it enough."

She winks at me again. "That's a good start." Then she motions with her head at Mia. "She's next."

I close the door and turn back around. Mia is right there waiting for me. "I'm sorry I gave up on us," I tell her, following my mother's orders.

"When you didn't answer my note…"

"Wait. What note?" There was a note? How did I miss that?

"The one I left in your suitcase."

Oh, my God. I open the closet door and it's still sitting where I put it the day it arrived, with the clear tape wrapped around it so no one would open it and the shipping label firmly attached. "I never opened it."

"Why not? Why would you not…"

"I don't know. I just…couldn't. I was so sad and angry I just threw it in there and never looked at it again."

Mia takes a few steps closer and we stare at the suitcase together. "You were sad?"

How can she ask such a thing? "Devastated," I whisper. Just thinking about it makes me want to cry again. "And when I turned my phone back on…" I have to take a deep breath. She looks at me and I shake my head. "You didn't even try. And I know I was the one who left, but you didn't even try."

She grabs the suitcase, yanking it out of the closet. "Get a knife."

I go to the kitchen, grab a sharp knife, and hand it to her. "This should work."

She cuts through the tape and unzips it, pushes back the flap, and looks up at me. "Read it."

I kneel down next to her and pick up the folded piece of hotel stationery that's sitting on top of my clothes.

Samantha,

I understand that this all seems a little overwhelming right now, but please don't give up on us.

I never should've put you in the position I did. Now that I've had the opportunity to know you and love you...I should've realized that to get over you would take years. And maybe nobody ever does. Maybe Gabe will always love you and so will François. Maybe after basking in the beauty that is you—no one is ever the same.

I know I won't be.

I'm forever changed by you. I see the world differently now. It's bigger and brighter and full of adventurous possibilities.

I've lived most of my life with my nose to the grindstone (my grandmother's favorite English metaphor) trying to make my parents proud and also, I've recently realized, trying to make up for the fact that I'm gay and will probably never be the daughter they'd hoped for.

You've lived your life in spite of your family and I've lived my life for mine.

I realized today that if I had to make a choice, I would choose you. Because you give me joy. And I need joy. I need life and you are life to me. You are everything to me.

And so, I'm begging you to please give us another

chance. It's your decision. It's your call. I won't force you.
Just know that I'm here, waiting for you.
  Love,
  Mia

I sit on the floor next to her, both of us leaning against the wall, me with the letter in hand and both of us wiping our tears away.

"I would've found this tonight when I pack for my trip." I turn and look at her, resting my hand on her thigh. "You'd really choose me over Gabe?"

"I already have." She covers my hand with hers. "I yelled at him. I even hit him. And then I kicked him out of the hotel room and went looking for you, but you were gone."

She closes her eyes and starts to cry. I wrap my arm around her and rest my cheek against her head. "I'm so sorry." I say it over and over again, just like my mother told me to. I hold her even tighter as she starts to sob. I've been crying for weeks, but I get the feeling this is the first time she's let it all go.

CHAPTER TWELVE

I got us out of the house for lunch. I knew if we stayed in my apartment, we'd eventually fall into bed, and that's not what we need. Not first, anyway.

What we need, is communication—and lots of it.

In New York, it's not easy to find a quiet place to eat and talk. All the restaurants are small, with the tables packed tightly next to each other. In my time living here, I've been present for several confessions of adultery and too many breakups to count. And by "present" I mean having the unlucky pleasure of being seated next to those people.

That's why I chose a place that has old-fashioned high-backed booths for our lunch today. We can talk freely here. Mia didn't eat much at breakfast, so I decide to keep the conversation light until she's eaten most of her soup.

She clung to me on our walk to the restaurant, her arm wrapped firmly around my waist. And it wasn't just casually walking arm in arm, she literally didn't want to let go of me.

I'd built it up in my mind over the last three weeks, her side of this. She never called or texted because she knew in her heart it was better this way. She didn't need me tearing her family apart. She didn't want to risk something happening between Gabe and me if we were around each other again. And also, I'd imagined that she wasn't hurting at all. Oh, how wrong I was.

She sets her spoon on the plate and wipes her mouth with a napkin. I decide it's now or never, so I take a deep breath and dive right in. "I know there are a lot of things I need to work on." I look for a reaction before I continue. She seems so fragile right now. It's almost as if now that she's allowed herself to feel the pain of what happened, she's feeling all of it—all at once. "I haven't been in a real relationship in a while."

"I know. It's been a while for me, too."

She had told me about her last relationship and how badly it ended four years ago. They were close to being engaged and then one day her girlfriend came home and told her she'd fallen in love with someone else. Mia said she hadn't dated much since.

The thing is, I never told her about my last serious relationship. Yes, she knows about François, but that was in my twenties. In my thirties, which technically I'm still in, I did something horrible. And that's why I haven't told her about it.

"I need to tell you something."

She shakes her head. "No, you don't. I know what I want, and nothing you tell me will change it."

"What if it would? What if it's bad enough…that you would?"

She studies me for a moment and then says, "Tell me."

"I had an abortion."

I expected some sort of reaction from her, and maybe she's purposely not trying to react. I can't really tell, so I keep going. "I didn't tell him. The father, I didn't tell him I was pregnant."

Her eyes search mine for a few seconds. "I'm sorry. That must've been difficult."

I nod and look away. I can't hold her stare. "His name was Mike. He wanted to get married. I couldn't. I didn't love him enough to marry him and have his child. I couldn't just hand over my life to him like that." I look at her again. "I know that makes me a terrible person."

"No, it doesn't. I mean, if you were in a serious relationship you probably should've told him, but the decision was ultimately yours."

"I don't think he would see it that way."

She's studying me again. I focus on a chip in the Formica table, making it a little bigger with my fingernail.

"Okay, look," she says. "If I could actually get you pregnant, I wouldn't see it that way either. I would want the child we created together whether it was planned or unplanned. And I'd probably talk until I was blue in the face, trying to get you to keep it and marry me."

"And you'd hate me if I never gave you that option. Just like Mike would hate me if he knew. Hell, he hates me anyway. You'll end up hating me too. You might as well save yourself the trouble."

It's the truth, isn't it? She hit the nail on the head. I'm selfish. Always have been. Always will be. I manage to get my fingernail far enough under the chipped Formica to send a nice-sized piece flying across the table. Mia picks it up and tosses it on her plate. "What the hell is going on here? Are you trying to sabotage us again? Prove yourself unworthy of my love? Because I have to say, Sam, it's getting kind of old."

I furrow my brow in confusion. "What are you talking about?"

She leans in, resting her elbows on the table. "If you want me, fight for me. Those were your words. And here I am, fighting for you, but you don't want a fight. You want a battle."

"I don't even know what that means."

"It means you want to keep fighting me until I'm battle weary. Until I have so little strength left that I have to give in and say, yes, you're right, Samantha…you are unworthy of my love. And then you win and Gabe wins and that fucking town wins because every one of you was right all along. This"—she wags her finger between us—"was never going to work."

"Mia…"

"No, I think this is a good idea, actually. Let's go down the list of reasons why I'm unworthy of *you*." She thinks about it for a second, tapping her finger against her chin. "I'm not a tall, dark, handsome, wealthy man. In fact, I'm not any kind of a man and you're straight, so that's a pretty big one. Also, after my last relationship ended in a blaze of glory, I had to see a therapist. I guess you could say I was somewhat unstable at that point. I can't guarantee it won't happen again, so that seems pretty big. Did I mention I'm a woman?" she says. "Yes? Well, let me say it again…"

I can't take any more of this, so I slide out of the booth.

"Oh! We have a runner! How far will you get this time, Sam, before you realize that there's no escaping this? Because believe me, when you didn't reply to my note, I wanted to forget you. I wanted to completely wipe you from my existence. Just scrub my brain and my heart clean. In fact, I begged God to help me forget. But it didn't work. Nothing worked. I'm just stuck with this gaping hole in my heart, now. But go ahead, Sam. Run like hell and see how far you get!"

Not even the high-backed booths could've blocked that out from our lunch neighbors. I notice the woman in the next booth staring at me, wondering what my next move will be. I don't want to give her the satisfaction of knowing, so I lean down with my hands on the table. "Well, that was a nice speech, but I was only going to the restroom."

I don't know if that's true or not. Maybe I *was* headed out the door, but after she said what she said, I wasn't about to leave. I splash some water on my cheeks and then make the mistake of looking at myself in the mirror. I could say that I never think about my unborn child, but that would be a lie. I don't judge anyone who has to make the heart-wrenching decision to have an abortion, but for some reason, I've never been able to forgive myself.

I wasn't trying to prove myself unworthy by telling Mia. I just wanted her to know the whole truth, which seems silly now. The abortion weighs heavy on my mind sometimes, but that doesn't mean it has to weigh heavy on hers. I'm such a moron sometimes.

I grab a paper towel and blot my face, keeping my eyes focused on my cheeks. If I look myself in the eye again… Don't. You'll cry if you do. Shit.

Five minutes later, I manage to pull myself together enough to go back out into the restaurant. The table is empty, money sitting on top of the bill. I walk outside and look both ways. Mia is leaning up against the wall of the next building. She sees me and then starts walking the other direction. I catch up to her at the crosswalk.

"Maybe if we both agree." She keeps her eyes on the crossing signal. "We could shake on it, even…and then maybe the universe will free us of this absurd connection."

I guess she's made up her mind. The light turns green so I start walking, not really caring if she follows me or not.

"Samantha."

I don't answer her. I just keep walking until we're across the street and then I stop and turn around, offering her my hand to shake. "You say the words."

She looks down at my hand and hesitates, but then she takes it. "We agree to let each other go so we can get on with our lives and live in peace." She looks up and our eyes meet. "Agreed?" she asks with a shaky voice.

"Agreed." I give her hand a firm shake and then let go.

I tuck my hands in my coat pockets and walk next to her, keeping a good foot between us. I'm so pissed off right now, I could scream. I could just fucking scream. This is such bullshit! Just shake on it and we're suddenly free of each other? If only it were that easy!

She must be relieved to have it all over with because she's certainly not trying to take it back. Maybe this is what she wanted all along. Maybe she came here so *she* could be the one to break up with me. Well, she's not getting off that easy. I take my hand out of my pocket and grab hers, holding it tightly.

We walk another block like that, holding hands and not saying a damn thing to each other. At the next crosswalk, I let go of her hand and wrap my arm around her shoulder. She glances at me and then quickly looks away, but I'm not letting go. She'll have to push me away if she doesn't want this much contact. When the light turns green, she wraps her arm around my waist.

Another block goes by, and as we wait for the next light to turn, she starts to cry. I pull her closer, wrap both hands around her shoulders, and kiss her head.

By the next block, I also have tears in my eyes, because we're almost home and I honestly don't know if we'll be saying good-bye for the last time.

She suddenly pulls away from me, so I tuck my hands back in my pockets and keep walking close to her. She takes a tissue from her coat pocket and wipes her nose, then presses her fist to her mouth. I can see her chest heaving. God, this hurts like hell.

She's gasping for air behind her fist, so I look up at the sky and ask a god I don't even believe in for help. I feel a snowflake land on my cheek. "It looks like we're going to get snow."

She nods her head, keeping her eyes on the sidewalk. "Yeah," she manages to whisper through her tears.

"Wanna get married?" I come to a dead stop, unable to believe what just came out of my mouth. I look up at the sky, wondering if that's how God answers prayers. Maybe he just throws things into your mouth, so you have to spit them out. I look at her and wait for an answer.

Her fist is no longer covering her mouth. Her cheeks are tear-stained and her eyes are glistening and the snow is starting to fall heavier now, sticking to her long, dark curls. If I had a dream girl, she would be it. A sad, confused beauty who's looking at me like I'm completely insane, and just when I can't look at her anymore and lower my gaze to the sidewalk, I hear her say, "Yes."

"Yes?" I have to repeat it, just to make sure I heard right.

She nods and smiles and I think I even heard a little giggle. "Yes," she says again.

I remove absolutely every inch of distance between us and touch her cheek, wiping a tear away. "I mean it. I'm not messing around here." She nods and I don't waste any time. "Okay. Come with me."

I hail a cab and tell him to take us to the nearest jewelry store. I'm in full fighting mode now. Fighting for us. Fighting for who we know we can be together if we can just block out all the noise and focus on why we *should* be together—not why we shouldn't.

She looks over at me and her eyes fall to my heaving chest. Yes, I feel like I could hyperventilate right now. I mean, this is freakin' huge, what we're about to do, and I'm the one who instigated it and I'll be damned if I'll let either of us go back on it. I put my hand on her knee and give it a squeeze. "It's okay," I reassure her, but really, I'm trying to calm myself down.

Luckily, it's a short cab ride and I'm grateful for the cold air hitting my lungs again. I grab her hand and I'm about to drag her into the jewelry store, but she stops me. "Wait."

"No. No waiting. We can't use our brains right now, only our hearts...and I love you, so just come with me," I beg.

She takes a tissue out of her pocket and dabs my forehead. "You're sweating. I just want you to take a minute and breathe, okay?"

God, she's gorgeous when she smiles and those dimples pop out. I can't help myself. I have to lean in and kiss the right one and then the left. "I love you."

She wraps her arms around me and it calms me right down. I melt into her again, just like I always do when she holds me. I don't miss the broad shoulders of a man. Her shoulders suit me just fine. And I love that we're the same height. I don't have to crank my neck up to kiss her. I love her scent, too. She's feminine in every way, from the sway of her lower back where my hands are currently resting, to her soft, plump lips that I'm about to kiss.

This will be my life now. A woman. A woman who turns me on like no man ever has. A woman who can boss me around if she wants, dominate me, tell me what she wants and I'll move heaven and earth to make sure she gets it. A woman. A wife.

Thank you, God.

"I'm ready if you are," she gently tells me.

I take her left hand and kiss her ring finger. "Let's do this."

❖

I had to make it official. Do it right, so to speak. And saying *wanna get married?* while standing in the middle of the sidewalk wasn't how I wanted Mia to remember me proposing to her. But, knowing her, that's probably the moment she'll cherish more than me taking her to the rooftop of my building and getting down on one knee right in the same spot where I took the selfie that changed our lives forever, but I did it anyway. And then we took another selfie, with her disgustingly large diamond solitaire sitting so pretty on her finger.

She wanted to get a ring for me, too, but I asked her to wait until we get married. I need this moment—where I'm the one who puts the ring on her finger. I'm not sure why. Maybe so I'll hold myself to it, knowing it was all me who made this happen and I cannot—will not—back out.

I can't imagine that happening now. I can't imagine I'll leave her side much at all. She's mine, now. Mia Rossi is my fiancée, and one day soon, she'll be my wife. The importance of that, the sheer magnitude of that statement, doesn't scare me at all anymore. The second I put that ring on her finger, my perspective completely changed. It was as if everything had switched places. My fear, my hesitations, my ability to run from her—it all seems so absurd now. And my commitment to her feels so solid, I can't imagine anything or anyone getting in our way. It's us now. Never just me. Always us.

My mom keeps taking Mia's hand, inspecting the ring and wagging her eyebrows at me. She's done it three times since we sat down for dinner. Yes, it's a big diamond, but I'm only getting married once. Besides, I think she's damn proud of me for following her advice.

It seems right that my mom is the first person to know since it was she who gave me the courage to jump in with both feet. I sent the selfie to her and she immediately called and yelled in my ear and cried over the phone. Then, she insisted on taking us to dinner. Her treat.

"So, what's the plan?" she asks.

Mia and I look at each other and both shrug our shoulders. "Not sure," Mia tells her. "We haven't had time to think about it."

"I have." They both look at me, my mother with her signature one eyebrow raise and Mia with both eyebrows in the air. I take her hand in mine. "How would you feel about going to Puerto Rico with me and getting married there?"

"I think that's perfect," my mother says, before Mia can say anything. "As much as I'd like to be there to see my daughter get married, there are family issues to consider." Her eyes go to Mia. "You want this to be the happiest day of your life, with no distractions."

"You're right," Mia says. "My parents will understand. And Gabe will do whatever it is he's going to do. In fact, I don't even care if he knows I'm getting married."

"Tell him," Mom urges. "Give him the chance to do the right thing. And if he doesn't, then it's his loss."

When did she get so wise? Maybe she always was and I just refused to listen. I reach across the table for her hand. "I love you, Mom."

"I love you too, honey. Be happy. Live your life well together. And come home every once in a while," she says with a wink.

❖

Mia doesn't want me in the room with her, so I'm pacing in the living room while she talks to Gabe. So far, there hasn't been any yelling, so that's a good thing. She's been in there so long I'm starting to worry that maybe he's successfully talking her out of it.

I stop dead in my tracks when I hear the door open. She tucks her phone into her back pocket and stands a few feet away. "Gabe gave me his blessing, and then my *actual* father gave me his blessing and my mother cried, but good tears. She's happy for me. And I gave my boss my verbal two weeks' notice, which starts after the New Year, and after I type up a written resignation, I'm all yours."

I try to act casual. "So, we're doing this? We're really doing this?"

She raises her eyebrows. "I hope so because I just spent…" She looks at her watch. "Like, an hour on the phone telling everyone I'm getting married."

Okay, now I can be the happy idiot. I run to her and grab her and kiss her and giggle in her ear and tell her how much I love her and then I slowly push her back toward the bedroom.

"What are you doing?"

"Taking you to bed."

"We should wait," she tells me, looking very serious.

I stop pushing and just hold her around her waist. "For what?"

"Our wedding night."

"Oh," I whisper. "Seriously?"

She's thinking about it, so I decide to lean in and kiss her neck and nibble on her ear. "Have you decided yet?" She doesn't answer, so I pull back enough to look at her. I think she's in a happy trance. Her eyes are closed and she's smiling.

She opens her eyes and looks at the ring on her finger again. "I've always wanted one of these. I just can't believe you're the one who gave it to me."

"Childhood dream come true?"

"That would make you my Princess Charming. Are you ready for that?"

I take a deep breath. Am I ready for that? Am I ready to be everything she needs me to be? Am I ready for that family I know she wants? The only way to know is to ask myself another question. Am I ready to go back to my old life? The one without Mia in it? The one where I jump from one man's bed to another and travel alone, racking up miles so I can travel alone some more?

The answer to that question is definitely *no*.

"One kid and one dog," I tell her. "No cats. I hate cats. And no white picket fence. We live in the city…a bigger apartment, but still the city." She takes my hand and leads me to the bedroom. "What are you doing?" I ask.

"I'm going to make love to my fiancée."

I guess that was the right answer.

❖

Fifteen Months Later

I'd forgotten what it's like to feel whole. In fact, I don't think I've ever known that feeling. I think I was always looking for something that was just beyond my reach. And I was wrong about myself. I did have holes, I just wouldn't acknowledge them. And the reason I know that now is because Mia has filled them, and I am whole again.

Tomorrow, our lives will change forever. Mia is being induced and we'll have a beautiful baby girl. We'll be parents.

We traveled the first three months of our marriage. I told her she couldn't get a new job until I'd shown her my world, so pretty much the world. The travel was so different with her. Everything took on new meaning and a new beauty. She soaked it all in, tasted everything I put in front of her, and made sure we took photos and selfies and posted them for everyone to see. I've truly never seen so much joy emanating from one person as I saw from her on those trips.

And she's still joyous. She lights up a room and giggles all the time and I'd like to think it's because she's married to me. I'd like to think I've made her whole too.

I'm so lost in thought, I jump when Gabe opens the roof door. The whole family is here for the birth, including my mom and Juliet. Our tiny apartment was getting stuffy with everyone eating and laughing and playing some board game, so I came up here to escape for a few minutes and catch my breath.

"You okay?" Gabe asks, leaning against the wall next to me.

"Yeah," I tell him, even though I'm anything but okay.

"She'll be fine. They'll both be fine."

Him just saying the words makes me burst into tears. I'm so scared that something could go wrong and I could lose her.

Gabe wraps his arm around me. "She has the best doctors in the world. The baby is strong and healthy. You have nothing to worry about."

"Did you worry?" I ask, looking him in the eye.

"Did I worry?" He laughs. "God, I was such a mess with our first. They had to kick me out of the room because I was crying and telling Janey how sorry I was that I did this to her."

That makes me giggle, but then he gets serious again.

"It was this last one that scared me the most, though. Janey didn't want me in the room. She was angry…"

I put my hand on his arm. "I know."

I don't want him to have to relive what we all went through that Thanksgiving. We didn't know it at the time, but while Mia and I were getting married, Janey was giving birth alone. She had kicked Gabe out of the house, but it only lasted a month. It's been over a year and they're fine now. Solid.

The roof door opens again and it's Mia this time. I can't believe she climbed those stairs. Gabe and I both rush over to her. "What are you doing, sis?" Gabe takes her arm and helps her to a chair.

Once Mia catches her breath she looks at me. "I came to find my wife." She furrows her brow. "What's wrong?"

"She's worried about you doing stupid things like climbing a flight of stairs!" Gabe shouts.

I quickly wipe my eyes and smile at Gabe, grateful for his concern. "Can you give me a minute with her?"

He nods and gives Mia a stern look. "Call me if you need help going back down."

Once he's gone, I pull up a chair next to her and rest my hand on her belly. "How's she doing?"

She ignores the question. "You've been crying. Did Gabe say something?"

I shake my head. "No. I just…I'm feeling a little overwhelmed by it all. And I'm scared…about tomorrow."

"Honey." She cups my cheek and leans in for a kiss. Her lips are so soft. "We're going to be fine."

"I can't lose you. Now that I have you, I feel like I would shrivel up and die without you." I lay my head on her stomach and cry a few more tears while she runs her fingers through my hair.

"Will you promise me something?"

"Anything," I tell her.

"Promise me that every year on her birthday, you'll tell her the story of us, so she'll know how special she is and how much she's loved."

I sit back up and look her in the eye. "Can I leave out the part where I was too drunk to remember having sex with you?"

She giggles, making her tummy bounce up and down. "You can leave out *all* the sex."

I want to straddle her and kiss her deeply, but it wouldn't really be conducive to romance since she can barely breathe and doesn't currently have a lap to sit on. Instead, I pull her up from the chair and rest my hands on her tummy. "I'll also tell her every day how much I love you, just so she knows she'll always have both of her mommies."

She wraps her arm around my shoulder and leads me back to the roof door. "And I'll tell her at least once a week that she has to go to bed on time, so I can do naughty things to her mommy."

"Ooh, I like that one."

EPILOGUE

Chloe knows the clean version of our story very well. And even eight years later, I still tell her how much I love her mommy.

"Mom?"

"In the kitchen!"

Chloe comes in and sits at the breakfast bar. "Where are you going all dressed up?"

"I told you last week. I have to fly to California today. Now, do you want fried or scrambled?"

"I want a protein smoothie." She opens her notebook and starts doodling in purple ink. "And I hate it when you travel."

"Oh, come on, honey. It's only once a month or so now. And besides, I have to pay the electricity bill. You don't want the lights going out, do you?"

"I know you're lying."

I turn around with my jaw hanging open. "I do not lie to you."

"Grandma Helen says you do."

"What are you talking about?" I put the blender on the counter in front of her so I can look her in the eye while I make her smoothie.

"Last time you said the lights might get turned off, I called Grandma and asked her for money. And she told me that Mommy makes plenty of money being a doctor and that you're just using scare tactics to get me to behave."

"Really, honey?" Mia says, coming out of the bedroom looking hot in her tight navy-blue skirt and white silk blouse. Yes, my wife still has expensive taste in clothing. She kisses Chloe's head and then walks over to me, grabbing me around the waist and pulling me to her. "You're scaring our child?"

My eyes find their way down to her cleavage, and a surge of lust runs through my body. Our eyes meet and hers widen. She knows what I'm thinking. "Chloe?" She calls to our daughter, keeping her eyes on me.

"Yeah?"

"Mommy and I need fifteen minutes." She grabs my hand and drags me out of the kitchen.

"Am I going to be late for school again?"

"Eat some cereal!" I yell as our bedroom door is being slammed behind me.

Mia pushes me up against the wall and unzips my trousers. "How long are you going to be gone?"

"Two days." I throw my head back against the wall when I feel her hand slide into my underwear.

"Two days is too long."

I lean forward and kiss her deeply. She slides into me with two fingers and I groan into her mouth. She gives me her tongue again as she pushes into me over and over. My knees want to buckle, so she presses her body against mine, pinning me to the wall.

"I don't want you to come," she whispers, pushing into me again. "I want you to do that tonight…in your hotel room…when I call you."

"God, I love you," I whisper.

She slowly removes her hand and gently massages my clit in a teasing way. "Tell me the story of us."

"Um…" I take a breath and try to focus. "We met in a bar nine years ago…"

"The dirty version," she whispers.

"You got me drunk and seduced me…and we fucked all night. And the next morning…oh God." My hips start to move in rhythm with her fingers.

She slows down her movement. "And the next morning, I wanted to fuck you again…but we both had meetings and you couldn't remember anything."

"So, you let me go…but I couldn't forget you. I had to see you again."

She stops her movement. "And then you ran away from me."

I take her hand out of my pants and lick my own juices off her fingers while she watches. "And then I sent you a selfie."

"Send me a selfie again, Sam. Tonight. Something I can look at while we…"

"Have phone sex?" I ask. She nods.

And then I tell her something she needs to hear every once in a while. Something I'm more than happy to tell her. The truest words I've ever spoken. "You're my wife, Mia Rossi. The mother of our child, Chloe Rossi-King, and the only person who will ever touch me the way you just touched me. And I will never…ever…run away from you again."

She runs her hands over my shoulders and down my arms to my hands, bringing them to her mouth and kissing my wedding ring. "I thank God every day for you. I sit at my desk and look at your picture and wonder how in the world I managed to marry someone so amazing and beautiful and talented. And I know…" She pauses for a second, looking me in the eye. "I know that Chloe wouldn't be who she is…so smart and loving and kind and quick-witted and all the things that make her our child, if it weren't for you. You're such an incredible mom and wife. And I'm so happy to be married to you, Samantha King." She pulls me in for a kiss. "Come home safe to us. We would both die without you."

❖

Before I met Mia, I was never very concerned about my personal safety. I traveled to places I probably shouldn't have. I hitchhiked my way through Europe. I jumped out of planes and surfed in any ocean, not even thinking twice about it.

Now, as I find my seat in first class, I try to send good vibes to the pilot. *Please fly safely. I have a wife and child who need me.*

I didn't know how good it would feel to be needed, to be loved so much that someone (Chloe) cries when I leave her, even for just a few days. I didn't know that family is everything. Now I understand why Gabe wanted this for his sister. He knew what it would mean to her. He knew how she'd feel if she never had it. And every time I see him, I remember his words to me:

Who will tell the story of your life to future generations? Who will remember you ever existed?

Our daughter will. She knows the story. And she'll tell it to whoever will listen.

FORGET HER NEVER

.

CHAPTER ONE

H as anyone ever told you that you drink too much?"

Abby stiffened. She looked around to make sure the woman sitting a few seats down was actually addressing her. Surely she wasn't. Was she? But the woman was staring right at her. Great. Abby took another sip of her drink. "Strangers, acquaintances, even a few lovers." She set her drink down with some force. "But never a call girl."

The woman smirked. "Nice."

"Hey, you had that coming."

"Maybe so, but you still drink too much."

Abby turned on her stool and gave the woman a once-over, purposely letting her eyes linger on what she could only imagine were pretty nice breasts under that tasteful little black dress. She liked what she saw, even if she didn't care much for the woman's pickup line, if that's what it was. "Care to join me?"

"No, I'm waiting for my pimp. You know how it is," the woman said with a shrug. "If I don't pay him every night, things get ugly."

Abby couldn't help but laugh out loud. "Okay, you win."

The brunette with the pretty green eyes leaned in a little closer. "Yeah? What do I win?"

"Let me buy you a drink." Abby waved her hand, trying to get the attention of the bartender.

"I'd rather pick my prize."

Abby's eyes widened in surprise. "Oh, this should be interesting. Yes, by all means, pick your prize."

"A date. You and me on a riverboat tomorrow night."

Unimpressed, Abby swung her stool back toward the bar. "Those boats have terrible food."

"Not the boat I'm thinking of."

Abby took the swizzle stick from her drink and rolled it on her tongue while she considered the offer. Did she really care about the quality of the food on a damn boat? Not really. She gave the woman another glance. "Just dinner? Or do I have to put out?"

"Only if I make you laugh."

Abby tried not to laugh, but it snuck out. "Okay, maybe I *have* had too much to drink."

"Or maybe I'm just that funny."

"Maybe," Abby said with a shrug. "But like you said, I'm a little tipsy. Now, a hot chick who can make me laugh when I'm sober would be a rare package indeed."

The brunette slid off her stool and moved closer. "Not so rare. I'm looking at one right now. Maybe I should take a picture and post it on Instagram. I wonder how many likes I'd get?"

Abby looked away in disbelief. "You wouldn't post that on Instagram."

"Twitter, then." She made a show of taking her phone out of her purse.

Abby suppressed a grin. "And what would the tweet say?"

"Good question. Let's see. How about, 'With any luck, this hottie will be doing a walk of shame tomorrow morning'?" She held up the phone as if she was about to take a photo. "Hashtag wish me luck."

Abby shook her head. "Okay, you really are funny."

"You didn't LOL." The brunette steadied her phone. "Okay, smile."

Abby gently pushed the phone away. "I was laughing on the inside."

"So, how about a ride home?" She tucked her phone back into her clutch. "And I'm Kendall, by the way."

Abby threw her swizzle stick back in her drink. "Wait. Did we just backslide? First you ask me out on a mediocre date to, what was it? Medieval Times?"

"A boat." Kendall raised her eyebrows and half smiled. "On the river."

"Right. The backslide. You wanted to take me to see Riverdance and now you just want to take me home and—"

"Wait." Kendall put her hands up in defense. "It's just a ride home. No ulterior motives."

Abby wasn't buying it. The offer was tempting, but she'd never pictured herself with someone older than herself. Not that she really knew how old what's her name was, but there were laugh lines around those gorgeous eyes. "Thank you for the offer, but I can take care of myself."

Kendall leaned in. "Right now you can. But in about three minutes, that last shot of tequila is going to hit you hard."

"You've been stalking me?" Okay, now it was just getting weird.

"Not stalking, just admiring." Kendall threw a couple of twenties on the bar to cover the bill. "Please, I'd really like to make sure you get home okay so we can go on that mediocre riverboat tomorrow night."

Abby huffed at the thought. She was definitely not going on some damn tourist riverboat with this rude woman. "It's nice of you to offer, but I'm very capable of hailing my own cab."

"I don't doubt that you are, but I have a driver waiting right out front."

This woman is relentless! "Thanks, but I'd feel safer in a cab." *And just take no for an answer already, would you?*

"A cab it is. May I at least ask who we're hailing a cab for?"

Abby hesitated for a second, then shook the offered hand. "Abby." She forced a smile and slid off the stool.

"Easy, there." Kendall grabbed Abby's hand to steady her. "Take a second to get your bearings."

Abby wasn't about to admit it, but that last shot of tequila had indeed been a very bad idea. She grabbed on to the bar to steady herself as the room around her swayed. After a deep breath, she gave Kendall an unconvincing nod. "Okay. I'm good."

Kendall smiled. "Take my hand, and I'll lead you through the crowd."

Abby did as she was told. It was for the best since the room had gone from a gentle sway to a slow spin. She watched Kendall motion to her driver as she hailed a cab. Abby tried to get it together. She could do this. She could get home without making a complete fool of herself. It would just take a few deep breaths. She took those breaths and got in the cab.

"Scoot over," Kendall said. "I'm going to make sure you get home."

"I'm fine," Abby snapped back.

Kendall went to the other side of the cab and got in. "You don't look fine," she said. "Have you given the driver your address?"

Abby furrowed her brow. "No. Not yet." She gave the driver the address and looked behind them. "Is your driver going to follow us?"

"Yes. I'll need a ride home once you're safe and sound."

"Oh." Abby turned back around a little too fast, causing her to grab on to the door with one hand and Kendall's leg with the other. The movement of the cab was seriously conflicting with the movement in her stomach. "I feel sick."

The cab driver immediately pulled over and screeched to a stop. "Not in my cab, lady. Get out!"

Abby jumped out of the cab, spotted a trash can on the sidewalk, and ran to it. Kendall also got out, giving the cab driver the opportunity to squeal away. "Oh, thanks!" she yelled.

Abby wanted to crawl under a rock and die. She was throwing up into a trash can on the street. Could it get any worse? She saw fancy black heels on the ground right before she heaved out the last of the contents of her stomach. She wiped her mouth with the back of her hand and stood. Kendall was there with a napkin. "You'll feel better soon," she said.

"This is so embarrassing." Abby wiped her mouth again and tried to hold back the tears. "I don't usually do this." Ever. This had never happened to her before. Not even in college.

Kendall rested her hand on Abby's back and gave it a gentle caress. "Now you know why I wanted to help you home."

Abby didn't see anything in Kendall's eyes but true concern. "Right, you were watching me. Or stalking me. Or whatever."

"Admiring. I was admiring you," Kendall said. She looked up and down the street. "We lost our cab, but my driver is right there. What do you say we get you home?"

Abby nodded her agreement and followed Kendall to the SUV. They both got in the back seat and sat mostly in silence, with Abby giving the driver brief directions when necessary. She felt so humiliated. The truth was she hardly ever had more than one drink when she'd frequented that bar or any other. She wasn't usually so rude, either. This woman, Kendall whoever she was, had caught her in a bad moment. She'd apologize and hopefully never see her again. That's how this night would end.

The driver helped Abby out of the car and over to the curb where Kendall was waiting. "Thank you," Abby said, barely able to stand the bad taste in her mouth. "And I'm sorry I called you a—" She didn't want to say it again with the driver standing right there. "Anyway, thank you for the ride."

Abby tried to walk past her, but Kendall gently took her by the arm. "I'll walk you to your door."

"That really isn't necessary."

"Please, let me."

Abby searched Kendall's eyes again, wondering what her motives could be. Again, she only saw genuine concern, so she gave her a nod. In the elevator, it took everything she had to not lose what little was left in her stomach. She managed to get her keys out of her purse but couldn't quite get the key in the lock.

"Here, let me." Kendall took the keys from her and opened the door, pushing it open wide enough for Abby to walk through but not walking in herself. "Drink lots of water. And I'll see you tomorrow night at seven."

Abby shook her head. "Surely you don't want to—"

Kendall smiled. "Be ready at seven."

CHAPTER TWO

A bby opened the door. Feeling rather shy and hesitant, she said, "Hello again."

"Hello." Kendall looked her up and down. "That gorgeous dress you're wearing tells me you're planning on going out tonight, but your eyes are saying something different. Have you changed your mind?"

"Did I throw up on you last night?" Abby blurted the question out and then bit her lip while she waited for an answer. She couldn't remember if she actually hit the trash can or the sidewalk. And God help her if she hit the sidewalk and ruined this kind woman's expensive looking shoes.

"Not on me per se, just near me."

"Oh God." Abby covered her eyes. "Did you have to send your dress out for dry cleaning? I'd be happy to pay for it."

"I would have anyway. Vomit or not," Kendall said with a smile.

"I don't believe you."

Kendall shrugged. "Okay, yes, it was gross. You threw up all over me."

"Oh, my God." Abby covered her eyes again, this time with both hands. Throwing up in public? On someone? A beautiful someone? Was someone kidding with this shit? She was better than that. So much better than that. She was a professional woman, living and working in New York City. Not some bar-hopping drunk who didn't know when enough was enough.

"I'm kidding," Kendall said. "It wasn't that bad. The way you ran to that trash can was impressive. I'd say you were on the track team."

"I wasn't. And I'm sorry. I don't usually drink like that." Abby looked away, embarrassed. "Obviously."

Kendall gave her a gentle smile. "Hey, I might have had one too many too if I, you know, had bombed so badly trying to pick up a beautiful woman."

"You saw that?" Abby needed a rug to crawl under. Or better yet, a hole in the ground she could fall into right about now. Picking up women in bars—or anywhere for that matter—wasn't a skill she'd managed to hone. In fact, she was terrible at it when she was sober and obviously not much better when drunk.

"Maybe you need a better pickup line," Kendall said.

"Oh, like asking a woman if anyone's ever told her she drinks too much?"

"Hey, that line's a winner. I'm standing here, aren't I?"

Abby narrowed her eyes. "I threw up on you. Why would you want to go out with me after that?"

"And right before that, you called me a call girl." Kendall grinned. "Oh, and you also intimated that taking you on a riverboat would quite possibly be the worst date you could imagine. So yeah, I was intrigued."

Abby eyed her for a second and then shook her head. "I forgot about the riverboat."

"Get your coat." Kendall gave her a wink. "I'll wait."

❖

Kendall stood at the bottom of a gangplank and motioned for Abby to walk ahead. Abby started but quickly turned back. "You said we were going on a riverboat."

"We are." Kendall pointed a finger at the Hudson. "This is a river." Then she pointed nonchalantly at the rather large yacht in front of them. "And this is a boat." She put her hands on Abby's hips. "Eyes forward. I really don't want to ruin another dress trying to pull you out of the water."

Abby whipped around. "I knew it! I ruined your dress last night, didn't I?" She didn't mean to step so far into Kendall's personal space, but there they were, almost nose to nose. It was too dark to see what Kendall's eyes were telling her, but Abby caught a hint of sweet perfume and minty breath. She let her eyes fall to Kendall's lips. It had been a while since she'd felt another woman's lips on hers. She missed everything about it. Nothing turned her on like a soft, wet tongue dipping into her mouth for a little taste.

"I was just teasing. My dress is fine." Kendall gently turned Abby back around and kept her hands on her waist.

Abby took a breath and tried to shake herself out of her musings. "This is a private yacht, not a riverboat." She took a few careful steps up the gangplank.

"Oh! My bad."

Abby stopped halfway up and turned around. "Well, this is a night of firsts. A private yacht. An older woman—"

Kendall put her finger on Abby's lips to silence her. "Hey, watch it. I can't be that much older than you, but that doesn't mean you need to ask my age. Not yet."

"Thirty-six," Abby mumbled past the finger.

"Yes, that is correct. How did you know?"

Abby laughed. "That's how old I am."

"Fine." Kendall sighed. "If you must know, I'm forty-seven. And a half."

Abby grinned. "So, forty-eight?"

Kendall turned Abby back around and urged her up the gangplank. "I saved you from yourself last night. Surely you can cut me some slack on the age thing."

Abby would most definitely cut this beautiful woman some slack on the age thing. She'd never dated an older woman, but there was a first time for everything.

She boarded the yacht, expecting to find a party going on, but the only people she saw were wearing uniforms. The first gentleman bowed slightly. "Ma'am, welcome to *The First of Many*. Would you care for a drink?"

Abby glanced back at Kendall and smirked. "The first of many drinks? Probably shouldn't go there again."

"How about a glass of wine? I have a great selection."

"*The First of Many* is yours?" Abby looked around the very expensive-looking yacht.

Kendall rested her hand on Abby's lower back. "May I choose something for us? A nice pinot noir to start?"

It didn't go unnoticed that Kendall had avoided the question, but Abby didn't want to push it. She put up a finger. "Just one glass."

Kendall signaled to her bartender. "The sixty-one, Sergio." She took Abby's hand and led her to the upper deck. "You'll tell me if you get chilly?"

"Of course." Abby glanced at their intertwined fingers before turning her attention back to Kendall's green eyes. "But I don't think that will be a problem."

Sergio came back with a bottle. He poured them each a glass of wine. "The normal route, ma'am?"

"Yes. Thank you, Sergio." Kendall offered Abby a glass and held her own up for a toast. "Here's hoping I can make you laugh tonight."

Abby gave her a quizzical look.

"Last night, you asked if you had to put out tonight, and I said—"

"Only if you make me laugh," Abby said as she nodded. "Now I remember."

Kendall cleared her throat. "So, a guy walks into a bar with an alligator."

Abby started to giggle in spite of herself.

"Well, that was easy," Kendall said. "I didn't even have to get you tipsy."

"I was laughing at your ridiculous attempt to get me to laugh, not the actual joke. It doesn't count."

"I would love nothing more than to hear you laugh all night. And don't worry about the other thing. I won't hold you to it."

Kendall took Abby by the elbow and led her to a sofa. "We should sit while the captain embarks." She waited for Abby to sit first. "Please, wherever you like."

Abby sat in the middle of the long sofa and crossed her legs, swirling the wine in her glass. "So, is it?"

Kendall sat and turned toward Abby with her legs crossed. "Is it what?"

"Is it the first of many?"

Kendall smiled and held up her glass for a toast. "The first of many times I make you laugh? God, I hope so."

Abby clinked their glasses together. "Are you going to deflect my questions all night?"

"Will you be here all night?"

God, this woman had a non-answer for everything. Abby grabbed the seat when she felt the boat move. She'd been on the ferry a few times, but never on a smaller boat like this. As if you could really call this boat small. She smiled at Kendall, trying to hide any anxiety she was feeling.

"It's okay," Kendall said. "Once we get going, it'll be smooth sailing."

Abby was trying to take it all in. She needed to adjust to her surroundings and react appropriately. She was on what appeared to be a very expensive yacht with an extremely attractive woman. How did she end up here after making a complete fool of herself the night before? And was this something Kendall did on the regular? She needed more information, but she had her doubts that she'd get a straight answer about anything. "That guy, Sergio, asked if you wanted to take the normal route. Does that mean this is normal for you?"

"Hmm," Kendall said. "If I say yes, you'll think I'm in this for one thing. And if I say no, you'll call me a liar."

Abby gave her a sympathetic frown. "You can't win."

"Not with that question. Ask me another."

Abby's eyes fell to Kendall's lips. They were naturally plump. Not the fake plump that looked as if someone had attached a tire pump to them. No, Kendall was obviously born with the most sensuous, kissable lips Abby had ever seen. "What's that shade of lipstick called?"

"It's called You Get My Jokes," Kendall teased.

Abby stifled a snicker.

"See?" Kendall said. "I speak the truth. Ask me another."

Abby tucked her long, dark hair behind her ears. "Okay. What's on the menu tonight?"

"Riverboat food. What else would you like to know?"

"Your last name."

"Squires."

Abby put out her hand as if they were in a business meeting. "Mine is Dunn."

Kendall reached out and pulled Abby's hand to her mouth and gently kissed it. "It's a pleasure to meet you, Abby Dunn."

Abby's heart skipped a beat. "It's nice to meet you too," she whispered.

Kendall took Abby's cold hand and rubbed it between her own. "You're getting chilly. Stay right there, and I'll grab a blanket for us."

It was a clear, crisp, early autumn evening. Abby looked but couldn't see any stars in the sky. It didn't matter. The New York skyline was beautiful, and the woman walking toward her with a blanket was absolutely stunning in her navy-blue dress and camel hair coat.

Kendall sat and wrapped the blanket over their legs. "Better?"

"Yes, thank you." Abby's tummy did a little flip when Kendall smiled at her. She turned away, feeling shy all of a sudden. Was this woman even real? She'd never been treated so well on a date before. Even back when she'd dated men, they were never as chivalrous and attentive as Kendall was being. It felt too good to be true. And it probably was.

Kendall pointed out landmarks and talked about the different buildings as they made their way past Lower Manhattan. It was obvious she'd grown up in the city and knew it well. Abby found it fascinating since she hadn't lived there for very long. She listened intently, adding a comment here and there, but mostly, she was content to drink her wine and listen to Kendall Squires talk about the city she loved. She had a pleasant voice, and she used her hands when she spoke. Abby found she didn't want to take her eyes off Kendall, even when she would point to a landmark.

Sergio stepped outside with a plate of appetizers. "Excuse the interruption, ladies. We have Osetra caviar to begin this evening if that would be satisfactory?"

Kendall looked from Sergio to Abby. "Are you okay with caviar?"

"Absolutely."

"Personally, I'd prefer buffalo wings, but Sergio is a snob about these things."

Abby looked at Sergio, and he lowered his head, trying not to laugh. "Caviar is fine, Sergio."

Kendall put her hand on Abby's knee and gave it a gentle squeeze through the blanket.

Abby smiled. "I love good caviar. And something tells me this will be good."

Kendall leaned in and lowered her voice. "Only the best for the drunk girl I picked up in a bar."

Abby covered her eyes for a second as the awful memory came forward. "Is there any chance we could pretend we met tonight?"

Kendall put a dab of caviar on a blini and offered it to Abby. "And forget that you called me a call girl? Not on your life."

"I'm sorry about that. I misspoke." Abby looked around at their surroundings. "I should have called you a high-class call girl."

Kendall grinned. "Thank you."

After enjoying an incredible meal in the dining room, Abby leaned back in her chair and studied Kendall for a moment. She hadn't been able to get much personal information out of her, but she did get her to admit that *The First of Many* was indeed her yacht. Abby could play the secretive game too, although it wasn't really necessary since Kendall hadn't asked any personal questions.

Don't ask, don't tell seemed to be the theme of the evening. Abby could deal with that as long as Kendall kept looking at her the way she was looking at her—as if she was the most beautiful woman she'd ever laid eyes on.

When had any woman looked at Abby that way? Men, sure. They weren't hard to please. But women were different. They didn't usually let their desire show so openly as Kendall Squires did. Abby had to admit that it felt good, and she didn't want it to stop.

Kendall didn't break her gaze while she sipped from her glass. "You look like you have something on your mind."

So many things were on Abby's mind. Like, where was the bedroom? And what was under that high-necked, navy-blue dress? And what cruel designer made a neck that high anyway? And also, what did her skin smell like? And underneath that well-spoken, high-class façade, was this the kind of woman who would let herself go in bed? A woman who would let herself be devoured? Because that was what Abby would do, given the opportunity. She would devour Kendall Squires, if that was even her real name.

"Just one question," Abby said. "What were you doing in that bar?"

Kendall looked a bit perplexed by the question. "I imagine I was doing the same thing as you. Having a drink."

"What I mean is, I wouldn't take you for the type to hang out in bars looking for drunk girls to hit on."

"True. Stumbling across a drunk girl was just a bonus."

"Would you please be serious?"

Kendall leaned on the table, resting her chin in her hand. "Maybe I am being serious. Did it ever occur to you that maybe I really was looking to get laid?"

"Most people don't do that with yachts and caviar," Abby said.

"Don't they? Well, maybe I'm just willing to work harder than most."

"That's just it. You don't have to," Abby said. "Any woman… or man, if you like both, would be so enamored, simply by your voice and your touch and those eyes and your graciousness and your witty comebacks and those lips and those eyes."

Kendall grinned. "You said eyes twice."

Damnit, she did. And those eyes were searing into her, and if she didn't look away, she'd get lost in them forever. "My point is—"

"Oh, there's a point! I can't wait," Kendall said, her chin still resting in her hand and her face looking so gorgeous Abby was tempted to swipe the dinner table clean and climb across it and kiss that cute smirk right off Kendall's lips.

"Kendall." Abby liked the way the name sounded coming from her own mouth. "Why would someone like you go to a bar that's obviously way out of her neighborhood—unless you live downtown, which judging from all of this, I seriously doubt—and pick up a stranger?"

Kendall leaned back in her chair and sighed. "I guess I can't use a witty comeback for this one, can I?"

"You could. But wouldn't it feel great to just tell me the truth?"

Kendall pushed her chair back and stood. She offered her hand to Abby and waited for her to stand too. "The truth is, I'd love to have dessert with you out on the deck." She ran her other hand over Abby's shoulder and pushed her hair out of the way. Abby shivered under the touch. Goose bumps popped up on her arms. Kendall ran her hand down Abby's arm. "And I promise to keep you warm."

Abby was already warm. Kendall had a gentle but purposeful touch. She knew what she was doing. And it was working. God, was it working. "Yeah," Abby said. Because really, who gave a damn about anything other than how Kendall's warm, soft hand was caressing her arm? "That sounds nice."

"I'll meet you out there." Kendall walked away, presumably to find Sergio. It was obvious that making himself scarce was a key part of the steward's job description. Abby took advantage of the opportunity and let her eyes rake over Kendall's body as she walked away. Because Kendall Squires was definitely a woman worth watching—whether coming or going. *Coming.* Abby knew that would be a sight to behold. She tried to keep those images out of her head as she walked out onto the deck.

CHAPTER THREE

Abby dipped her spoon into the chocolate mousse and offered it to Kendall. "I don't know what your chef does to this, but oh my God."

Kendall took a bite and moaned her approval. "He's a genius. Found him in Greece."

They were snuggled in close under a large blanket on a double chaise lounge. Steam rose off the hot tub in front of them as Manhattan faded in the distance. Abby wondered if that hot tub would be their next stop. Or maybe she just hoped it would be.

Kendall was wealthy, obviously. Well-spoken. Well-traveled. Abby turned the spoon over and ran it over her tongue, getting any chocolate mousse Kendall had missed. And again, those eyes were on her, watching her every move. It was unnerving. And sexy as hell. Abby had so many questions, but there was only one she dared ask. And so, she asked it again. "So, tell me. What were you really doing in that bar?"

Kendall adjusted the blanket she'd wrapped around the two of them. "Are you warm enough?"

Abby set the dessert down and turned so they were face-to-face. "You either need to tell me, or you need to kiss me."

"God, you're beautiful," Kendall said. "The moment I saw you, I was just so taken."

Taken. Abby liked that word. And she had a feeling Kendall, if given the chance, would take her to all kinds of interesting places tonight. She leaned in and let their breath mingle. "Kiss me," she whispered.

With the lightest of kisses, Kendall worked her way from Abby's cheek to her ear. "Don't you want to know the truth?"

Abby's eyes shuttered closed. "Will the truth hurt?"

"The truth," Kendall whispered as she placed soft kisses on Abby's neck, "always hurts."

Abby's breath caught. She turned and met Kendall's gaze. "Then lie to me."

It didn't feel like a lie when their lips met. It was slow and gentle and real. Abby felt that kiss from her head to her toes. She slid her fingers into Kendall's hair and pulled her closer, deepening the kiss. She wanted this, and she didn't care what happened tomorrow or the next day. Tonight was everything. Tonight, she hoped, would last for days.

Kendall pulled away first, a sly grin firmly planted on her lips. She reached across Abby and dipped her finger into the chocolate mousse. She brought it to Abby's lips, and without hesitation, Abby took the finger into her mouth and sucked it clean.

Abby did the same thing, dipping her own finger into the mousse. She tried to control her breathing while Kendall sucked on her finger, but it was an impossible task. Her chest heaved as she tried to catch her breath.

"Does this turn you on, Abby?" Kendall dipped into the mousse again and spread a dab on Abby's bottom lip.

"*You* turn me on." Abby wanted to say her name again. "Kendall." She licked the mousse off her own lip.

"Hey, that was for me." Kendall put another dab on Abby's lip and took it into her mouth. She sucked the chocolate off and dipped her tongue into Abby's mouth, giving her a taste. She pulled back before Abby could deepen the kiss.

Kendall was going slow. Too slow. Keeping the kisses shallow. Teasing Abby. Or maybe it was something else. *Permission.* The thought of what might happen if she gave it caused Abby's breath to catch. "Take me," she said.

In one quick move, Kendall straddled Abby and pushed her

hands over her head. Kendall was being gentle, but at the same time, Abby's hands weren't going anywhere. Kendall kissed her again. This time with an urgency that wasn't there a few seconds ago. Kendall intertwined their fingers, and Abby held on for dear life as her body caught fire.

She needed her hands. She wanted to touch Kendall everywhere. Feel her skin. Run her fingers through her hair. But Kendall was holding her down and devouring her mouth. That was fine. It was more than fine. It was perfect. Abby would get her chance, but for now, she would relax and let Kendall Squires do whatever the hell she wanted to do. And right now, she wanted Abby's neck.

"Oh God, yes," Abby whispered. *Take me.*

Just when Abby couldn't stand it anymore and wanted to break free so she could wrap her hands around Kendall's ass and pull her closer, Kendall let go of her hands and sat up. She slid her finger into the gold zipper pull on the front of Abby's dress. "I've been wondering all night if this dress was for me," Kendall said.

Yes, Abby had worn the dress on purpose. The heavy gold zipper went from cleavage to hem. It was by far the sexiest black dress in her closet. She hardly ever wore it, but the truth was, she wanted to feel sexy tonight. "Maybe," she said with a shrug.

"Maybe? Hmm." Kendall toyed with the zipper but didn't pull it down.

Abby watched the perfectly manicured finger run its way down the zipper to her stomach. The nail was short and painted a shade of blush. God, this woman could be a tease. She imagined that finger running down her bare skin. All the way down until it found the edge of her panties. Just a moment ago, she'd sucked on that same finger. And now, she wanted it inside her.

"It's for you, Kendall."

"I love it when you say my name." Kendall tugged on the zipper. She pulled it down just enough to reveal a black lacy bra. "Oh," she whispered in a long breath. "Abby Dunn, you are positively gorgeous." She tugged the zipper lower still, revealing Abby's stomach, and then her belly button. "How did I get so lucky?" She unzipped it all the way and pushed it aside.

Abby's breathing had become shallow. Her stomach was rising and falling a little too quickly. Kendall's eyes were raking over her body, taking it all in. She put her hands on Kendall's bare thighs and dug her fingernails in. "I think I'm the lucky one tonight."

Kendall hiked her tight dress over her ass and moved up a little bit, then let her weight rest on Abby's center. She ground against her, causing just enough friction to make them both moan with pleasure.

Oh, my fucking God. Abby couldn't believe what was happening. A beautiful, sexy woman was grinding her pussy against her, and she seemed to be getting very turned on. And God knows Abby was getting turned on. She gripped Kendall's thighs, moving a little higher with each passing second. Wetness was building. She could see it coating Kendall's red thong. Maybe the *taking* would be done by her tonight. But she wouldn't ask for permission.

As quickly as Kendall had straddled her, Abby pushed Kendall's thong aside and plunged a finger into her. Kendall's eyes widened in surprise and then darkened. She rode Abby's finger, keeping eye contact.

Abby wanted to sit up so she could push in deeper, but the view was too good. Kendall's breasts were bouncing under her dress and the look in her eye—well, Abby knew pure, unadulterated lust when she saw it. "More," Kendall said. "Please, Abby. More."

Abby slid two fingers in. Kendall gasped and tilted her head back. Abby needed to be deeper. She sat up and wrapped her arm around Kendall's waist, then pushed in as deep as she could. Kendall let out a strong moan and grabbed Abby's shoulders.

She would fuck this woman all night, right out in the open, if that's what she wanted. But the dress needed to come off. Abby grabbed hold of the neckline and tugged. "Can we take this off?"

Kendall slowed her movements. "We should—"

"No," Abby said. "Don't stop. I just need all of you."

Kendall leaned over and kissed Abby's cheek. "You can have all of me." She grinned and motioned toward the cabin. "Inside."

❖

"Your zipper is caught. I can't seem to—" Abby yanked on the zipper, but it only got worse. The delicate fabric was caught, and it wasn't coming loose anytime soon. "Shit."

Kendall looked over her shoulder. "This dress isn't coming off me unless you un-catch that zipper."

"I know. It's like it was painted on you." That, and the high neck that was definitely not wide enough to go over Kendall's head were a real problem. Abby ran her hands down Kendall's body, letting them land on her hips. She leaned in and kissed the small patch of skin, just above the broken zipper. "You smell so good." She snaked her arms around Kendall's waist and pulled her closer. "I'm sorry I broke your dress."

"It's always an adventure with you, isn't it?" Kendall covered Abby's hands with her own.

"Was it expensive?" Abby didn't need to ask. The dress was one of a kind, she had no doubt. Between last night's dress, the one she might or might not have thrown up on, and this one, she probably owed Kendall a couple grand. Not that she'd ever Venmo Abby for the money. That wasn't her concern. Besides, she did okay. She had the money in the bank. No, it was that she couldn't stop being an idiot in front of this fabulous specimen of a woman.

Kendall turned around in Abby's arms. "We could call Sergio."

"No! God, no! He'll think I'm...not smooth."

Kendall grinned. "After what happened last night you're worried about not being smooth?" She lifted Abby's chin. "Although, what you did outside just now? That was pretty smooth."

Abby blushed. "That may have been my only moment of greatness."

"I doubt that." Kendall put her finger in that gold zipper pull again and gave it a tug.

Abby grabbed her hand. "My dress doesn't come off until we can get yours off."

"Well, that's a shame." Kendall backed away. She sat on the edge of the bed, crossed her legs, and motioned with her finger up and down Abby's body. "Because I think you could have another moment of greatness right now."

Abby folded her arms. "Oh, yeah?"

"Nothing turns me on more than watching a beautiful woman undress."

Abby smirked. "That's a nice way of saying you want me to strip for you."

"Mmm," Kendall said with a grin. "I guess it is."

"I've never done that before," Abby said defiantly. She was, under no circumstances, going to play stripper. "Besides, there isn't even any music." Oh God. Abby watched in horror as Kendall picked up a remote that had very conveniently been sitting on one of the bed pillows. She pushed a button and soft, sexy music filled the cabin.

"I'll be your first," Kendall said. "I kind of love that."

Abby lowered her gaze for a moment because if she kept looking at that gorgeous woman sitting on the bed, with her sexy green eyes and those legs that she so desperately wanted to have wrapped around her—

"Jesus, Abby. You are just—" Kendall paused and took Abby in. "Captivating. Even if you don't see it, I do," she said.

Abby had on the perfect dress for it. She just needed to find her inner porn star. Except without the porn. She looked over at the delectable, thoroughly edible woman across from her. Okay. Maybe with the porn. "If I do this—"

"Anything," Kendall said without hesitation.

"Scissors." Abby pointed at Kendall's dress. "We cut it off if we have to."

Kendall glanced down at her dress. "This dress isn't—"

"From Marshall's. I know. But that's my price."

"I was going to say 'off the rack.'" Kendall smiled and picked up the phone by the bed. "Sergio, please find a sharp pair of scissors and leave them outside the door." She sat back down on the edge of the bed.

Rich people and their sex games. But if it got Abby what she wanted—to get Kendall out of that dress? She slid her finger into the zipper pull and slowly tugged it down to her breasts. There wouldn't be any dancing, but she could take a few sexy steps closer, but not too close.

Kendall's eyes were all over her, taking in every inch of her body. That gave Abby a thrill. At first, she wanted to get this over quickly, but now, she thought it might be fun to drag it out. Maybe she wouldn't unzip the dress all of the way. Maybe only halfway, and then take it off her arms and let it hang around her waist. Why reveal everything so quickly?

Abby's hair hung in loose curls over her breasts. Even if she removed her bra, they'd still be somewhat hidden by her hair. She unhooked the clasp and held her bra out to the side with two fingers. She was going to drop it on the floor, but she had a better idea. She sauntered over to Kendall and wrapped the bra around her neck like a scarf, then sauntered back to her original position.

Kendall pulled the bra off her neck and held it to her nose. "Nice move, Ms. Dunn."

Wait until you see what I do with my panties. Abby had no idea what she'd do with her panties when she took them off. What would a real stripper do? Fling them across the room? Twirl them on her finger? Let Kendall slide them down her legs? Abby liked that last one.

Kendall's eyes were locked on Abby's chest. She hadn't noticed that her hair had fallen to the side, revealing her left breast. She pushed her hair on the other side out of the way as well, and got a slow, appreciative hum in return.

She didn't think it would happen, but Abby was actually getting turned on by all of this. She had a feeling that when she removed them, her panties would be wet. She slowly unzipped her dress enough that it slid over her hips and fell to the floor.

Kendall motioned Abby toward the bed with her finger. "Come here."

Abby approached her, wearing nothing but panties and heels.

Kendall took a long look and said, "Turn around."

Abby did as she was told. Kendall's hands felt warm on her hips. She was held in place as Kendall slid one side of her panties down and placed a kiss on her ass. It was a gentle kiss at first, warm and wet. Then it became more urgent, with the sucking and a little bite that made Abby gasp.

Abby was getting impatient. She wanted Kendall's hands to be everywhere all at once. On her breasts, inside her, holding her down like she'd done outside. It was time to be taken by this amazing woman. She turned back around so she was facing Kendall. She tucked her thumbs into her panties, ready to push them down.

"No," Kendall said. "Let me."

Abby took her hands away and waited. It was clear Kendall Squires liked to take her time with a woman, but Abby couldn't wait much longer.

Kendall ran her finger along the hem of the panties, causing goose bumps to pop up on Abby's arms. "Tell me what you like."

Abby hadn't ever been brave enough to tell a lover what she really wanted. Maybe she'd just been with the wrong women. Kendall seemed like the right woman. She lifted Kendall's chin so they were eye to eye. "Now is not the time to be gentle with me."

Kendall stood. She locked eyes with Abby for a few seconds, then grabbed her head and kissed her hard, shoving her tongue in Abby's mouth. Abby gripped her shoulders as they kissed. When Kendall pulled back, Abby nodded. "Yeah, like that," she said, her chest heaving.

Kendall led Abby to an empty wall and held her against it with her body while she pushed her panties down. "Are you wet? I don't want to hurt you."

"You won't hurt me," Abby said. Her chest heaved against Kendall's. "Look at my panties."

Kendall bent and helped Abby step out of them. She stood back up, holding the panties with one finger. "I guess I don't have to worry about that."

Abby grabbed the panties and tossed them aside. She took Kendall's hand and held it against her pussy. "Fuck me." Kendall pushed in hard with two fingers. "God," Abby moaned. She gripped on to Kendall's shoulders and wrapped a leg around her hips, giving her better access. Kendall pushed three fingers in and increased her speed.

Abby knew there were other people on the boat. She didn't want to be too loud, but goddamn, it had been too long since she'd felt this. "Fuck," she whispered. "Don't stop."

Kendall didn't stop. She gave Abby exactly what she needed, then turned her around so she was facing the wall. She bit and sucked on her back while she fingered a nipple with one hand and her clit with the other.

Abby's legs were shaking. She leaned back against Kendall, her forehead covered in sweat. This was everything. A woman she barely knew was giving her everything. She stilled and then came hard in Kendall's arms. She finally fell to her knees. Kendall fell with her, holding her and kissing her cheek.

Abby had no words. She didn't need any. Kendall was whispering in her ear, telling her how beautiful she was. How sexy she was. And Abby took it all in, believing every word.

CHAPTER FOUR

A bby opened her eyes and blinked a few times. She wiped the drool from her mouth and rolled onto her back. The ceiling was moving, but she knew she wasn't hungover. She sat up and scanned the room. It all came back in a flood of memories. She'd given herself to a beautiful stranger, but that stranger was nowhere to be found. Her shredded dress was there, stuffed into a small trash bin that had conveniently been placed by the door for removal.

Abby's clothes had been laid out on the other side of the bed—a blatant invitation for her to get dressed and get the hell out, she imagined.

God, what had she done? She sighed and rubbed her eyes, no doubt making the mascara smears even worse. She'd had the best sex of her life, that's what she'd done. *Don't forget the striptease, Abby.* And then there was a cutting off of a very expensive dress. Abby had done some pretty fine work there, turning that dress into a pornographic work of art.

Abby had wanted it to be a slow reveal, and it was. She'd carefully cut two openings around Kendall's breasts. The bra was still there, so she'd cut openings in that too. God, Kendall's breasts were magnificent. Abby had her way with them for a good five minutes.

Then, there was the opening she'd cut to reveal Kendall's belly button. She and her tongue spent some time there as well.

And the final, long cut, straight up the front of the dress, revealing every inch of that beautiful woman. A woman who had at some point snuck away from the scene of the crime.

Abby got out of bed and headed for the bathroom. "Walk of shame, here I come."

Carrying her coat in one hand and her heels in the other, Abby went out onto the deck. Sergio was there, waiting for her. "Good morning, miss. Can I get you a coffee or tea for your journey home?"

Abby didn't need an interpreter. There would be no fancy breakfast waiting for her. No mimosas. No caviar omelet with a croissant slathered in strawberry jam on the side. Abby grabbed her stomach to cover up the growling noise. A croissant did sound good. "Just a cab."

"Yes, miss." Sergio took a small envelope out of his pocket. "Ms. Squires wanted you to have this."

Abby stared at the envelope. It couldn't possibly be what she thought it might be. If it was, she was definitely *not* touching that envelope. "Please tell me that isn't money, Sergio."

Sergio shuffled from foot to foot and cleared his throat. He ran the envelope through his fingers. "It doesn't feel like money."

Abby covered her eyes in embarrassment, letting her heels dangle in front of her face.

Sergio bounced on his feet and let out a short but nervous laugh, still keeping his eyes averted. He offered the envelope again. "I apologize for the misunderstanding."

Abby took the envelope. It was too late to get out of there with her dignity intact, but she could at least be gracious. She offered Sergio her hand. "Dinner was lovely, Sergio. Thank you again."

She couldn't get off the boat fast enough. Once she was on solid ground, she slid into her heels, and even though it was a warm morning, she put her coat on. No one wanted to walk around in a cocktail dress at 8 a.m. Not even in New York City. She hailed a cab and threw the unopened envelope in the nearest trash can.

❖

Abby chewed on the end of her pen as she stared at the blueprints. She turned away from the conference room table and stared at the design pinned to the corkboard.

"Don't do this, Abs. We have to present it tomorrow." Julie leaned forward in her chair. "Seriously, Abby. Do not mess—"

Abby put her hand up, silencing her assistant. "It's too small. The client won't like it."

Julie put her face in her hands and shook her head. "What's with you this week?"

Abby turned back around. "I don't know what you're talking about. And get Syd up here. I need her opinion on this one." She collected her paperwork and was about to leave when the intercom beeped.

"Abby, are you in there?"

"Here," Abby said. "What's up, Beth?"

"You have a visitor. She wouldn't give her name. She just said Sergio sent her."

Abby froze.

"Abs? You okay?" Julie turned to the intercom. "Beth, tell her—"

"No," Abby said. "It's fine. Beth, please put her in my office. I'll be right there."

"Anything I should know about?"

Abby shook her head. "No. It's personal." She headed for the door. "Put the client off for a day, and get Syd up here. We need a bolder statement in the lobby."

She walked slowly to her office, buttoning her blouse a little higher as she went. Just knowing Kendall was in the building had made her chest and neck turn bright red. One more button wasn't going to cover it up, and on top of that, it looked silly. She quickly unbuttoned it again and took a deep breath.

"Hi," Kendall said with a big smile.

Abby closed the door but didn't let go of the handle. "Hi." She didn't return the smile.

Kendall's smile faded. "Look, I know it was rude to leave you like that."

"Oh. Well, Sergio and I bonded." Abby walked over to her desk and stood in front of it. "We're like this now," she said, crossing her fingers.

"I left my number," Kendall said. She took a tentative step closer. "And a note."

"Yeah, that kind of fell in the trash can before I had a chance to read it."

Kendall put up her hands. "Okay, I get it. I should've woken you up and said good-bye."

"That would've been nice. Otherwise, a girl might think she was nothing but a cheap fuck."

"I had a meeting."

"Yes, I'm sure you're a super important and powerful woman." Abby couldn't keep the sarcasm from seeping out. "So busy you couldn't take ten seconds and nudge me awake."

"I know, and I can't stop thinking about it. Why do you think I showed up here unannounced? Abby, I'm not a total stalker. I wanted to apologize."

Abby crossed her arms and leaned back on her desk. "Well?"

Kendall took a step closer. "I woke up, and all I could think about was how badly I wanted to snuggle up with you and talk about silly things until we got so hungry that we had to order breakfast, which we'd have in bed, of course, while we talked about more silly things. And then more snuggling and probably, hopefully, definitely more sex. Except that none of those things could happen, and I knew that, so I...you know...left."

"Why couldn't those things happen?"

"I just..." Kendall looked away. "I told you. I had a meeting."

"Right. A meeting. Well, I'm pretty sure I've got one of those right about now, too."

"Abby?"

"What, Kendall?"

"It was a rotten thing to do, and I'm sorry."

"Okay then. Now you've apologized," she said with a glare.

"Good. Now that we've gotten that out of the way, let's talk about why I'm really here."

Abby raised her eyebrows in surprise.

"It's an intervention. Your drinking is still an issue, but it's your sex addiction that really has me worried."

Abby looked away. She tried to hold back her amusement, but damn, this woman was so quick to disarm her. She put her hand over her mouth and giggled quietly.

Kendall stepped forward, removing the distance between them. "I guess this means you're putting out again."

Abby couldn't keep her eyes where they belonged. They wandered to the buttons on Kendall's silk blouse. She imagined herself ruining yet another expensive piece of clothing. Those buttons would pop fairly easily, she surmised. And the skirt wouldn't be a problem. God, she could fuck Kendall right here on her desk. Right now. *Just lock the door first.* But Kendall wasn't getting off that easily. So to speak.

"No. I'm still mad at you," Abby said. Kendall smirked, and yeah, maybe it wasn't a convincing no, but there was no need to smirk. "I'm serious," Abby added.

"Okay." Kendall folded her arms and stared Abby down for a few seconds. "What if I promise it'll never happen again—the leaving without saying good-bye thing?"

Abby sighed. It should never have happened in the first place. And how could she possibly know if Kendall Squires kept her promises? "How did you find me?"

"You told me that you're an architect, so it wasn't that hard. What you didn't tell me is that you're an award-winning architect." Kendall slid her hand around Abby's waist. "Imagine how turned on I was when I found out."

Those lips that she'd gotten to know pretty well were right there again, begging to be kissed. And Kendall smelled so good, Abby was sure she could get high off the scent. The door wasn't locked, but maybe she could steal a quick kiss.

"Abs?" Syd stopped dead in her tracks. "Sorry, I didn't know you had company."

Kendall took a step back. "I was just leaving." She grabbed a pen off Abby's desk and scribbled something on a sticky note. She made the "call me" sign with her hand and winked at Abby before she left the office.

Syd stood outside the door and watched Kendall walk down the hall. Abby's heart was racing. She covered her red chest with her hand and cleared her throat. "Get in here, Syd."

"Are you hitting that?" Syd closed the office door and sat. "Please tell me you're hitting that."

Abby ignored the question. "I need you on the Taylor project."

Syd slowly shook her head. "Oh, no. Not until you tell me what I just walked in on."

Abby sat and slid the entire pad of sticky notes into her purse. "Nothing. She's a friend. Now, back to work."

"She's hot."

"She's too old for you," Abby said. "And way too sophisticated."

Syd leaned back in her chair and feigned shock. "You know I like older women, and are you saying I'm not sophisticated?"

"Considering you just asked me if I'm 'hitting that'? If the sensible shoe fits."

Syd was the most talented intern Abby had ever worked with, but she completely lacked any sense of style. She had a long, lean figure and amazing blue eyes, but they were completely overshadowed by baggy, out-of-date jeans and a haircut that was so wrong for her it made Abby sad just to look at it.

"If you want to get a woman like that, you need to up your game," Abby said. "You still dress like a poor college student, and that haircut…"

Syd ran her fingers through her short, dark hair. "My friend cuts it for me."

"Your friend the hair stylist?"

"No," Syd said. "My friend the nursing school student." She put up her hands. "Okay, I get your point. Maybe you could refer someone who is an actual hair stylist."

"And?" Abby motioned with her finger up and down Syd's body. The faded polo shirt was definitely not from this century.

"And maybe take me shopping?"

"Me?" The request surprised Abby. She really liked Syd as

a colleague, but becoming friends with her was a whole different story. Abby hadn't made any close friends since she'd moved to the city. Plenty of acquaintances, but finding real friends in New York had been a harder task than she'd expected. "Yeah, I could do that. We'll start with the hair."

❖

"Hi, it's Kendall. You haven't called me, so I'm calling you. The weekend is coming up, and I'd love to spend Saturday with you. I can't stop thinking about you, which never happens to me. That sounds vain, so just nix that. I had a great time with you…no, nix that too. Abby, you gorgeous creature, I want you in my bed again. So, call me, okay? Don't make me beg. Save that for the bedroom."

Abby had missed the call earlier in the day, but she'd listened to the voice mail left on her office phone several times before leaving work. It was after eleven by the time she'd gotten home, put on her pajamas, and climbed into bed. She held her phone in one hand and the sticky note with Kendall's number in the other.

Against her better judgment, Abby typed in the number and waited. She got a generic voice mail message, so she ended the call. She closed her eyes, and just as she was about to fall asleep, her phone rang. It was the same number.

"Hello?"

"Now I have your cell, so you should just give in and see me this weekend."

Abby couldn't help but smile. Kendall had one of those soft, sexy voices. "Hi."

"Hello, beautiful. Long day? You sound tired."

"Yeah. I have a Friday deadline," Abby said.

"Perfect. You'll be all mine on Saturday."

Abby was too tired to put up a fight, even though her instincts were telling her that she should. "That sounds nice."

"What would you like to do?"

"Anything. Nothing. Lie in your arms while you lie to me."

"I haven't lied to you since…at all, actually."

Abby turned over and lay on her side, tucking the phone between the pillow and her ear. "You just haven't told me anything."

"I find it hard to believe you haven't googled me yet," Kendall said.

"Why would I Google someone I'm trying to forget? The last thing I need is to find out you're married to some kinky rich guy who likes to watch his wife bang chicks through a two-way mirror. Oh God, I'm not going to find a sex video of us online, am I?" Abby grinned, feeling slightly amused with herself. "I expect royalties for that, you know."

"Wow. I'm a call girl, and you're a porn star. Maybe it's meant to be. Regardless, while I hate to cut into a potentially lucrative income stream, there were no double mirrors or videos involved."

"What about the other thing?" In her heart, Abby already knew. Which was why she couldn't bring herself to type *Kendall Squires* into the search bar.

"Am I married to a rich man? Absolutely not," Kendall said.

Abby sat up in bed. There was no avoiding it any longer. "Okay, so the old money is yours, but you're married, right?"

Kendall didn't reply. Abby threw the phone number on her bedside table and waited for a response. She finally broke the dead silence. "No witty comeback?"

"No witty comeback," Kendall replied.

Abby closed her eyes and shook her head. "I knew it. I knew it when you said the truth would hurt, but after three glasses of wine, I guess I wanted your body more than I wanted the truth."

"And now?"

Abby took a deep breath. She'd promised herself she wouldn't do this again and yet, here she was. "I've been here before. I really have no interest in making this a trend. Hashtag Abby fell for another hot, straight, married woman."

"I really want to see you again, Abby. Please don't end this."

"Don't call me again." Abby ended the call and flopped back on the bed, putting both arms over her eyes. "When will I ever learn?"

CHAPTER FIVE

Two Months Later

Did company Christmas parties have to suck as hard as they did? Abby looked around the restaurant, noticing that everyone had a date or a spouse on their arm. Everyone except her. She walked over to the bar and ordered another glass of wine in the hope that she'd stop thinking about Kendall for two minutes. How had the woman managed to work her way so deep into Abby's consciousness after only one date?

It was the perfect date, that's how. With the perfect woman, except for one minor—well, not so minor—detail.

Syd walked up behind Abby and tapped her shoulder. "Hey, you."

Abby turned around and looked Syd up and down. "Not bad, Syd. Not bad." Syd was rockin' one of the outfits Abby had picked out for her on one of their shopping trips: black skinny jeans that complemented her long legs, a gray cashmere sweater, and black ankle boots. Her hair was a shorter, cleaner cut with long bangs that she pushed to the side. Syd looked fantastic, and Abby felt proud. "Who's your date?"

Syd glanced at the table behind her. "Just a girl I met at a club. She's sweet."

Abby narrowed her eyes. "Sweet, huh. Not feeling it?"

Syd leaned in close and took a beer from the ice bucket. "Feeling something. Just not for her."

Abby's eyes narrowed again. She wasn't sure what Syd meant by that. "Oh. Okay."

"What about you, Abs? Where's the hottie you said you're not involved with?"

Abby picked up her martini and took a long sip. "I have no idea what you're talking about."

"The sexy, older—"

"Stop," Abby said, giving her a warning look.

"Okay." Syd put up her hands and leaned on the bar so they were face-to-face. "Hey, I've been meaning to ask you if you'd ever considered dating someone younger than you."

"How much younger?"

Syd let out a nervous laugh. "Um…well, you're thirty-six, and I'm twenty-six, so…"

Abby coughed on her drink. "You and me?"

Syd grabbed a napkin and handed it to her. "Yeah."

Abby laughed. It was the most absurd thing she'd ever heard. They were friends and colleagues, not—Syd turned to walk away, but Abby grabbed her arm. "Syd, wait."

"It's okay, Abs. I get it. I'm just going to get my date and call it a night."

"You haven't had dinner yet. Syd." Abby took her by the arm and led her to a corner where they could talk privately. She didn't know what she would say, but she wasn't about to let Syd leave like this. "Look, it's just that we work together. And we're friends. And I really like having you as a friend."

"And there's someone else?"

Abby sighed. She didn't want to lie, but was it a lie? Kendall was always right there, invading her damn thoughts. Invading her dreams. She'd been back on that yacht with her quite a few times, reliving every moment and imagining new moments where they woke up together, had breakfast in bed, and made love well into the afternoon.

Then there was the issue of getting involved with a work colleague. It could be career suicide if you hooked up with the wrong person. Besides, she was Syd's mentor. Not her boss, technically, but still, it seemed wrong.

"It's complicated," Abby said. "But yes, there's someone else."

Syd glanced back at the party happening behind them. "I should get back to my date." An awkward few seconds passed before she said, "I'm glad we're friends too, Abs. Maybe after payday, we could go clothes shopping again?"

Abby breathed a sigh of relief, grateful she'd dodged a bullet without ruining a friendship. "I'd love to. Now, go take care of your date. She's not just sweet; she's damn cute, too."

Syd smiled. "Yeah, she is. And she really likes my cool outfit." She put air quotes around the word *cool*. "I guess I have you to thank for that."

Abby winked at her. "Go get 'em, Tiger."

❖

Abby said good-bye to the few people who were sober enough to notice her absence and left the party early. She pulled her coat collar a little higher on her neck and tucked her hands in her pockets. It was a cold night, but she felt like walking.

Syd seemed to bounce back after their conversation, laughing and cuddling with her date during dinner. Abby, on the other hand, strongly felt the sting of being alone for yet another holiday season.

She didn't notice at first that there was a black SUV following her until she stopped at a crosswalk. She looked to her right and then to her left. She did a double take when she saw the back window roll down. Her tummy did a flip-flop thinking it was Kendall, but a man leaned forward and put his hand out, waving someone else over to the car.

Abby tried hard to hold back the tears. She stood frozen at the crosswalk as people pushed past her. She couldn't go home alone. Not now. She turned right, knowing there was a hotel close by.

"Do you have any rooms?" Abby rubbed her cold hands together as she waited for the clerk.

"One left. It's a deluxe suite with a balcony. Seven hundred per night."

She slid her credit card across the counter and pulled her phone out of her purse. "What's the room number?"

"Ten sixteen."

Abby quickly sent a text. *NYLO on 77th. Room 1016.*

❖

It only took Kendall sixty-seven minutes to knock on the door. Abby knew because she'd been staring at the clock, wondering if she'd show up. She opened the door and gave Kendall a weak smile. "Hi again."

Kendall didn't return the greeting. She walked into the room and looked around, then turned to Abby. "You summoned me. No one summons me."

"I didn't summon you. I simply made you aware of my location. What you chose to do with that information was up to you. Wine?" Abby went to the small table and picked up her glass. She took a sip and waited for a reply.

Kendall set her purse down but didn't remove her coat. "Why am I here?"

Abby sat on the end of the bed and crossed her legs. She'd spent sixty-seven minutes staring at the clock, but she hadn't thought to come up with a good story. She could tell Kendall that she was horny and wanted to fuck, but Kendall was too smart for that. She'd hear the sad tone in Abby's voice. She'd see the tears that were lying in wait, just under the surface. The truth was the only option, hard as it would be to admit.

"I was at my company Christmas party, and all I could think about was you," Abby said. "It sounds so stupid, but I found myself wishing you were my date tonight because those parties suck, and everyone had a date or a spouse, but I didn't. Because I can't stop thinking about a married woman."

Kendall took a step closer and softened her stance. "Why am I here?"

Abby took another sip of wine and kept her eyes on the red liquid as she swirled it in the glass. "I've been the other woman before. With Heather, I knew that taking her to a Christmas party was definitely *not* an option. But that first night on the yacht, you talked about dating me, so I need to know." She raised her head and met Kendall's gaze. "Could I have asked you to go with me tonight?"

Kendall sighed. She started to say something but stopped herself. After a moment of silence, she shook her head and whispered, "No."

Abby's gaze fell to her wine again. "Because some married couples have arrangements, you know? Like ground rules. They can sleep with other—"

"Abby," Kendall said, interrupting her. "Why did you bring me to a hotel room that's a five-minute cab ride from your home?"

"Just answer the fucking question," Abby said. She shook her head, disappointed that she'd let her feelings show.

"You didn't ask a question. I did."

Abby threw her hand in the air. "Because it seemed better than going to a bar and drinking away the pain, okay? Feel better now that you know the truth?"

"No," Kendall said. "I feel better because I'm breathing the same air as you. That's why I feel better. I've missed you."

"I don't even know you! You won't *let* me know you, but you're in my head constantly, and I don't know what to do about it."

Kendall took off her coat and threw it on a chair. "Ask me." She went to the bar and poured herself a glass of wine.

Abby followed Kendall's every move. She could ignore her head and just follow her heart, she told herself. Just get up and push Kendall against a wall, forgetting the hard reality of their situation. Have unbelievably great sex again and then set up a weekly secret rendezvous. She'd done it before. But Christmas was just around the corner and she wanted more. She wanted Christmas Eve and Christmas morning and all the other things Heather never gave her. All the things she knew Kendall couldn't give her either, and yet, here she was, trying to convince herself otherwise. She focused on her wine again. "Who are you married to?"

"Her name is Isabelle."

Abby's head shot up. "You're married to a woman?"

Kendall turned around, glass of wine in hand. "You thought it was a man?"

"Yeah." Falling for straight women, that was Abby's M.O. This revelation definitely surprised her.

"Maybe if you hadn't hung up on me."

It didn't change anything. Man or woman, Kendall was still married, and on some level, this was even worse. This was just straight-up cheating without the excuses straight women could make, like trying to find their true selves. "Why were you in that bar where we met?"

Kendall set her glass down and leaned against the bar with her arms folded. "Same reason you were there. I wanted a distraction."

"So, this wife of yours...I take it it's complicated?" Abby ignored the pounding in her head along with the unopened bottle of water sitting on the bedside table. She finished the wine in her glass and held it out for Kendall to fill again.

"Very complicated." Kendall emptied the bottle into Abby's glass.

"That's what Heather said too. And then I realized that 'complicated' actually meant valuable. Her husband held more value than I did."

Kendall pulled a chair over to the bed and sat so she was facing Abby, knees to knees. "I'm going to try and say this without sounding like a complete asshole."

"Don't try, just say it." Abby wanted honesty even if the truth was ugly.

"Okay. Do you want someone who can be your date at a stupid company Christmas party, or do you want someone who can rock your world and make you forget about all those people who had boring dates and spouses who complained about having to go to that party the whole way there? Because I guarantee you, Abby, they all got drunk as soon as they could and ninety-five percent of them are not having sex right now."

Abby let that sink in for a moment. Kendall was probably

right. She didn't know anyone at work who seemed truly happy in their marriage. "Syd was hoping to get laid tonight. In fact, maybe I should introduce the two of you. She thinks you're hot, and she sure seems to have a thing for older women."

Kendall blinked a few times, then stood. "Okay, I don't know who Syd is, but I think we're done here."

Abby squeezed her eyes shut. She'd invited Kendall here, so why was she being such an asshole to her? "I'm sorry. I shouldn't have said that."

"No, you shouldn't have." Kendall put her coat back on.

"The hardest part about being with Heather was knowing that after she'd been with me, she went home to her husband's bed. Do you and your wife still…" Abby shook her head to try to clear it. She was starting to slur her words.

Kendall took the wineglass from Abby's hand and sat next to her on the bed. "Has anyone ever told you that they'd give you the world if they could?"

Abby nodded. "Heather told me that all the time. Isn't it convenient that the people who tell you that have a huge out? I would if I could, but I can't, so I won't. And the really sad part is, all I wanted…all I ever wanted was to wake up with her in the morning. Just once, wake up and see her lying there next to me." She looked at the ceiling and shook her head. "I'm such a fool."

"I'm sorry," Kendall whispered.

Abby squeezed her eyes shut again, trying to fight back the tears. "It's okay. I still have a great career ahead of me, and I hear next year's Christmas party is going to be stellar. Lots of pretty girls serving drinks. I love being in a male-dominated industry. Have you ever been to one of their conventions? It's like a gay girl's dream come true. Tits and ass everywhere."

Kendall rested her hand on Abby's arm. "Abby."

"No. Really, Kendall." Abby's eyes widened. "By this same time next year, I won't even remember this. I mean, it's not like you're the only gorgeous woman in this city who has a great sense of humor and also fucks like a champ. They're a dime a dozen, right? I'll find her, right?"

Kendall stood and lingered for a moment. Eventually, she picked up her purse and went to the door. Resting her hand on the handle, she stopped and turned around. "I hope you find her, Abby. I hope you find her and marry her and have babies with her. That's what I hope."

Abby couldn't hold it in anymore. Her eyes filled with tears as Kendall walked out the door. She couldn't leave it this way, with so much unsaid. She got up and ran to the door. She opened it to find Kendall a few doors down, leaning against the wall. She looked distraught, but Abby stayed where she was. "I won't, Kendall. I won't find her and marry her because there's only one you. And you're right. Christmas parties suck, no matter who you work for. And Isabelle…whoever she is…is one lucky woman. And she better wake up every morning happy as fuck to be alive. Because if you were my wife, that yacht would be called *My First and Last*."

Abby stumbled back into her room and fell on the bed, face first, crying into the pillow. Her last thought before she fell asleep was *Please, God, let me forget her.*

CHAPTER SIX

January had been especially cold. Abby stood by the stove in the break room, making her third cup of hot tea and dreaming about summer, when Julie came in. "You have a walk-in."

"Give it to Syd." Abby had been buried for weeks. She was lucky if she left before nine each night, and Syd had been right there beside her, making sure the project would be finished on time. Abby continued to mentor Syd, and that included how to handle prospective clients.

"I'm pretty sure you'll want to take this one yourself," Julie said excitedly. "Abs, it's Isabelle Wright! She asked for you!"

"Never heard of her."

Julie lowered her voice. "Don't let Denny hear you say that! She's one of the most important developers in New York. Seriously, Abby, how have you not heard of Isabelle Wright?"

Abby scowled. "Take it easy, would you? I've been in New York all of six months, and literally every other person I've met is the most important developer in New York."

"Well, this is the only one you'll find dripping in diamonds. She's the principal of Altafor."

"Oh God." Abby might not have memorized the name of every CEO in town, but she had certainly heard of Altafor. You couldn't walk down a street in Manhattan without running into one of their projects. "Why on earth did she ask for me?"

"I didn't ask, Abs. I thought you knew her. I just asked her to wait in the conference room."

Abby checked herself in the mirror by the door and walked down the hall. She opened the door and immediately put out her hand. "Ms. Wright? Abby Dunn. It's a pleasure to meet you."

Abby waited for the woman to take her hand, but she just stood there, looking her up and down. Abby lowered her hand. "I'm sorry. Maybe Julie misunderstood. Were you looking for someone else?"

"Do you know who I am, Ms. Dunn? Or do we need to pretend for a moment before I cut to the chase?"

"Of course I know who you are, Ms. Wright." *I've known for at least thirty seconds.* "Would you care to sit?"

"I'd rather stand."

"Okay." Abby stood on the opposite side of the long table. "How can I help you?"

Isabelle tilted her head. "Wow. You really don't know who I am, do you? When you sleep with married people, is it too much trouble to find out who their wives are?"

"Excuse me?" Abby's eyes widened. "Ms. Wright, I really think you have me confused with someone else. If you knew me, you'd know that I'm not interested in your husband or anyone else's."

"My husband? You really are a piece of work. If you seriously don't know who the other half of Altafor is, you're as bad a lesbian as you are an architect."

Abby's heart dropped. The pieces were coming together. Not the least of which was the piece where Kendall had apparently told her wife about their night together. "Oh, my…"

Isabelle's expression transformed into a spiteful grin. "Well, Abby Dunn, I know exactly who you are. You screwed the wrong woman, and now, I'm about to make or break your career."

"I had no idea," Abby stammered.

"Well, let me educate you," Isabelle said with a sneer. "Your boss, Denny Milkin, has been courting me for years, and by courting, I mean doing everything he can to get me to notice his little firm, which I haven't, until now." Isabelle glanced at the door. "I'm certain your entire office knows we're meeting right now. How will it work out for you if I let Denny know you're the reason he'll never see any of my business?"

Abby started to interject, but Isabelle held up her hand. "It was a rhetorical question, dear. Now, I'm here to make a deal. I'll invite Denny to bid on our new Chelsea project, and you will stay the fuck away from my wife. Otherwise, you can kiss your career good-bye."

Abby's mouth opened, but nothing came out.

"You may speak now," Isabelle said.

"I haven't seen her," Abby whispered. Her heart was pounding so hard she could barely speak.

"Excuse me?"

"It was just the one time," Abby said with a little more strength in her voice.

"Well, that must've been one hell of a fuck." Isabelle threw her clutch purse on the table and sat.

If Abby hadn't been so thrown off by this unexpected turn of events, she would've heartily agreed that it had indeed been one hell of a fuck. One that she couldn't seem to forget, no matter how hard she'd tried.

"You're obviously way out of your league, Abby. Risking your career for a fuck. You do realize it could all go away like that?" Isabelle said, snapping her fingers. "You know, we actually have more in common than you think." She leaned forward in her chair. "I'm an architect by trade too. That, and our taste in women, are where the similarities end. You see, my voice in this city matters. I get what I want. One phone call, three words spoken, and you are done in this town."

Fire Abby Dunn. The words rang in Abby's ears as if Isabelle had actually spoken them. *So be it.* Isabelle Wright was about to get an earful as well. "Do you love her?"

Isabelle gasped. "Excuse me?"

"When was the last time you told her?"

Isabelle stood and grabbed her purse. "Do you really think I'm going to let a drunken bar tramp lecture me on love?"

A bar tramp? That was something Abby hadn't ever been called before. And now she was sure it wasn't Kendall who had told Isabelle about their encounter. It must've been the driver, or maybe Sergio had spilled the beans. Definitely not Kendall. And being called that only strengthened Abby's resolve.

"Isabelle—do you mind if I call you Isabelle?" Abby didn't wait for an answer. "The only thing to do with a woman like Kendall is to worship the ground she walks on. It sounds like somewhere along the way, you forgot that."

Abby was just guessing. Basing her assumptions solely on what she'd experienced with Kendall on the yacht. She'd pegged her for a hopeless romantic within the first fifteen minutes. Someone who knew how to treat a woman and reveled in making her feel beautiful and special. And when they made it to the bedroom, well, let's just say Abby had been using that night to take care of her needs ever since. Kendall was a kind, caring, giving lover who couldn't seem to get enough of Abby's body. Isabelle didn't strike Abby as the kind of person who would return Kendall's love. Her passion, maybe, but not her love.

"Isabelle, I am sorry about what happened with Kendall. If it counts for anything, and I suspect it doesn't, I didn't know who she was, and I didn't know she was married because I chose not to ask. That's on me." Abby stood and pushed her chair back. "If it makes me a lesser lesbian that I don't recognize the city's gay power couple…well, it sounds like that bothers you more than it does me. But none of that gives you the right to threaten my career."

Isabelle walked over to Abby and leaned in, getting well into her personal space. "If you value your job, you'll end it for good. Consider this your one and only warning."

❖

Abby never did respond well to threats. Also, it bothered her that Kendall's last memory of her would forever be that of a sad-sack drunk girl who cared way too much about office Christmas parties. Isabelle's little visit seemed like a good opportunity to change that. She wasn't sure she'd get any response when she'd sent the text asking Kendall to meet her, but the response was immediate: *Of course. Where are you?*

Abby's face lit up when she saw Kendall walking toward her. She tried to suppress her grin, but it was no use. She was truly happy to see that beautiful face again. "Cream. No sugar." She offered Kendall one of the coffee cups she was holding.

Kendall took off her gloves and tucked them in her coat pocket. "How did you know?"

"On the yacht, we had coffee after dinner."

"Good memory." Kendall took a sip. "Mmm, I needed this. Thank you."

Hearing Kendall hum her approval took Abby right back to that night on the yacht. She desperately wanted to lean in and taste those lips again. She did lean in, but she kissed Kendall's cheek instead. "It's good to see you."

Kendall looked surprised. "After the last time, at the hotel, I didn't think I'd ever see you again."

"I know. Me neither." Abby took Kendall's arm. "Let's walk." It felt so natural, so good to be in Kendall's presence again, Abby was tempted to forget everything she'd planned to say and steal Kendall away for a day. Take her back to that hotel and rip her clothes off this time instead of cutting them off.

She glanced at Kendall, taking in her beauty, her grace, her sexy smile. Her hair was slightly different, maybe a little bit shorter. Abby had pulled on that hair. Not too hard, just hard enough to gain access to that smooth neck. Kendall had gasped and then moaned. And moaned again. And eventually whispered Abby's name in her ear. *I'm coming, Abby*, she'd said. And then she came undone in Abby's arms. And Abby wanted to hear her name come out of that gorgeous mouth again. She wanted it more than anything.

"It's good to see you," Kendall said.

Abby would have returned the sentiment, but she couldn't see enough of Kendall at all. The wool coat was covering up her dress, and some very expensive-looking boots covered her legs. Abby wanted more. She wanted to feel Kendall's arm where she was holding it instead of the thick coat. Why couldn't it have been a warmer day?

"Thanks for meeting me on such short notice," Abby said.

Kendall smiled. "Yes, well, you're the only person in the entire city who has the power to summon me. I dropped everything to be here."

Oh, why did she have to say that? Abby pulled her one-time lover a little closer. Even though they could never be anything to each other, it meant something that Kendall still seemed to care about her. Maybe she wasn't alone in thinking that their one night together had been special. But Abby needed to stay strong. She had things to say, and thinking about the past wouldn't help her get through this conversation.

"Before you tell me why I'm here, can I say something?"

"Of course," Abby said, grateful she didn't have to jump right in.

"It's difficult for me to fully regret what I did," Kendall said. "Because I will never regret knowing you, but I do want to apologize for the pain I caused you. It wasn't fair—"

"To sweep me off my feet and then tell me you're married?" Abby said, interrupting her. "No, you're right, that wasn't fair." She kept hold of Kendall's arm. "And I appreciate you not taking advantage of my drunken state in the hotel room that night after the office party. That's twice now you've saved me from myself."

"The only thing I wanted to do that night was take away your pain, but I was the cause of it. Well, me and a woman named Heather. I really despise her, even though I know I'm not much different."

"You're very different," Abby said. "The situation might be similar, but you're nothing like Heather, which is why you're rarely far from my thoughts." It was a big admission, but Abby wasn't there to lie. She wanted to get everything out on the table. And she would if she could keep her head in the game and not in Kendall's bed on that damn boat. "And even more so today," Abby added.

"Why today?" Kendall asked.

"Your wife just paid me a visit."

Kendall stopped short in the middle of the busy sidewalk, forcing people to walk around them. "What?"

"Isabelle. She came to my office. She's really quite beautiful." Abby took Kendall's hand and led her to a park entrance, getting them out of the heavy foot traffic. She wanted to intertwine their fingers and pretend that this happened every day—a walk in the park on a crisp winter afternoon. But she let go and kept walking.

"What did Isabelle want? Was it business?"

"Not exactly. I guess I really should've used Google sooner. Then I wouldn't feel like such an idiot right now." Abby took a deep breath, trying to calm her frustration. She should've done so many things differently. The minute Kendall revealed her last name on the boat, she should've excused herself and gone to the restroom with her phone in hand. She should've found out everything she could about the woman right then and there. But she didn't want to know. It felt too good, being in Kendall's presence. By the time she knew the truth, she was afraid googling Kendall would have made it even harder to stay away.

"There were threats," Abby said.

"Wait. What?" Kendall stopped again. "She threatened you?"

Abby urged her forward, interlocking their arms. She was afraid that if she stood for too long facing Kendall, she'd lose her resolve and pull her in by the lapels. She'd tell her how cruel she was right before she kissed her. Fuck Isabelle Wright. She was a bitch anyway.

"Do you have any idea how she even knows who I am?" She took a sip of her coffee and glanced at Kendall.

"Abby, I didn't—" Kendall's mouth gaped open as she shook her head. "I have no idea how she knows. She hasn't said anything."

"I knew it wasn't you. Or at least, I assumed it wasn't once she called me a bar tramp."

Kendall sighed. "I guess I need to fire a certain driver."

"Tell me about Isabelle." Abby wanted Kendall to say something good. She wanted assurances that Isabelle had some redeeming qualities. She wanted Kendall to express her undying love for her wife and tell her that their night together was a big mistake that she would always regret. If she heard those words, she could say what she needed to say. But Kendall didn't respond.

"Okay," Abby said. "I'll tell you what I know. Kendall Squires and Isabelle Wright marry right out of college, joining two of

Manhattan's oldest and richest families. Together, they build a real estate empire. And their first yacht was indeed the first of many. Or three, to be exact. But who's counting?"

Kendall narrowed her eyes. "I see you and Google are friends now."

Abby continued. "They donate millions to their alma mater and several of their favorite charities. They're on more boards than even they can count, and no charity ball is considered a success until they walk into the room."

Kendall cleared her throat. "If you say so."

"They haven't had any children. No one knows why. And Isabelle's latest passion project has her spending several months of the year in Italy, where she's immersing herself in the language and culture while restoring an old winery in Tuscany. I'm guessing that's where she was when we met."

Kendall leaned in and lowered her voice. "Now you just sound like a stalker."

"Maybe. But I understand now that it's complicated. And even though your wife threatened to have me fired, I certainly don't blame her for wanting to keep you. And honestly, no one has ever fought like that to keep me, so I have no doubt she really loves you."

Kendall stopped walking and turned to Abby. "Is that what you wanted to tell me? That Isabelle loves me?"

Abby shook her head. "No. I wanted to tell you to go home to your wife and renew your vows or something. Figure out why the hell you got married in the first place. And if it's too late for that, then get divorced. But don't keep breaking hearts. I know I'm not the first girl who fell for those green eyes and that stupidly sexy smile."

There. She'd said what she came to say. And now she was staring into those amazing eyes, and it took everything in her to not pull Kendall in and kiss her the way she'd been dreaming about since their one night together.

Kendall broke eye contact and sighed. "Now you sound like a friend."

A friend who knows what you taste like. A friend who knows what kind of perfection is under that coat. A friend who— Abby needed to get out of her damn head. She forced a smile. "I'd love it if we could be friends. Although if I were Isabelle, I'd make sure that never happened."

Kendall slowly shook her head. "I can't believe—" She stopped and straightened her shoulders. "I'll make sure you don't lose your job. Don't worry about that."

"I hate my job."

"What?"

Abby shrugged. "I transferred to the New York office to get a fresh start. I needed one after the Heather debacle, you know?"

Kendall's eyes misted over. "And then you met me. God, Abby. I'm so sorry."

"I know," Abby said with a nod. "But like you said, it's hard to regret everything."

"So, you're going back to San Francisco?"

"They worked me twelve hours a day there too. Besides, I like New York. The only question is whether or not this is the place to start my own business." She shrugged. "Or maybe I should go back to New Mexico and design dental offices and strip malls."

Kendall took their cups and threw them in the trash. She took hold of Abby's hands. "You're too good for that. This is the place you need to be. And I'll help you. Just friends. I swear. But I'd love to help you. In fact, what if I promised that you'll have a client the day you open your doors."

Abby shook her head. "I can't touch my boss's clients. And even though Altafor isn't a client, he's desperate for you to sign on. It'd be a mess."

Kendall grinned. "I'm not talking about me. I know developers all over the country." She brought Abby's hands to her lips and kissed them. "Please, Abby. Let me help you live this dream. My dreams have all happened. Professionally, at least. These days, Iz and I are just re-icing the same cake."

It was a generous offer, but Abby was hesitant to take it. She wanted to know about the dreams that weren't realized. The personal ones. She wanted to not cringe when Kendall called her wife by a nickname. *Iz.* Whatever. And she really wanted to figure out how to say good-bye. Well, kind of. But not really. "I don't know, Kendall."

Kendall pulled her into a hug. "Just let me get you your first client. After that, it's up to you."

Abby accepted the hug and held on a little longer than she should have, breathing in Kendall's scent and basking in her warmth. The truth was, she didn't want to let go. "Honestly, it's a big move, and I'm petrified, but I know I'll be happier if I do it."

"It's done, then." Kendall pulled back from the hug and squeezed Abby's shoulders. "It's going to be great. *You're* going to be great."

Kendall's excitement was contagious. Abby grinned and said, "I guess I'm staying in New York. And apparently, I have a friend."

"Apparently, you do."

CHAPTER SEVEN

It had been five months since Abby had handed in her resignation at work. Three months since she'd officially opened her doors for business. And one week since she'd decided maybe it wasn't the dumbest thing she'd ever done. She had her second client and a possible third. She'd be okay. At least for the next six months.

She was putting the final touches on a scale model of her latest project when Kendall knocked on the doorframe. "You need a bigger office."

Abby's eyes lit up when she saw what was in Kendall's hand. "Is that coffee for me?"

Kendall casually took a sip. "No, it's mine."

"I'll buy it from you. The new coffeepot broke." Abby turned her back to the model and tried to scoot past it, but she knocked over two trees with her ass. "Damnit!" she shouted.

Kendall giggled. "Baby's got back."

Abby reached into her pocket and pulled out a five-dollar bill. She handed it to Kendall and grabbed the cup from her at the same time. She took a sip and then kissed Kendall's cheek. "It was mine all along. I can taste the cinnamon."

Kendall threw the bill on the desk and put the little trees back where they belonged. "It's a beautiful building."

"I hope so. It's the sole reason I haven't slept in a month." Abby sat in her chair and took a long sip of her cinnamon mocha. "And God, this coffee is everything right now."

"Do you know what the condos will go for?"

"Nine-fifty and up."

Kendall turned around and smiled. "Nice work."

"Coming from you," Abby said with a wink. "I'll take it."

Kendall grabbed a folding chair and set it right next to Abby's office chair. She sat and looked around the old, run-down office. "I sure wish you would've taken me up on my offer. This place is a dump."

"We've had this conversation."

"I know, I know. You need to do it on your own." Kendall shook her head. "Such a stubborn woman."

"How's it going? Are you staying on the straight and narrow?" Abby asked, trying to change the subject.

Kendall gave her a wicked side eye. "You're taking this friend thing a little too far, don't you think?"

"What? I can't check up on you and make sure you're not riverboating?" Abby put finger quotes around the last word.

"Hmm." Kendall shook her head. "No, you can't."

"Fine," Abby shrugged. "But I gave you up because you're married, not to give you license to fuck around with someone else."

Kendall looked away and said, "That's the last thing I want to do."

"Well, that's good, right?" Kendall didn't reply, so Abby nudged her. "What's wrong?"

Kendall gave her a half-hearted smile. "You said riverboat, and it reminded me of the night I met you."

Abby covered her eyes. "You mean the night I threw up on you? At the bar?"

"*And* you called me a hooker."

"Call girl. I said call girl."

"Because that's so much better?"

"Not really." Abby sighed deeply. "And now, here we are, sitting in my shitty little office, not having sex. God, we're a couple of winners."

It came out before Abby could stop it—the frustration of the last few months nicely wrapped up into two sentences. They'd managed to stay in contact, mostly over the phone. Abby had tried to keep their in-person visits to a minimum because it was just too hard to look at Kendall and not see what they could be together, not feel everything she felt every time they were breathing the same air, as Kendall had put it. Breathing the same air, like they were right now.

Abby had wanted to take Kendall up on her offer to rent a nice office in one of their buildings at a discount but thought it best to keep her distance. The building, along with everything else, belonged to both Kendall and Isabelle. The last thing Abby needed was another run-in with the wife. She was under enough stress with starting a new business, and she didn't need the woman trying to sabotage her efforts.

Abby hated the office she'd rented. It was cold, drafty, and way too small, but she'd never admit that to anyone. She'd make do. And keep her distance. It was the smart thing to do.

They sat in silence for a minute, Abby sipping on her coffee and Kendall fiddling with a loose string on her jacket. "You know, you always look like a million bucks in your designer clothes," Abby said. "Do you ever just kick back in sweats and an old college T-shirt and binge watch Netflix?"

Kendall searched Abby's eyes for a moment and said, "Come to Cape Cod with me tomorrow and find out."

Abby furrowed her brow. "What's going on?" The sadness in Kendall's voice worried her.

Kendall quickly shook her head. "Nothing. I have to go to Cape Cod, and I thought it might be fun is all."

Abby stared at her intently. She wanted to say, *Yes! I'd love to go to Cape Cod with you.* But she knew it would be a mistake. "I can't go to Cape Cod with you."

"Why?"

It was a firm question from Kendall. That also worried Abby. "You…Kendall, you know why."

Kendall stood, walked over to the far wall, and leaned against it with her arms folded. "Why?" she asked again, this time even more sternly.

Abby set her cup down and closed her office door. She stood

in front of Kendall with her hands in her back pockets. "You know why."

"*Tell* me, damnit! Why can't I take my friend to Cape Cod? That's what friends do. They go places and do things!"

Abby's gaze fell to the floor. Did Kendall really not understand? Were all these lingering feelings she was having one-sided? She didn't think so. She'd felt the spark, the fire, the longing, every time they met for coffee, which had only been a few times, but it was enough to remind Abby that she was living on the edge when it came to this woman.

"I don't trust us," Abby said, keeping her eyes on the floor.

"Oh, come on, Abby. We've been doing this friend thing for months. You think we can't take a little trip together?"

Abby lifted her gaze. "Just barely. We've been doing this friend thing, but just barely."

Kendall looked away in frustration. "I don't even see you that way anymore. You're my friend. Period."

Abby let out a little laugh. "Okay."

Kendall pushed past her, their shoulders brushing. "I'll see you when I see you, then."

Abby caught Kendall's arm as she tried to leave. "Okay," she whispered.

"Okay?"

"I'd love to go to Cape Cod with you. It'll be fine, right? Just two friends, doing what friends do." Abby's voice didn't sound convincing.

"Yes," Kendall said. She searched Abby's eyes and then looked at the hand that still had hold of her arm. "No, you're right. We would drive to Cape Cod, and I'd get to know you better and fall even more in love than I already am. And you're probably a backseat driver anyway, so…"

Abby let go and folded her arms. "And then there's that great restaurant by the water where we'll drink too much wine and laugh too much, and since it's Friday night, they'll probably have a live band."

"And dancing with you is so awkward because you just don't have any rhythm," Kendall added.

"Of course I have rhythm," Abby said with a huff.

"I can only imagine," Kendall replied, feigning innocence as she bit her lip.

Abby stared at her intently for a few long seconds. "You're in love with me?" she asked, her voice cracking as she said it.

Kendall looked away. "And then there's the cute little bed and breakfast that only has one room left, and it's a queen bed, so there's no getting away from cuddling." She paused for a second and then made eye contact. "Yes."

Abby backed away and leaned on her desk. She gripped the edges so tight, her fingers turned white. "You need to leave," she whispered. Kendall took a step toward her, but Abby held up her hand. "Please. Just don't touch me."

Kendall didn't listen to her. She wrapped her arms around Abby and pulled her to her chest. "Don't push me away," she said as she kissed her head. "Please don't push me away."

Abby's breathing became shallow. She closed her eyes and buried her face in Kendall's chest. Her hands worked their way up Kendall's legs, over her ass, and onto her back. She gripped Kendall's blouse in her fingers as her lips found skin. She inhaled deeply, and her body instantly reacted to Kendall's scent, overwhelming her with a feeling of euphoric comfort. She rested her forehead on Kendall's chest and wrapped her arms around her waist. "I love you too," she whispered.

Kendall stayed there for a least a minute, holding Abby and caressing her hair. When Abby looked up and their eyes met, Kendall seemed to choke back her emotions. "I can't. I can't do this to you again. It's not fair. You deserve better."

Abby kept hold of Kendall's hand as she backed away, not wanting to let go. Not ever wanting to let go. "It sounded nice, Cape Cod."

Kendall took another step back and let go. "I'll stop by again sometime."

Abby could hear it in Kendall's voice that she didn't mean what she'd just said. She ran for the door as it closed. It took every ounce of her strength not to open it and run down the sidewalk to catch Kendall. To kiss her and tell her she could do it. She could be the other woman again if that's what it took to keep Kendall in her life. She bent over and held on to the handle, her gut wrenching in pain.

Abby's knees hit the floor. She sucked in air, trying to hold back a sob. Being just friends wasn't an option. It never was.

CHAPTER EIGHT

Kendall sat next to her wife on the upper deck of *The First of Many*. It would be their last night together before Isabelle left for Italy again. Spending it on the yacht had been Isabelle's idea. It was the one place in the city where they never discussed business. They had a rule; when they were on the boat, they put work aside.

Of course, Kendall couldn't remember the last time Isabelle had been on the boat with her. It had probably been last summer— or maybe two summers ago. She'd have to look at her calendar to know for sure. But what good would that do? Kendall didn't need a calendar to know how far they'd grown apart.

"I told you we have to be in Paris a day early next month, didn't I?" Isabelle reached over and ran her fingers through Kendall's hair. "An August wedding in Paris is perfect. Is anything more romantic?"

Kendall stirred from her thoughts after a moment. "What? Oh, yeah. Cousin's wedding. Rehearsal dinner. Got it."

"Kendall, don't be mad. I'm going to Italy, not the moon. Time will fly by. You'll see." When Kendall didn't respond, Isabelle nudged her gently. "You're a million miles away."

"No," Kendall said. "Not a million. Just 5.2."

"What does that mean?"

"Abby's apartment…is 5.2 miles away."

Isabelle took her hand away. "Why are you telling me this? Are you sleeping with her again?"

Sleeping with her, Kendall internally scoffed. *I'd give anything just to sit across from her and share a coffee again.*

There was no question that the night she'd shared with Abby on this very same boat was so seared into her memory, Kendall could probably recount every minute of it. Abby was one of a kind. An unforgettable woman. And the last few months of getting to know her as a friend had only solidified those feelings. Why Abby was still single, she couldn't for the life of her understand.

Kendall was still undecided about whether or not she would try to reestablish a connection with Abby. She wanted to so badly, but she knew Abby was right—they had just barely been managing the "friend" thing. The memories of what they'd shared together that night were always right there, simmering beneath the surface of every conversation.

Kendall had noticed the longing looks from Abby. She'd noticed when Abby's eyes lingered a little too long on her lips, her hands, her legs when she'd worn a dress. And keeping her distance had been difficult. But more difficult was the thought of losing Abby forever.

And then, Kendall went and ruined everything by inviting her to Cape Cod. They both knew what would happen. Abby had been the one brave enough to say it out loud. And all Kendall could do was walk away. For good.

Kendall turned to Isabelle and said, "No, Iz. I'm not sleeping with Abby. But I miss her. And I'm not going to spend another three months alone while you're in Italy."

Isabelle stood and paced for a moment, then stood in front of Kendall with her hands on her hips. "This is what you tell me the night before I leave? That you're going to screw the bar tramp while I'm gone?"

Kendall remained calm, even though Isabelle's nickname for Abby pissed her off no end. Her driver, who was no longer her driver, had been all too happy to tell Isabelle the story, painting Abby as a so-called *bar tramp*. Kendall felt guilty about so many things, but that one cut her to the core. Abby didn't deserve it.

After finding out about Isabelle's little visit to Abby's office, Kendall had gone home and told her wife the truth; that she'd had a one-night stand, but it hadn't turned into anything more. She also told Isabelle that she and Abby had a friendship. That prompted an immediate divorce ultimatum from Isabelle; it was obvious she didn't expect Kendall to call her bluff. When Kendall did, she backed down and agreed to the friendship. Kendall replayed the conversation in her mind daily, wondering when they would have a version of it that ended differently.

Kendall had been waiting for her wife to admit that she'd had her own indiscretions. Waiting for her to cancel her trip to Italy. Instead, she'd watched Isabelle pack and prepare for her trip with undiminished excitement. And Kendall wondered when it was that they had both become such good liars.

"I know you have someone there." Kendall surprised herself with how calmly she could say the words.

"What are you talking about?"

Kendall set a hard gaze on her wife. "In Tuscany. You have a lover in Tuscany. For going on two years now." Isabelle turned away. "Tell me I'm wrong, Iz."

"I won't go."

Kendall shook her head. "Izzy..."

"No, Kendall. I won't go." Isabelle straddled Kendall, pressing their foreheads together. "I'll stay here with you. It's you I love. It's you I need."

"No," Kendall said. "You haven't needed me for a very long time."

"That's not true," Isabelle whispered. She placed a gentle kiss on Kendall's lips.

Their relationship had always been so passionate, in the bedroom and out. They loved hard, played hard, and even fought hard. And then a few years ago, Isabelle had started going to Italy, and they'd slowly grown apart. Their only shared passion now was their business.

The distance hadn't made the heart grow fonder. Kendall found herself feeling bitter every time Isabelle left her in New York to run their business all alone. It wasn't what she wanted. They were a team. Until they weren't.

"You'll still go," Kendall said. "Isabelle, even if we made love tonight, you'd still go tomorrow."

"I won't." Isabelle stood and pulled her wife up with her. "I promise."

Kendall backed away, needing space. She glanced at the large suitcase sitting by the cabin door. If Isabelle stayed, it would only be for one reason: to keep Kendall from filing for divorce. It wouldn't be because she wanted to stay. Her heart would still be in Italy. Kendall knew that, and anything Isabelle said wouldn't change that fact.

"Iz, why are we still doing this?"

"Doing what?" Isabelle asked innocently.

"This. The boat." Kendall made a sweeping motion around the deck before turning to Isabelle and gesturing between them. "You and me."

"We're trying. This is what marriage is, Kendall. Or have you forgotten that amongst your many indiscretions?"

The comment annoyed Kendall. Isabelle knew Abby had been the only one. As for Abby, well, Kendall could have just about killed Sergio when he asked about "the usual route." The truth was, Kendall did take that route regularly. What Abby didn't know was that, apart from the crew, she always took the trip alone. It was the only place she felt safe enough—and solitary enough—to think about what her life had become.

"No, Iz. It's not. Nothing about this is a marriage anymore. All we do anymore is grow further apart."

"I've loved you since college. That hasn't changed."

"Yes, Iz, it has," Kendall answered softly.

Isabelle looked away. "You were a hot mess back then, but I adored everything about you. You just had to look at me, and I would giggle."

Isabelle was on the verge of tears. Kendall always hated that.

She couldn't bear to see her Isabelle upset. "I literally charmed your pants off," she said, trying to lighten the moment. "And to think my mother thought sending me to charm school would help me find a man. Boy, was she wrong."

Isabelle laughed. "Yes. I remember her face when we told her we were getting married."

"Her face stayed that way for months. Like she'd seen a ghost and smelled a fart all at the same time."

"I see the charm school didn't help much on any front." Isabelle laughed again. "Oh my God, what we've been through with our parents."

Kendall nodded. "We got through it together. And we held on tight for the longest time."

The truth was, she and Isabelle had to fight everyone in their lives to be together. Both families were devastated and angry. They had threatened not only physical harm but also disownment. But Kendall and Isabelle stood their ground. They were in love and just young enough to believe that love did indeed conquer all. And in their case, it had. Almost. After several years, the families came together and agreed that their daughters' happiness was more important than pride. That was the story. In reality, they recognized that joining their two families would further cement their legacies in the greatest city on earth.

Isabelle's expression saddened. "What happened to us?"

"We found different dreams to dream."

"Oh God!" Isabelle slapped her forehead. "You built a house on Cape Cod for us, and I've never seen it. I'm so sorry I haven't made the time."

"And you've built a life for yourself in Tuscany that doesn't include me."

Isabelle stepped forward and took her wife's hand. "Come with me. You'd love it there if you just gave it a chance."

"Someone has to run our company, Iz. I can't just leave town for months on end. And besides, if you really wanted me there, you would've asked me before today."

Isabelle rubbed her face in frustration, then clasped her hands together. "If you know there's someone in Italy, why aren't you begging me to stay?"

"Is that what you want? To see me beg?" Kendall asked, her voice getting higher. "Is your ego really that big, Izzy, that you'd have me beg you to stay and then still leave? Because you *are* leaving, aren't you? No matter what I say, you're leaving tomorrow."

"Why won't you at least try?" Isabelle pleaded.

Kendall threw her hands in the air. "Because it won't change the fact that we're both in love with someone else. Marcella? Is that her name?"

Isabelle's jaw dropped. "What?"

"Is it that shocking to hear her name come out of my mouth?"

"No," Isabelle said. "The other part. You're in love with her?"

Kendall didn't respond.

"I'm staying."

"Isabelle."

"No, Kendall. I'm staying. Conversation over." Isabelle went into the cabin and slammed the door shut behind her.

❖

The conversation was not over, but Kendall waited a few minutes, hoping Isabelle would calm down. She stepped into the master suite and shut the door behind her.

"Tell me about her." Isabelle wiped her nose and tossed the tissue on a small pile she'd created.

Kendall sighed. "I really don't want to make this harder than it already is."

"I just want to know about her. She drinks too much, and she's pretty. That's hardly a reason to leave me."

Kendall shook her head. "I'm not going to talk about Abby."

"Why?" Isabelle yelled. "Why is it so hard to tell me what you found so goddamned fascinating about her?"

"Okay, she wasn't so full of herself that she couldn't see past her own nose. Are you fucking kidding me with this, Izzy? You were practically living a double life, and you want to know about Abby? Why don't you tell me about Marcella and fucking *Tuscany*!"

Isabelle seemed to consider it for a moment. "How about if I just show you?"

Kendall couldn't believe what she was hearing. "You seriously want me to meet your lover?"

"No. I want to show you the place I fell in love with so you can love it too."

Kendall was taken aback. Appalled even. This was ridiculous. Isabelle was well aware that she did not share her love for Italy. They'd had conversations, arguments, all-out fights over the place. Kendall had finally caved and told Isabelle she could spend a month there without her. That month turned into three months, which then turned into a semiannual event. Except that "semiannual" wasn't the right word because it meant twice a year, not half the year. Maybe someone should tell Isabelle that. Kendall couldn't believe they were having this conversation, but if Isabelle really wanted to know, then she'd answer the original question. Fuck Italy.

"Abby Dunn is funny. She makes me laugh. I make her laugh. She's smart and passionate. I met her when she was having a really bad night, and I *still* wanted to get to know her better." Kendall stopped and covered her mouth with her hand. Just talking about Abby made her emotional. She felt guilty for what she'd done, not because of Isabelle, but because of how it had torn Abby apart. Kendall had offered her the world, but she couldn't deliver. She hated herself for that.

"You knew about Marcella, and that's why you slept with her?"

Kendall recalled the meeting with the private investigator. He'd been so matter-of-fact about it, laying out the facts as if they meant nothing. She decided to do the same. "Marcella Scarpio. Thirty-five years old. Former model. Comes from a prominent Italian family. Never married, but she has a five-year-old son. Her Pinterest feed is full of baby clothes, nursery décor, pregnancy advice, etcetera. My guess is, she can hear her biological clock ticking, and she wants a sibling for her son. She speaks English fluently, which is probably very helpful, considering your Italian is still a work in progress."

Izzy held up her hand. "Okay, enough." She paused for a moment and said, "You didn't answer the question."

"I answered half of it. I knew about Marcella. But if you really think I just found out about your lover and got one of my very own to even the score, you know even less about me and this marriage than I thought you did."

"Just tell me you love me more than that woman," Isabelle said. "Tell me I'm not giving up half of my life for nothing."

"That's kind of the point here, isn't it, Izzy? At some point, I became only half of your life. And I can see it in your eyes—you don't want to stay here with me. You will, if you think it'll save our marriage, but you don't want to. You want Italy."

"Fine. You can have your little flings. I won't stop you, but I keep this ring on my finger. I am Kendall Squire's wife, and that will never change."

"Is that what Marcella is to you? A little fling? Or does she believe it's more than that?"

Isabelle looked away. "It doesn't matter what she believes."

"You have her believing that one day, you'll leave your wife for her. She believes you're her future. She's just waiting, hoping that the next time you show up, you'll be free of all of your entanglements. And the sick truth is, I probably would've done the same thing with Abby had she let me. I'm so disgusted with both of us, Izzy. When did we become such self-centered egomaniacs?"

"That woman can't possibly be worth—"

Kendall put up her hand. "That woman is so much better than both of us." She took a deep breath. "I'm calling it, Iz. Our marriage is over. You can beg and plead and make the threats I have no doubt you'll make, but do it through email because I can't look at your face anymore. I can't look into your eyes and not see all of the lies you've told. And I can't keep pretending this marriage is still real. It's over. Let it be over."

❖

Being alone in their penthouse apartment wasn't new for Kendall. And it was no surprise to her that Isabelle took off for Italy a few days prior, just like she'd planned to do.

As Kendall walked around the apartment they'd lived in for almost fifteen years with a tumbler of whiskey in her hand, it was overwhelming to consider that the life they'd built together was coming to an end. All of the art they'd collected together hung on the walls, each one with a story behind it. All of the books on the shelves, all of the vinyl records, all of the curios and souvenirs from their travels—they all held a memory, a story of their life together. And now, it would all be sold or put into boxes to rot away in storage.

Tomorrow, she'd have to call her lawyer. She'd have to tell her family that the marriage she'd fought so hard to have all those years ago was over.

Would it be selfish to call Abby? What would she say if she did? Just saying the words *I'm getting a divorce* didn't seem like enough. It could go on for years if Isabelle fought it, and Kendall had no doubt she would.

She poured more whiskey into the tumbler and turned off all the lights in the apartment. She set the glass on the nightstand and crawled into bed. It would be another night full of regret. Another night of wishing she would've asked Abby out to lunch instead of dinner on a "riverboat." Another night of replaying conversations that never happened over and over in her head. The conversation where she told Abby the truth, that she was unhappily married. The conversation where they talked about their careers and their families and what foods they liked. The conversation that would end with a hug and a promise to do it again sometime. In the imaginary version of Kendall's life, Abby was never the other woman. Not even for a night. They were friends when the divorce happened. Good friends. Friends who were in love with each other. Who would start their life together in the way they both deserved.

Kendall rolled onto her side and squeezed her eyes shut. She couldn't change the past. She could only do better in the future. Abby was doing well for herself. And if Kendall really was her friend, if she truly cared about her happiness, she'd leave well enough alone.

CHAPTER NINE

Abby's new office manager greeted her at the door with a coffee. "You're late."

Abby dropped her briefcase and took the cup. "We talked about you stating the obvious this early in the morning, Cheryl."

"I know it makes you grumpy, but what's the use in updating your calendar every night if you just ignore it?"

Abby hadn't been herself lately. She was overwhelmed with work and really needed to hire someone, but she didn't have time to set up interviews. There was also the minor detail of cash flow. She had more than enough business, but it wasn't as if everyone paid up front. Secretly, she loved her office manager's compulsive punctuality, but she wasn't willing to give her the satisfaction. Besides, she really wasn't that late. "What did I miss?"

Before Cheryl could answer, Syd poked her head out of Abby's office. "It's just me. I won't keep you long."

Abby gasped and opened her arms. "Syd! What are you doing here?"

Syd hugged Abby and with a sheepish grin said, "I thought we could celebrate the one-year anniversary of my new haircut. I brought donuts."

"Oh God. You're a saint." Abby led Syd back to her office. "Has it really been a year?"

"On October seventh of last year, my life was forever changed."

Abby looked her up and down. "And you're still dressing sharp, I see."

"Yeah," Syd said with a cringe. "It's going to kill me to admit this, but the new haircut and clothes really have helped with the ladies."

"Glad to hear it. You're a total catch." Abby closed her office door behind them. "How are you? How are things at the firm? Have they given you my job yet?"

Syd sat and slid a donut across the desk. "Your favorite. And no. They went outside the firm."

"*What?* Oh God, Syd, I'm so sorry. I told them I thought you were by far the best choice."

"I know you did. I also know from Cheryl that you're super busy, so dig in."

"*Too* busy." Abby ignored the donut and kept her eyes on Syd. She looked downtrodden, which wasn't at all like the ambitious go-getter she remembered. "What's wrong, Syd?"

Syd fidgeted in her chair. "Well, it's just that you always gave me credit for my work, and this new guy...he just makes me work my ass off and then acts like everything was his idea. I mean, he literally steals my concepts. And I just wanted to see if you happened to have any words of wisdom for me."

Abby leaned forward in her chair. "Yeah, I do. Quit."

"Quit?" Syd's voice raised an octave. "You think I should just—"

"Yes, I do. Give your two weeks' notice, then come and work for me at your current salary for two years. After that, I'll consider making you a partner."

Syd ran her hands over her neatly pressed trousers. "Are you sure you're busy enough?"

"I'm drowning. I had no idea I would get two more projects so soon. Frankly, I would have poached you sooner, but when I left, Denny had assured me the job was yours. I had no idea he hadn't come through. Idiot."

Syd took a deep breath and slowly blew it out. "People thought you were crazy when you left."

"And they'll think you're crazy too. But you're not, Syd.

You're smart and talented, and you shouldn't let some idiot steal your work."

"Two years and we're Dunn Riley Architects?"

"Has a nice ring to it, doesn't it?"

"I mean, it's no Riley Dunn."

Abby grinned. "Don't push it, or I'll show your next date a picture of you when we first met. Oh, that depressed, despondent hair."

"Come to think of it, Dunn Riley is perfect. Sounds like a Pritzker winner," Syd said, referring to one of their field's top awards. "And you're right. I didn't come all the way from Ohio just to let someone else get rich off my talent."

Abby stood and put out her hand. "Shake on it?"

Syd stood and grinned. "I can't believe I'm saying this, but I'll give my notice this afternoon."

❖

Two months after Syd had been hired, it was obvious that the offices weren't working for anyone. Cheryl was miserable sitting at her small desk in the foyer, where the cold air from the unheated hallway blew in under the door. It was fine during the summer months, but now Cheryl was bundled up as if she was going Christmas caroling.

Syd's office was ridiculously small. She had been kind about it, but every time Abby walked in, she cringed. They wouldn't last much longer like this, but Abby was having zero luck finding something that was affordable and also available when her one-year lease ran out in a few months. She slammed her laptop shut and sighed.

"Everything okay?" Syd asked, poking her head in Abby's office.

"We need to move." Abby closed her eyes and rubbed her temples.

Syd stood behind Abby's chair. "Is Cheryl complaining again?" She gently squeezed Abby's shoulders.

"Oh, that feels good." Abby pulled her hair to one side, giving Syd better access. "She has every right to complain."

Syd rubbed Abby's shoulders, digging in with her thumbs. "What are you doing tonight?"

Abby leaned back in her chair. "Oh my God, that hurts so good. Nothing, I hope."

"Why don't you let me give you a real massage? Your shoulders are a mess." Syd leaned next to Abby's ear. "We could order in and watch a movie afterward."

"Are you trying to get my clothes off?"

"Is it working?" Syd dug in a little harder on the tight muscles.

Abby laughed. "Almost, but no. And it never will. Don't make me hire an HR department. We don't have the space."

Syd couldn't help herself, Abby knew that. She was a flirt. Always had been. Abby didn't mind as long as Syd didn't take it too far. She was still of the mind that keeping their relationship somewhat professional was for the best. They were friends, and they spent some time on the weekends together, but Abby hadn't confided in Syd the way a best friend would. She hadn't told her about Heather. Or Kendall.

Kendall. Abby put her hand on Syd's to stop her. She had to think. Maybe this could be the solution to her office space problems. Kendall had made the offer before, telling Abby she could rent office space at a discounted rate. In Manhattan, no less. Maybe Abby could take her up on that offer now. The only problem was, they hadn't talked in months. Not since the day Kendall had invited her to Cape Cod.

Abby stood, still deep in thought. Would it be too risky to contact her? Kendall hadn't so much as sent a text since that day, and maybe there was a reason for that. Maybe Kendall had to cut Abby out of her life completely to make her marriage work. Abby realized she was being ridiculous. She needed to make it work on her own. Besides, it wasn't as if Abby could just pick up the phone and say, "Hey, it's been months, and I still intend to have no contact with you, but that cheap office sure would be handy right about now." No. That wouldn't do at all.

"Earth to Abby."

"What?"

"You stood up and froze."

"Right. What were we talking about?"

Syd laughed. "Um, it wasn't important. But I did want to ask you about something. A woman."

"A woman?" Abby immediately felt on guard. Oh God, had she said Kendall's name out loud? God, she hoped not.

"Vivienne Parks. She was in the meeting last week."

Abby frowned. "Sit down."

"What?"

Abby pointed at the chair. "Sit." She sat behind her desk and leaned forward, giving Syd an earnest stare. "Just because a client shows interest—"

"A potential client," Syd said. "She's not ours yet."

Abby wanted to shout, *She's twice your age! And married!* She'd noticed the way Vivienne had looked at Syd, as if she'd just found a new toy to play with. She'd ignored it because Syd hadn't seemed to show any interest in return. She'd actually been proud of Syd, who was normally delighted to act like a player whenever she had the chance.

"I tried to play it professional the other day, but she called and wanted to have lunch," Syd said.

"Lunch." Abby shook her head. "Okay, look. You don't want this for yourself because if there's one thing I know about you, Syd, it's that you want to find real love. And you're never going to find that if you keep looking at older women who aren't right for you. Date someone your own age. Find the real thing."

"Why can't I have a little fun with a beautiful woman?"

Abby sighed. "Two reasons. The first is that you have a big, wide open, and inexperienced heart."

Syd interrupted her. "Exactly. What better way to get some experience than with someone who's, you know, experienced?"

"Too experienced. The second reason is a biggie. Surely you noticed that giant rock on her left hand. Syd, I know you. Yes, you're an insufferable flirt, but I happen to know what you really want is to find love. And one day, I suspect you'd like people to respect your marriage, so maybe you should do the same."

Should she divulge the truth? If Syd knew, would she avoid the same mistakes Abby had already made? She wasn't ready to talk about Kendall. She couldn't do that without breaking down, but maybe she could talk about Heather. "There was a woman. A married woman. A straight, married woman. Her name was Heather, and I was in love with her." Saying the words brought up more emotion than Abby thought it would. She tried to shake it off, but tears filled her eyes. "It's wrong, and it's not worth it," she whispered. "Trust me. I know."

CHAPTER TEN

Syd rode the elevator of a client's high-rise office building. She had just dropped off some plans and was mired in thought about the project. Abby had given her total control, and she loved it. She could have daydreamed about the future building all day, but she was interrupted by the only thing she loved more than a beautiful building. A beautiful woman. As the woman stepped into the elevator, she nodded and smiled at Syd, then turned around and hit the button for the lobby. Syd knew immediately who the woman was. No one would forget that face. "You're Abby's friend." The woman turned around but didn't say anything. "I remember seeing you in her office." Syd offered her hand. "I'm Syd Riley. I work for Abby now."

Kendall stared at the hand for a few seconds and then took it. Instead of introducing herself, she said, "How is she?"

Syd saw a look of pain wash over the woman's face. "She's good," she said, wondering why the woman suddenly looked so sad.

"Good. That's good." Kendall released Syd's hand and turned back around.

Questions raced through Syd's mind as they rode. She desperately wanted to know who this woman was to Abby. She remembered walking in on them in Abby's office and immediately thinking they were lovers. But Abby had denied it and then never mentioned the woman again.

"Your name wouldn't happen to be Heather, would it?"

Kendall didn't turn around immediately. The elevator stopped, the doors opened, but no one was there. When the doors closed again, she turned around. "What made you ask that question?"

"Just a hunch," Syd said with a shrug.

"Abby's not with her again, is she?"

Syd shook her head. "I don't think so. But then again..." Syd wondered if Heather was really a thing of the past. Maybe that was why Abby refused to give her a chance. Maybe she was still having an affair with Heather but just didn't want to admit it.

"Then again, what?"

"Nothing," Syd said. She shouldn't be talking about Abby's personal life. What was she thinking?

Kendall grabbed Syd's arm. "Tell me, please. If Abby's not doing well, if she's struggling, I need to know."

"What's your name?" If Syd was going to have a conversation with this woman, she wanted a name.

"Kendall Squires. We're friends. Used to be...friends."

Syd furrowed her brow. She'd heard that name before when she was first interning with a company downtown. "The developer?" she asked. Altafor had been a major client for that company. "I worked on the Cascade project. I was just an intern back then, but I worked closely with your wife, Isabelle. She's an amazing architect."

"Oh," Kendall said. "I know she was very pleased with how that building turned out. If you had anything to do with it, then consider me grateful."

"Grateful enough to let me buy you a cup of coffee?" Syd wasn't about to miss out on such a big opportunity. If they could get Altafor as a client—well, Syd would be asking for that partnership a lot sooner than Abby expected.

Kendall paused for a moment, then gave Syd a quick nod. "Sure. There's a coffee shop in the lobby."

❖

Kendall wondered how long this Syd person had been in love with Abby. The admiration was written all over her face. Syd was trying to give her the hard sell by talking up their work and Abby's incredible talent, but there was more to it than that. This girl was in love with her boss.

Kendall sat back and crossed her legs, leaving one hand on the table. It didn't go unnoticed that Syd checked out her legs. She was young. She'd learn to be a bit subtler. Syd seemed smart too. She knew whose name to drop and which buildings in the New York skyline to talk about. Abby had hired well. "So, it sounds like you're staying busy at this new little company," Kendall said.

Syd's eyes lit up. "We're bursting at the seams! I mean, we're so busy we'll have to expand soon."

"Yes, I've been to your office. It doesn't really speak to who you are as a company."

"So, you're already a client, then?"

"No," Kendall said. "We haven't had the pleasure of doing business with the Dunn Company."

"Well, it's the Dunn Company for now, but soon it'll be Dunn Riley," Syd said proudly.

"She's making you a partner?" Kendall asked, surprised.

"She said in two years, but if I can bring in some awesome clients..." Syd smiled, leaving the statement hanging out there.

"I see." Kendall leaned forward. "You know, if your company was willing to rent office space in one of my buildings—a long-term lease, of course—I might consider sending some business your way. Nothing big, but something."

Kendall had put all of their big projects on hold until the divorce was final. In fact, it was her attorney's office she'd just been visiting when she ran into Syd. Of course, everything with the divorce was much more complicated and taking a lot longer than she'd hoped. Isabelle's trip to Italy was a short one. She had come home, determined to get Kendall back. Part of her strategy, apparently, was to make the divorce so difficult, Kendall would have to reconsider taking her back. So far, it wasn't working.

"Syd Riley? Is that you?"

Kendall's eyes shuttered closed when she heard her wife's voice. And it sounded so peppy too. Unlike the loud, angry voice she'd just been subjected to in her attorney's office for what felt like hours. She opened her eyes and forced a smile. "Syd, I believe you and Isabelle have met before?"

❖

Syd felt as if this was quite possibly the best day of her life. Sexy Isabelle Wright, a fellow architect and lover of Swedish Fish, just walked back into her life again. "Hey, Swede. Long time no see." She leaned in and air-kissed Isabelle on both sides, the way she liked it. Once she'd found out that was how Isabelle greeted her friends, Syd had practiced the move with her roommate, who thought she was insane, but whatever. She had the move down pat.

Isabelle laughed. "I forgot about that nickname. And Swedish Fish have been replaced. My new love is this little Italian candy with an almond filling." She stepped back and held Syd by the arm. "Look at you. You're all grown up."

Syd blushed. She'd been new to New York when she met Isabelle and immediately developed a mad crush on her. That's when she realized she had a thing for older women. Isabelle was everything Syd wanted to be: driven, successful, and happily married.

Syd had learned everything she could from Isabelle. It was a huge project the company was designing for Altafor, so meetings were plentiful, and Syd made sure she was at every one of them. They worked so well together, Isabelle eventually requested that Syd be her first contact.

"Honey, this is the girl I told you about a few years ago," Isabelle said to Kendall. "So talented. And I see you've learned how to dress," Isabelle said with a laugh.

Syd blushed harder.

"What is this, Armani?" Isabelle asked, touching the lapel of Syd's short black jacket.

"Um…I don't really know. Abby picked it out for me."

Isabelle froze. She glanced at Kendall, then smiled. "Well, it looks great on you."

"Would you like to sit?" Syd asked, pulling a chair from another table.

"I absolutely want to sit." She glanced at her wife again and then asked, "Abby Dunn?"

"Yes," Syd said. "I was just telling Kendall that I work for Abby now, and if you saw her work…"

"Yes," Isabelle said, interrupting her. "I've seen her work." She glanced at her wife again.

"Oh! Well, we're no longer with Milken. We've opened a new firm. It's just the two of us right now, but we're growing really fast."

Isabelle kept her eyes on Syd. "She dresses you, which, I have to say, Syd, this sleek, cool look really works for you."

Syd smiled. The new clothes and hair had kind of changed her life. "Thanks."

"And you started a firm together. How exciting," Isabelle said.

"Abby started a firm," Kendall corrected.

Isabelle looked at Kendall. "Are you and Abby dating, Syd?" She kept her eyes firmly set on Kendall while she waited for an answer.

"Um." Syd hesitated. She wasn't sure what was going on with Isabelle and her wife, but there was some pretty obvious tension there. "We're colleagues, but I'm working on it."

Kendall abruptly stood. "It was nice meeting you, Syd."

She was out of the coffee shop so fast, Syd didn't even have a chance to shake her hand and give her a business card. She looked to Isabelle for answers. "Did I say something wrong?"

Isabelle gave her a tight smile. "Can I have your card?"

"It's the perfect solution. There is no downside. We get in a nicer building and possibly land a great client."

"No." Abby didn't look up from her computer. She was barely holding it together. How dared Syd speak on her behalf to Kendall, of all people.

"If you're going to make me a partner one day, you need to give me some say. You can't just dictate."

Abby slammed her hand on the desk. "It's *my* company, Syd. It's *my* ass on the line. And I'm not going to sign a long-term lease for office space we can't afford."

Syd stood and shook her hands at the ceiling. "*Gah!* You make me crazy sometimes, you know that? This is how we'll grow. The *only* way we'll be able to grow! We can't stay in this shithole and expect our clients to take us seriously!"

Abby heard a voice coming from her doorway. Isabelle Wright appeared, looking like a million bucks and then some. Of course. Good God, could this day get any worse?

Isabelle pointed with her thumb at the front door. "Your receptionist must be on a break."

"Isabelle," Syd said.

Abby watched Syd make some weird, awkward move at Isabelle. *Oh my fucking God, what is she doing?*

Syd pulled back and put up a finger, "I was going to do the air-kiss thing again, but then I wasn't sure if that was just a once-a-day thing or…"

Isabelle laughed. "I wondered what that was." An awkward silence lingered for what felt like six days until she said, "Do you mind giving me a minute with Abby?"

"No, of course."

"Don't go too far, Syd," Abby said, hoping the daggers she was trying to shoot from her eyes were hitting their mark. Syd seemed to swallow hard before she shut the door, which gave Abby some slight satisfaction.

"We meet again." Isabelle sat, crossed her legs, and smoothed out her skirt.

"What do you want?"

"No pleasantries? Not even for a future client?"

"Oh, please." Abby threw her pen on the desk. "Just say what you need to say."

"Fine," Isabelle said. "I think I mentioned before that I'm

also an architect, although these days, I don't have time to do the legwork. I let people such as yourself bring my ideas to life."

"What do you want, Isabelle?" She took it upon herself to take a good, long look at Isabelle's empty ring finger. She had noticed it immediately, but now Abby stared openly.

"Oh, that," Isabelle said, spreading her fingers out. "It's messy right now, but we're working through it. And if we're being honest, which I hope we can be, that's really why I'm here."

Abby rolled her eyes. "I have a busy day, so if you don't mind getting to the point."

"I just happened to hear you arguing over office space when I walked in. You need more space, and I need my wife to forget you ever existed. We have a building in Brooklyn. The top floor is available. It's not Manhattan, but it's a hundred times better than this place."

So. Abby was somehow still a threat. Would this ever end? Would she ever be able to forget that Kendall Squires existed? This was Syd's fault for sticking her nose where it didn't belong. Maybe she was wrong about the whole partnership thing. She'd have to think long and hard about that, but right now, she had Isabitch Wright to deal with.

"I'll lease it to you for one dollar a year for five years. That should give you plenty of time to build your business into something respectable. All I ask in return is that you stay away from Kendall."

Abby stood. "If you've said all you need to say, I'd like you to leave now."

Isabelle seemed taken aback. "You won't even consider it? Do you have any idea what rent is like in a nice building?"

"I'm very aware." Abby slid her hands into her pockets and waited.

Isabelle also stood. "Okay. So, name your terms."

Abby shook her head in disgust. "My terms? Stop acting like your wife is worth nothing more than a few square feet in Brooklyn!"

Isabelle put up her hand. "Okay, you're right. I'll find you something in Manhattan."

Abby opened her door. "Get the hell out of my office."

Syd and Cheryl were standing outside the door with their mouths hanging open. Isabelle stepped up to Abby, getting well into her personal space. "If you change your mind." She slid her business card into Abby's shirt pocket.

Abby waited until Isabelle was gone before she went back into her office. "Get in here, Syd." She pulled her trash can out from under her desk and tore Isabelle's business card into tiny pieces.

"I'm guessing there are things you haven't told me," Syd said.

Abby glared at Syd. "Don't ever speak for me again. And don't ever try to air-kiss me like that."

Syd cleared her throat. "Right. No air-kissing." She took a step forward and leaned on the desk with both hands. "Now, will you please tell me what's going on?"

Abby's strength dissolved. She tried to hold back the tears, but there they were. "I'm in love with her wife," she whispered.

CHAPTER ELEVEN

Syd was about to make an enemy out of a potential client. She was nervous, and her hair hadn't cooperated this morning. The bangs that usually swooped nicely across her high forehead were hanging in her eyes. *Damn hair.*

She knew the whole story now. Abby had sobbed through most of it, but Syd got the gist. And Abby had been a total wreck ever since.

Something needed to change.

Syd straightened her jacket and adjusted her cuffs. She walked up to the security guard in the lobby. It was early, and he was sipping on his coffee. She felt as if her chances were good. "Syd Riley for Kendall Squires." As she said the words, she slid a box of donuts across the desk.

The guard looked at the donuts and then ran his finger down his list. "You're not in the appointment book today. I can't let you go up."

"She'll want to see me. Tell her it's about Abby Dunn."

"That's not my job, ma'am. You'll have to call her office and set up an appointment."

Syd shook her head. "I don't have time for that. Come on, man. It's Christmas Eve. I need to see her today."

"I'm sorry, ma'am. There's nothing I can do."

Syd pushed her bangs away and lowered her voice. "I have cash."

The guard chuckled and slid the donuts back to her. "I think it's time to escort you out of the building."

"No, wait!" Syd said, putting up her hands. "Okay, maybe that was out of line, but I'm desperate here." She lowered her voice again. "A friend of mine is hurting like hell, and only one person can do anything about it. That person is in this building. So, please, just bend a rule today. For her."

The security guard stood there with his arms folded. "Are you about to cry?"

Syd brushed her tears away. "No. I don't cry."

"Uh-huh." He slid the donuts back to his side of the desk, then picked up the phone. "What was the name, again?"

Syd blew out a sigh of relief. "Sydney Riley for Kendall Squires."

❖

Syd had never been in an office quite like the one she was currently standing in. The carpet under her feet felt like clouds, and the Christmas tree in the foyer was at least twenty feet tall. She tucked her hands in her pockets and tried to take in every little detail while she waited, from the placement of the wall sconces to the type of wood lining the walls. It looked exotic, whatever it was.

"You can have a seat if you like."

Syd looked at the nameplate on the desk. "Thanks, January. Is that really your name?"

Kendall's twenty-something administrative assistant smiled. "Yes." She glanced at the notepad she'd quickly written on when the security guard had called. "Sydney Riley. It is. My friends call me Jannie."

Syd walked over to the desk, noticing how light she felt with every step, partly because the carpet was so plush, but also because January Nielsen was a hottie. "My friends call me Syd."

January pushed her long, blond hair behind her ears and smiled even bigger, showing off her very straight white teeth and a cute dimple on her left cheek. "Nice to meet you, Syd."

"Syd." Kendall waved her into the office. "Jannie, please put Mary off for ten minutes."

"I'm on it."

There wasn't time to take in the view, even though Syd knew it would be awesome, forty floors up. She needed to stay focused, so she kept her eyes on Kendall. On second thought, maybe the view would be the better option. Kendall was wearing a tight ivory dress, and damn, was it hugging her in all the right places. Syd tried her best to look the woman in the eye. "It was shitty, what you did. And what Isabelle did was just as shitty."

Kendall stood behind her desk, her gaze falling at the harsh words. "I take it this isn't a friendly visit."

"Your wife thought she could bribe Abby with some crappy office in Brooklyn. And when did your wife turn into such a bitch, anyway? I used to think she walked on water—a fucking brilliant architect who would change this city's skyline. *That's* who I thought she was." Syd tended to swear when she got worked up. "Excuse my language."

Kendall moved toward a set of chairs. "Please sit, Syd." She also sat. "You just described Izzy perfectly, five, ten, twenty years ago."

"So, what happened to her? And why can't she just leave Abby alone? She's not the bad guy. You are."

"I know." Kendall clasped her hands together. "I've been trying to do the right thing. I promised myself I wouldn't contact Abby again until I was officially divorced. She deserves better than what I gave her."

"What you gave her is a broken heart."

Kendall lowered her gaze again. "Tell me about Brooklyn."

"She offered us office space there."

"In exchange for what?"

"In exchange for Abby forgetting you exist."

Kendall tried to hide it, but Syd saw her cringe. "Sounds like a good deal," Kendall said, barely above a whisper. "She should take it."

"She didn't take it," Syd said. "For some reason, God help her, she loves you."

Kendall stood and walked over to the window. "I love her too," she said. "But I'm also in the middle of a messy divorce that my wife happens to be contesting." She turned to face Syd again. "I can appreciate what you're trying to do here, but I really don't think this is the time or the place."

Syd stood. "You said you're getting divorced."

"I'm trying," Kendall said. "But like you said, Isabelle isn't who she used to be. She's making it"—Kendall paused and seemed to be choosing her words carefully—"difficult."

Syd tucked her hands in her pockets. She loved the style of pants Abby had picked for her. She had them in several colors now. They fit her long, thin body perfectly. They hugged her ass and sat just right on her hips. She was going to walk out of this office and ask January for her number, and she had a feeling she'd get it. In fact, she owed it to Abby to get it. She'd be proud of her. She'd give her a high five or a fist bump or something. But Abby would still be sad. And that was unacceptable.

"I'm leaving for Ohio tonight," Syd said. "And even though she won't say it, I know Abby is going to spend Christmas alone, just like she did last year. Probably in the office. She doesn't have a tree at home, but Cheryl and I decorated a small tree and put it in the office window because we knew that's where she'd be. We thought it would cheer her up, but literally nothing I do cheers her up because she's not in love with me; she's in love with you." Syd pointed at Kendall. "And you can bet everything you own that if Abby Dunn was in love with me, I wouldn't let her spend Christmas, or any other holiday, alone."

Kendall turned and looked out the window again, and as the seconds ticked by, Syd worried that she'd said too much and that her big, courageous move would only get her fired. But then, Kendall walked over to her and took her hand. "Thank you," she said.

And she didn't let go, either. She pulled Syd over to her coat rack, and quick-thinking Syd did the chivalrous thing and grabbed the wool coat, holding it open for Kendall. She also picked up Kendall's purse and held it out for her. "I take it we're going somewhere?"

Kendall grabbed Syd's hand again and led her out of the office and past January's desk. "Jannie, cancel Mary. Cancel everything."

Jannie stood. "Cancel Mary?"

"Tell her to go home and hug her children! And Merry Christmas! Your bonus is in my top drawer!" Kendall shouted.

Syd turned back to January, even though she was still being dragged out of the office. "Hey, can I have your number?"

Kendall stopped. She looked at January and then at Syd. "Go get it," she said, motioning with her head.

January smiled and quickly scribbled her number on a sticky note. She held it out and Syd took it. "New Year's Eve?" Syd asked.

January nodded. "I'll buy a new dress."

Syd proudly walked back to Kendall and held the note up. "I'm going to date your assistant. I hope you don't mind."

"We have to break into Abby's apartment. Help me do that, and you can *marry* her if you want to." Kendall didn't wait for a reply. She headed for the elevators.

"Wait. What?" Syd asked as she chased after Kendall.

Chapter Twelve

"Damnit." Syd was trying to get the key in the door, but her hands were shaking.

"Sergio can't hold that tree much longer, Syd."

"No, Ms. Squires. I can't," Sergio said with a grunt.

"I'm sorry, but I've never stolen someone's keys and made a copy and then broken into their house before." Syd hoped that when she came back from Ohio, she'd still have a job.

Sergio leaned the Christmas tree against the wall. "Let me try." He got the door open on the first try. "Voilà!"

Syd pulled all the shopping bags into the narrow hallway and helped Sergio haul the tree in. It would probably take up half of the small living room, but it was beautiful and smelled like Christmas. She crossed her fingers and held them up for Kendall to see. "Here's hoping she doesn't fire me."

Kendall laughed. "If she fires you, I'll hire you." She gave Syd a hug. "Thank you for all your help. My driver will take you to the airport."

Syd nodded and looked around one last time, then she looked at her watch. "You don't have much time."

"I have more helpers coming. We'll be fine." Kendall went to the door and opened it. "You better hurry or you'll miss your flight."

Syd was panicking inside. She'd acted like a moron in the office when she stole the key. Surely Abby knew something was up with all of her hemming and hawing and fidgeting. She lingered around for a painfully long time, waiting for Abby to excuse herself to get a coffee. Syd thought she'd die when Abby asked her to go get it for her. That never happened! "You can find a helping hand at the end of your arm," she'd said, prompting a puzzled look from her boss. Yup. She was definitely getting fired. Oh well, it was too late to worry now. "Take good care of her."

"I will," Kendall replied. "Enjoy your holiday with your family. And bring back some of those amazing cookies your mom makes."

Syd smiled. Her mom would be thrilled to know she'd been bragging about her Christmas cookies, and she'd probably send at least two dozen back with her. She glanced at Sergio, who had already started to get the tree in its base. "Sergio, don't forget to add water."

"Yes, miss."

Kendall rested her hand on Syd's shoulder. "We'll be fine. Now go, or you really will miss your flight."

"You have my number," Syd said as she backed out of the apartment.

Kendall laughed and pointed at the elevator. "Go."

❖

Sergio sat in the back of his boss's Escalade, watching the door of Ms. Dunn's office. He breathed a sigh of relief when the door opened just after five. He had to get home to his wife and mother. They'd kill each other if they were left alone for too long on Christmas Eve or any other day. Plus, he had to get to the jewelry store before they closed. He still needed to pick up his wife's Christmas present, which got quite a bit nicer thanks to the obscene holiday pay his employer had offered him.

"Okay, that's her," Sergio said. "Follow her."

The new driver pulled out into traffic and followed the taxi. Ever since Fritz had been fired, Ms. Squires had a hard time finding a driver she liked. This was number three. Sergio was hopeful about this one.

After following the taxi for a while, Sergio said, "Oh, no. No, no, no."

"What's wrong?" George pulled over behind the taxi and watched the woman they'd been following get out. She paid the driver and then went into the building.

"This isn't good." Sergio put his phone to his ear. "Ms. Squires! No, unfortunately, we're not almost there. Ms. Dunn stopped at a bar." Sergio cranked his neck. "Uh...it's called Blue something or other." He listened for a moment. "Yes, ma'am, I'll text the address. Yes, ma'am. Thank you. You too. And good luck with...I hope it goes well. Thank you, ma'am. Good night." Sergio ended the call and looked at George. "We can go home. But first, you're taking me to the jewelry store."

❖

The little bar in the Village was crowded. Abby ordered a shot of tequila and a margarita. She had to yell at the bartender, it was so loud in the place. There weren't any stools available, so she leaned on the bar and waited. When her drinks arrived, she downed the shot and looked for someplace to sit, but the place was packed.

"Abby? God, how long has it been?"

"Heather?" Abby was face-to-face with her ex-lover. "What are you doing in New York?"

"I'm here with a couple of friends, but Jesus, this place is packed. Apparently, they're having a Christmas Eve party for all the single folks who don't want to be alone tonight."

Heather stood close so they could hear each other. She was literally inches away, her long strawberry-blond hair brushing against Abby's face every time she leaned in to talk. "But this is a gay bar," Abby said. "You're in a gay bar, Heather. And where's Glenn?"

Heather laughed. "I guess it's been a while, hasn't it? And God, you look good enough to eat." Abby shook her head in confusion as Heather leaned in for a hug. "It's so good to see you, Abs, and I divorced Glenn and came out to my parents last year."

What the fuck? "Last year?"

"Yeah!" Heather shouted, looking as happy as Abby had ever seen her.

"*Last. Fucking. Year?*" Abby shouted. "And you didn't think I would maybe want to know that?" Abby turned to the bartender and asked for two shots of tequila. She was pissed as hell that Heather hadn't contacted her. "Well, I guess finally facing the truth about yourself deserves a drink." Abby scowled as she handed a shot glass to her ex. She didn't make time for a toast or any kind of lick-it-slam-it-suck-it ceremony.

"Would you like to join us? We're at a table in the corner," Heather said, pointing at her friends.

Abby was trying so hard to hold it together. She'd begged Heather to leave Glenn. She'd promised she'd be there for her every step of the way. They would build a life together, get married, and have kids. Heather always said that's what she wanted, but she just couldn't do it. She couldn't risk losing her parents' love. She didn't want to be gay. She'd come up with every reason in the book, all the while knowing Abby's heart was slowly breaking.

"Abby? Did you hear me?"

Abby wanted to slap that happy grin right off Heather's face. In fact, at that moment, she wanted to slap any married woman who'd ever broken another girl's heart. Instead, she simply declined the offer. "I'm good right here." She held up her margarita. "Merry Christmas."

"Merry Christmas," Heather hesitantly answered as she slowly backed away and then went back to her friends' table.

Abby was seething on the inside and drinking way too fast for her own good. When a stool opened up, she sat and ordered another drink. She'd turned on the stool and was watching Heather laugh with her friends when Kendall leaned on the bar next to her. "Has anyone ever told you they'd give you the world if they could?"

Oh, great! You too? What the fuck is going on? Abby nodded forcefully. "Yeah! All the time actually. In fact, two of them are in this bar right now!"

Kendall glanced in the direction Abby was looking. "Someone you know?"

"Yeah!" Abby yelled. "You could fucking say that!"

Kendall held out her hand. "You shouldn't be in a bar on Christmas Eve."

Abby's eyes ran down Kendall's body. She was wearing jeans and some type of Nordic ski sweater under her wool coat. "You look awfully festive. I guess you left the family Christmas party?"

Kendall kept her hand out, waiting for Abby to take it. "I have a taxi waiting out front."

Abby couldn't even. What. The. Fuck. First Heather and now Kendall? She was trapped in *Twilight Zone: The Christmas Special.* Heather, who couldn't even say the word *gay*, was laughing it up with her friends as if being in a gay bar was something she did every day of the week. And Kendall! Kendall, who had disappeared from her life, was in the same bar, using terrible pickup lines, just like she'd done over a year ago. What. The. Fuck.

Abby rolled her eyes. "Go be with your family, Kendall." Her eyes fell to Kendall's sweater and the cute little snowflakes bordering the zipper. "And their fucking Christmas sweaters."

Abby could see it all in her head. Kendall, Isabelle, and the rest of the family sitting for a portrait, all of them wearing their colorful Christmas sweaters. She had no idea what any of the family looked like, but she put imaginary faces on everyone. Kendall's mom, with skin too tight for her age and lots of jewelry weighing her down. Her dad with—

"What are you doing?" Abby squeaked as she was yanked off the stool. Well, not technically yanked, but Kendall had her by the arm. "You can't just…"

"I will carry you out of here if I have to," Kendall stated firmly, Abby's purse in her hand.

"And take me where?"

"You're drunk, and I'm not going to let you be drunk in a bar on Christmas Eve, so please don't fight me," Kendall begged.

"Don't fight you?" Abby yelled. "I haven't seen you in

months! Not since you invited me to Cape Cod and then left me forever!"

"I've been busy."

"Yeah? Well, your wife made time for me! God, you just think you can yell *jump* and *everyone* will ask how high!"

Kendall glanced around. People were starting to stare. "Please, just let me take you home."

"Not the yacht?" Abby shouted. "Not the first of fucking how many? And by the way, I don't need your pity, Kendall. So, just go home and eat your Christmas ham and drink your eggnog and kiss your wife in your stupid-ass ugly sweater!" It was actually a cute sweater, but that was beside the point.

Heather walked up behind them. "Is everything okay here?"

Abby backed up, her body hitting Heather's. "Kendall, this is Heather. She's single now." Abby turned around and laid a big, fat kiss on Heather's lips, then turned back around to Kendall. "And I'm not going anywhere with you."

❖

The key was upside down. Why was the key upside down on her key ring? Abby was drunk but not that drunk. She'd managed to get home on her own after telling both of the women who showed up on Christmas Eve to fuck the fuck off. She didn't say it in so many words—there was probably only one "fuck," maybe none—but they were both smart women, and they knew what a thinly veiled fuck off sounded like. Especially Kendall. A big fuck-you kiss on Heather's lips made it considerably easier to convince Kendall to leave her alone. As for Heather, well, she never cared about having Abby around in the first place.

She finally got the key in the door and stumbled into her apartment. "Holy fuck!" She stared at the tree for a second, then rubbed her eyes and opened them again. The gigantic, beautifully decorated tree was still there. And there were presents under it. Lots of them. And there was fucking Christmas music playing. And it smelled like a cinnamon nutmeg pumpkin pie forest. Apparently, she was still in *The Twilight Zone.*

She plunked the bottle of vodka she'd purchased on the way home down on the breakfast bar and slowly walked into the living room. She ran her fingers over the soft needle branches. It was a real tree with so many white lights, it lit up the whole apartment.

Abby sang along with Karen Carpenter, almost whispering the words as she picked up a present and shook it. The presents were real, too.

She walked into the kitchen and found a bottle of champagne sitting in a bucket of ice and a charcuterie board with crackers and cheese and olives. She cut a piece of brie off the wheel and set it on a cracker, then went into her bedroom. Feeling rather giddy, she plopped on her bed and called Syd.

"Merry Christmas, beautiful," Syd said in a low, sexy voice.

Abby giggled. "God, you're such a flirt. But you're also an amazing friend."

"So, you're home?" Syd's voice sounded full of excitement.

"Yes."

"And you're happy?"

"It was a very nice surprise," Abby said. "And now I know why you were acting so weird today."

"I wasn't," Syd said, feigning innocence.

"You're a sweetheart, Syd Riley. What did you do? Spend your entire Christmas bonus on all those presents under the tree?"

Syd was silent.

"You did, didn't you? What am I going to do with you?"

"Abby."

"Did you get me that purse I look at every time we walk past the Coach store?"

"Abby."

"Tell me which one it is. I want to open it first."

"It wasn't me, Abby."

"Liar. I know it was you. Who else would do this for me?"

"You can't get mad at me. Promise you won't fire me?"

Abby's smile faded. "What do you mean? What did you do?"
Syd didn't answer.

"Syd, you better start talking."

"Okay, fine." Syd sighed into the phone. "I stole your key and made a copy, but all the presents, the tree, everything, was Kendall."

Abby flew off her bed, the cracker and cheese flying in two different directions. "What?"

"Isn't she there somewhere? Hiding in a closet or something?"

Abby ran out into the living room again and looked around. "All of this was Kendall?" Even though she knew her hall closet was too full of junk for someone to hide in, she opened it just to make sure.

"I may have gone to her office this morning," Syd admitted. "I may have said some things."

"Like, what?" Syd was silent. "*Syd Riley!*"

"Okay! I may have told Kendall that you're, you know, head over heels in love with her still, and that you were going to spend Christmas alone. Again."

"*Fuck!*"

"Abs, you know it's true. You're miserable without her. And the great news is that her assistant is super hot, and I got her number. We're going out on New Year's Eve, so we'll probably have to go shopping first thing when I get back, okay?"

Abby was speechless and walking in circles. "Wha...you... how...*fuck!*"

"I need a cool suit. Probably Armani."

"Shut up, Syd! Just shut up for a second! This is not about you." Abby sat on the sofa and looked at the tree. There were red hearts and white angels and pinecones and silver snowflakes and little toy soldiers. It was quite possibly the most beautiful thing she'd ever seen. "What did I do?" she whispered.

"Abby?"

"No, Syd. You don't understand."

"What don't I understand? Kendall loves you right back. Can't you see that? She personally bought every single thing! Every present, every ornament. Even the wrapping paper. And she let me tell her off. She didn't even try to defend herself because she knows what she did to you was shitty. I even said that word. I told her it was shitty. And she took it all. And then she ran me all over town with her buying things so *your* Christmas would be special. If that's not love, then I don't know what is."

Abby tried to catch her breath so she could talk, but she was crying. "I'm such a fool."

"Why? What happened? Where is Kendall?"

Abby covered her eyes with her hand. "I don't know where she is, but I kissed someone else. Heather. I kissed Heather in front of her tonight."

Syd let Abby cry for a minute and then said, "Explain."

CHAPTER THIRTEEN

Abby stepped out of the hot shower and sat on the edge of the tub wrapped in a towel. She rested her face in her hands and cried a few more tears. She thought she was all cried out, but apparently, she wasn't.

Syd had stayed on the phone with her for a long time, trying to calm her down, trying to talk her through it. She thought she was okay, so she got in the shower, thinking she could fall asleep easier if she were clean and warm and didn't smell like a bar.

Maybe she could put on her headphones and fall asleep to music. She'd try that. And then she'd text Kendall tomorrow and apologize. She didn't want to contact her tonight. It was late, yes, but mostly, she was too ashamed. What an asshole she'd been!

Kissing Heather in front of Kendall? Why? What on earth had Abby hoped to gain from that? If the kiss was anything, it was confirmation. All those years spent hoping and waiting were spent hoping and waiting for a whole lot of nothing. Abby felt nothing thinking of Heather. She was suddenly grateful Heather hadn't sought her out. What if she had? What if Abby chose Heather a year ago, just so she wouldn't have to choose loneliness? She wouldn't have been in that bar. She never would have met Kendall Squires.

Kendall. She'd made her mistakes, but the thought that she'd seek Abby out in a bar wearing a Christmas sweater just to, just to what? Mock her? Remind her she was in love with a married woman? Why couldn't Abby see the good? The possibility? Why wouldn't she ask Kendall if she had left Isabelle?

Baggage, that's why. That not-so-teeny-tiny belief that she wasn't worth it. These were the thoughts running through Abby's head as she sat there. What if she had ruined everything?

Syd said Kendall would forgive her, but Abby wasn't hopeful. A woman like Kendall could be rejected only so many times before she'd walk away for good. Abby was pretty sure she'd met her quota.

She wrapped her wet hair up into a bun and looked at herself in the mirror. She'd beg if she had to. Forget texting. She'd call Kendall and beg for forgiveness. And not tomorrow. Tonight. She'd need to plug her phone in first, just in case it was a long conversation. She could only hope she'd keep Kendall on the line long enough to make it right or at least make it not quite so bad.

"You didn't answer."

Abby jumped when she came out of the bathroom and heard the words.

"Sorry. I didn't mean to scare you." Kendall held a key up and then put it on the sofa table. "This belongs to you."

Abby dropped her dirty clothes and stood there in her bathrobe, red puffy eyes and everything. "Syd?"

Kendall gave her a nod. "She called me. She's a good friend. You should keep her."

"The best." Abby bit her lip, trying to keep herself from crying again. Kendall was still wearing the ski sweater with little snowflakes on the collar and the cuffs. She matched the room. She was Christmas. She was everything. "I thought—"

Kendall kept her distance, standing several feet away. "You thought I'd snuck away from my family to have a little fun with you, is that it?"

Abby wiped her cheeks. "Your sweater."

Kendall looked at herself and smiled. "It's festive, isn't it?"

"Yeah," Abby said with a sort of giggle-sob, if that was a thing. "It's adorable."

"There's one for you too, if you want to put it on." Kendall took a wrapped present from under the tree and handed it to her.

Abby shook her head at her own stupidity and took the box. "Give me a minute."

"Wait." Kendall held up her hand. "Just let me say this." She took a breath. "At first, I thought Syd had somehow gotten it wrong—that maybe you didn't feel anything for me anymore—but I don't think you'd look like you were about to cry right now if that were the case."

Abby hugged the box to her chest, trying to hold back the tears.

Kendall took a step toward her. "The last thing I want to do is hurt you again. And I probably should've sent an email or something so you'd have the chance to refuse or at least think it through instead of trying to sweep you off your feet again with all this"—Kendall waved her hand at the Christmas tree—"madness." Her gaze fell to the floor. "Abby, if you want me to walk out the door and take the tree with me and send an email, I'll do it."

"And what would the email say?"

"Oh God. Well, I'd probably start with a bad joke. And then, I'd tell you that I tried, you know, with my marriage, but it's over. And I promised myself that I wouldn't contact you again until the divorce was final, but it's Christmas. And you love me. And I love you. And we can take it slow, but you're not waking up alone on Christmas morning ever again. And you're never going to another Christmas office party alone or spending Friday night alone or Sunday morning or any other day of the week if I can help it."

Abby smiled. "You're still trying to sweep me off my feet."

"Is it working?"

Abby shrugged. "I don't know. I kinda want to see you try to drag that tree out of here."

Kendall laughed. "I'll do it. If it'll make you smile."

Abby did smile. And then she held the box up. "I have a sweater to put on."

❖

They sat side by side on the floor in front of the tree, leaning against the sofa, Abby in her red sweater with little reindeer on the collar and cuffs and black leggings. The charcuterie board and two glasses of champagne sat in front of them.

"You always seem to catch me at my worst."

"Yeah, you really showed me with that kiss," Kendall quipped. "I've never been told off quite like that before."

Abby rested her head on Kendall's shoulder. "At least I didn't throw up on you."

"Oh, there's still time." Kendall put her hand on Abby's thigh. They sat in silence for a moment, taking in the Christmas atmosphere.

"When you walked into the bar, I'd just found out that Heather came out last year and didn't bother to tell me."

Kendall rested her cheek on Abby's head. "Had you been waiting for her?" She tried to ask the question casually, but her voice tightened up.

"I just thought if it ever happened, I'd be the first to know because she'd finally be able to have what we both so desperately wanted. But I guess she didn't want it after all. Me. She didn't want me. And realizing you really did waste years of your life being someone's side-piece is a punch in the gut."

"And that's when I walked in. Jesus." Kendall wrapped her arms around Abby, holding her close. "I'm sorry she made you feel that way, and I'm sorry you ever saw any of that in me."

Abby shed a few tears and then pulled back so she could look Kendall in the eye. "When did you leave Isabelle?"

Kendall knew what she was thinking. If Heather hadn't bothered to tell Abby about getting divorced, maybe Kendall had done the same thing. Abby wanted to know how long it took. She slowly shook her head. "No. You can't compare the two. It's not the same thing."

"Tell me."

Kendall cupped Abby's cheeks. "Honey."

Abby pulled Kendall's hands away. "How long?"

"I'm still in the middle of it, actually. We've been officially separated for four months, but Isabelle is fighting the divorce every step of the way. It's ugly, and I couldn't bear the thought of dragging you through it. After all you've been through, I think you deserve someone who is completely free to love you."

Abby fell back into Kendall's arms. "Give me a minute."

"I had to force myself to not call you or email you or go to you. Some nights I would have faxed you if anyone still had a fax machine."

"And yet, nothing on Instagram?"

Kendall laughed.

"No one has ever done anything this big for me before." Abby waved her hand around the room.

Kendall wrapped her arms even tighter around Abby. "I don't do small."

"Will you name a boat after me?"

"I'd rather name it after our child."

Abby raised her head off Kendall's shoulder and met her gaze.

"Too soon?" Kendall ran her thumb over Abby's tear-stained cheek.

"I was kidding."

Kendall shook her head. "I'm not."

"This is your idea of going slow?"

"Just dreaming about the future, I guess."

Abby smiled and kissed Kendall's cheek. "If you want to name it after our child, I thank God you already named a boat *The First of Many*."

❖

"I thought I told you to stay in bed."

"I couldn't. I missed you." Abby took a grape from the fruit plate Kendall was working on and popped it in her mouth. "You look adorable in my T-shirt." She slapped Kendall's ass. "And Merry Christmas, baby."

As Abby tried to walk away, Kendall caught her arm. "Where are you going?"

"I thought I'd shake a few presents. See if I could guess what they are."

Kendall pulled Abby back to her, wrapping her arms around her waist. "I was hoping to keep you in bed all day and open this present over and over." She ran her finger down a bare chest, opening the robe slightly.

"Mmm…that sounds like heaven. You don't have any family commitments today?"

"Are you trying to get rid of me?" Kendall nibbled on Abby's ear.

"God, no. I'd like to keep you forever."

"That can be arranged. But I have to tell you, it could be bumpy at first with the divorce."

Abby cupped Kendall's cheeks and looked her in the eye. "As long as you're getting one, that's all I care about."

"I'm getting divorced. End of story."

Abby took Kendall's hand and led her back to the bedroom. "That story, anyway. Ours is just getting started."

About the Author

Elle Spencer (http://ellespencerbooks.com) is the author of the best-selling Goldie Award finalist *Casting Lacey*. She is a hopeless romantic and firm believer in true love, although she knows the path to happily ever after is rarely an easy one—not for Elle and not for her characters.

Before jumping off a cliff to write full-time, Elle ran an online store and worked as a massage therapist. Her wife is especially grateful for the second one. When she's not writing, Elle loves travel, a good home improvement project, and reading lots (and lots) of lesfic.

Elle and her wife split their time between Utah and California, ensuring that at any given time they are either too hot or too cold.

Books Available From Bold Strokes Books

All of Me by Emily Smith. When chief surgical resident Galen Burgess meets her new intern, Rowan Duncan, she may finally discover that doing what you've always done will only give you what you've always had. (978-1-163555-321-5)

As the Crow Flies by Karen F. Williams. Romance seems to be blooming all around, but problems arise when a restless ghost emerges from the ether to roam the dark corners of this haunting tale. (978-1-163555-285-0)

Both Ways by Ileandra Young. SPEAR agent Danika Karson races to protect the city from a supernatural threat and must rely on the woman she's trained to despise: Rayne, an achingly beautiful vampire. (978-1-163555-298-0)

Calendar Girl by Georgia Beers. Forced to work together, Addison Fairchild and Kate Cooper discover that opposites really do attract. (978-1-163555-333-8)

Cash and the Sorority Girl by Ashley Bartlett. Cash Braddock doesn't want to deal with morality, drugs, or people. Unfortunately, she's going to have to. (978-1-163555-310-9)

Lovebirds by Lisa Moreau. Two women from different worlds collide in a small California mountain town, each with a mission that doesn't include falling in love. (978-1-163555-213-3)

Media Darling by Fiona Riley. Can Hollywood bad girl Emerson and reluctant celebrity gossip reporter Hayley work together to make each other's dreams come true? Or will Emerson's secrets ruin not one career, but two? (978-1-163555-278-2)

Stroke of Fate by Renee Roman. Can Sean Moore live up to her reputation and save Jade Rivers from the stalker determined to end Jade's career and, ultimately, her life? (978-1-163555-162-4)

The Rise of the Resistance by Jackie D. The soul of America has been lost for almost a century. A few people may be the difference between a phoenix rising to save the masses or permanent destruction. (978-1-163555-259-1)

The Sex Therapist Next Door by Meghan O'Brien. At the intersection of sex and intimacy, anything is possible. Even love. (978-1-163555-296-6)

Unexpected Lightning by Cass Sellars. Lightning strikes once more when Sydney and Parker fight a dangerous stranger who threatens the peace they both desperately want. (978-1-163555-276-8)

Unforgettable by Elle Spencer. When one night changes a lifetime… Two romance novellas from best-selling author Elle Spencer. (978-1-63555-429-8)

Against All Odds by Kris Bryant, Maggie Cummings, and M. Ullrich. Peyton and Tory escaped death once, but will they survive when Bradley's determined to make his kill rate 100 percent? (978-1-163555-193-8)

Autumn's Light by Aurora Rey. Casual hookups aren't supposed to include romantic dinners and meeting the family. Can Mat Pero see beyond the heartbreak that led her to keep her worlds so separate, and will Graham Connor be waiting if she does? (978-1-163555-272-0)

Breaking the Rules by Larkin Rose. When Virginia and Carmen are thrown together by an embarrassing mistake, they find out their stubborn determination isn't so heroic after all. (978-1-163555-261-4)

Broad Awakening by Mickey Brent. In the sequel to *Underwater Vibes*, Hélène and Sylvie find ruts in their road to eternal bliss. (978-1-163555-270-6)

Broken Vows by MJ Williamz. Sister Mary Margaret must reconcile her divided heart or risk losing a love that just might be heaven sent. (978-1-163555-022-1)

Flesh and Gold by Ann Aptaker. Havana, 1952, where art thief and smuggler Cantor Gold dodges gangland bullets and mobsters' schemes while she searches Havana's steamy red light district for her kidnapped love. (978-1-163555-153-2)

Isle of Broken Years by Jane Fletcher. Spanish noblewoman Catalina de Valasco is in peril, even before the pirates holding her for ransom sail into seas destined to become known as the Bermuda Triangle. (978-1-163555-175-4)

Love Like This by Melissa Brayden. Hadley Cooper and Spencer Adair set out to take the fashion world by storm. If only they knew their hearts were about to be taken. (978-1-163555-018-4)

Secrets On the Clock by Nicole Disney. Jenna and Danielle love their jobs helping endangered children, but that might not be enough to stop them from breaking the rules by falling in love. (978-1-163555-292-8)

Unexpected Partners by Michelle Larkin. Dr. Chloe Maddox tries desperately to deny her attraction for Detective Dana Blake as they flee from a serial killer who's hunting them both. (978-1-163555-203-4)

A Fighting Chance by T. L. Hayes. Will Lou be able to come to terms with her past to give love a fighting chance? (978-1-163555-257-7)

Chosen by Brey Willows. When the choice is adapt or die, can love save us all? (978-1-163555-110-5)

Gnarled Hollow by Charlotte Greene. After they are invited to study a secluded nineteenth-century estate, a former English professor and a group of historians discover that they will have to fight against the unknown if they have any hope of staying alive. (978-1-163555-235-5)

Jacob's Grace by C.P. Rowlands. Captain Tag Becket wants to keep her head down and her past behind her, but her feelings for AJ's second-in-command, Grace Fields, makes keeping secrets next to impossible. (978-1-163555-187-7)